THE KILLING TIME

GRIMM

THE KILLING TIME

GRIMM

TIM WAGGONER

BASED ON THE NBC TV SERIES

TITAN BOOKS

Grimm: The Killing Time
Print edition ISBN: 9781781166581
E-book edition ISBN: 9781781166598

Published by Titan Books
A division of Titan Publishing Group Ltd
144 Southwark St, London SE1 0UP

First edition: September 2014
10 9 8 7 6 5 4 3 2 1

A CIP catalogue record for this title is available from the British Library.

Printed and bound in the United States.

TITANBOOKS.COM

This one's for Barb and J.C. Hendee, two wonderful writers who published some of my first stories way back when. See what you started?

This novel takes place between "A Dish Best Served Cold" and "One Night Stand."

"I have seen many strange things, but such a monster as this I never saw."

"The Turnip," as per the Brothers Grimm

CHAPTER ONE

Dana Webber was getting a sack of groceries out of her car when she felt a prickle on the back her neck, an irritating scratchy-crawly sensation like tiny ants walking on her skin.

Someone was watching her.

She shifted the groceries to one arm, careful to keep her purse from sliding off her shoulder, then shut the door to her ancient station wagon. She still had hold of her keys, and she adjusted them in her hand so the ignition key jutted from between her index and middle fingers. Not much of a weapon, maybe, but it was better than nothing. She wished she had a small container of pepper spray hanging on her keychain, but she'd never trusted the things, had always worried they'd go off accidentally. Now she scolded herself for being so foolish.

She turned away from the car, stepped onto the sidewalk, and started toward her house. Their driveway was short and narrow, and right now Rich's Chevy—which was badly in need of a new transmission—was parked there, leaving her to park the station wagon on the street. And since the other houses in this neighborhood were all like the one she and her husband rented—old, small, built close together with tiny yards and even tinier driveways—lots of people parked on the street. It wasn't 8:30 yet, but cars lined the curb; she'd been forced to park almost a block from her home, and she'd been lucky to get that space. She didn't feel lucky at the moment, though. She might've had to walk only a block, but right now it felt as long as a mile. She imagined eyes on her, a watcher hidden in the shadows, tracking her movements with predatory fascination.

She told herself it was only her imagination. How many times had Rich told her the same thing when she jumped at every creak their old house made, woke startled in the night, convinced she'd heard a sound and that someone had broken in, only for Rich to get up, check, and find no evidence of a prowler? Too many times.

When she'd been a child, her mother had told her that her imagination was her greatest asset as well as her heaviest burden. She'd been a talented artist, covering her bedroom walls with detailed drawings and paintings of friends, family, and pets. But she'd also worried she was dying whenever she came down with a stomach bug, and when she'd got her first period, she might not have reacted as badly as Carrie White in Stephen King's novel, but it had still been something of a trauma for her. She was in her mid-twenties now, and while her imagination still got the better of her sometimes, in general, she'd learned to manage it.

She and Rich had been high-school sweethearts, and they'd married soon after graduation. She'd gone to work as a barista at a coffee shop near Portland Community College, while Rich found work with a landscaping company. She'd been taking classes on and off at PCC for a few years, but this semester she'd gotten serious and had decided to channel her artistic ability into a marketing degree. She wanted a job that was both creative *and* practical, and she viewed her new goal as a sign that she was finally, if reluctantly, growing up.

But now, walking down the sidewalk, holding her breath as she moved from one island of fluorescent light to another, she felt like a child once more, gripped by a fear she couldn't control.

Stop it! she told herself. This was a safe neighborhood. Sure, there was the occasional domestic disturbance and sometimes there'd be a party on the street that got too loud and went on too late, but that was about it. No robberies, no assaults, and certainly no murders.

A little voice, one that came from deep inside her, whispered, *There's a first time for everything.*

It was early November in Portland, and it wasn't all that cold out. Around fifty degrees, she guessed, maybe a bit lower. She wore a long-sleeved pullover beneath a denim jacket, and usually that was enough for her to be comfortable this time of year, but now she shivered as if she were freezing. *Just nerves,* she told herself, but it didn't stop her from trembling.

But instead of becoming calmer, the closer she came to her home the more her anxiety rose, and the stronger the prickling on the back of her neck became. Her breathing came in ragged gasps, and her pulse beat like the staccato *rat-a-tat-tat* of a snare drum. She felt an impulse to drop her groceries and run the rest of the way to her house, and she might have, if at that exact instant she hadn't seen the child step out from between a pair of parked cars ahead of her. Dana guessed the girl was in her early teens, if that. She was thin, with a round face and a head full of curly strawberry-blond hair. She wore a T-shirt with a rainbow design on the front, a pair of old jeans with holes in the knees, and no shoes.

Dana's anxiety drained away. The sinister watcher she'd

imagined was just a neighborhood kid, but something still didn't feel right. It wasn't that cold a night, but it wasn't yet warm enough to be going around without a jacket, and barefoot. Dana feared the girl was in some kind of trouble. She knelt, put the sack of groceries on the sidewalk, then hurried over to her.

"Are you okay, honey? Is something wrong?"

The girl stood in a patch of shadow between two streetlights, but now that Dana was closer, she could see that there was something off about the girl's appearance. For one thing, her facial features were remarkably uneven. Her left eye was set lower than her right, significantly so, and her left ear hung lower than it should, and it was tilted backward, giving Dana the impression that it might fall off any moment. The left side of her mouth drooped too, and the flesh on that side of her face sagged, as if the girl was a wax statue in the process of melting. But that wasn't all. Her curly hair was thinning, and her scalp was bare in several places. As Dana watched, a lock of the girl's hair above her drooping ear detached and fell onto her shoulder. The girl didn't react, and Dana wondered if she was even aware that it had happened.

Dana experienced a wave of revulsion and felt an urge to back away from the girl. But she ignored the impulse. The kid was clearly suffering from some kind of medical condition—one that maybe had affected her mind as well, given the way she just stood and stared at Dana without expression. This poor thing wasn't a threat. She needed help.

Now that she no longer had need of a weapon, Dana tucked her keys into her purse and stepped closer to the girl. She crouched down so she could look her in the eyes, hoping she wouldn't seem too threatening.

"Are you lost? Is there someone I can call for you?"

The girl didn't reply, but her gaze focused on Dana. She

took that as a good sign. It meant the kid wasn't completely out of it. Dana gave her a quick once-over. She didn't appear to be injured. There were no signs of blood or bruising. None visible, anyway. Whatever was going on with the poor thing, Dana couldn't leave her like this, standing out in the cold, confused, underdressed and barefoot.

Moving slowly so as not to startle the girl, she reached out and gently took hold of her hand. Her skin was clammy, and even though Dana didn't apply any pressure, the flesh seemed to give under her fingers.

She suppressed a grimace of distaste. "Why don't you come with me to my house? It'll be warm inside, and I'll make you a cup of cocoa while we figure out what to—"

Dana froze as the girl raised her other hand, flexed her fingers, and three-inch black spines jutted from her fingertips. Before Dana could react, the girl grabbed hold of her throat and squeezed, the spines sinking into her flesh with the ease of hypodermic needles. At first it felt as if her throat was on fire from the inside, but the pain quickly vanished, replaced by an almost pleasant numbness. *She's drugging me somehow,* Dana thought, panic rising in her chest. She felt the paralysis rapidly spread through her body, and she knew that she had to fight back and try to escape now, while some strength remained in her.

No longer was the girl's face expressionless. Her eyes were wide, filled with life and energy, and her lopsided mouth—which Dana saw was not so lopsided anymore—was stretched into a cruel, satisfied smile. And her hair had changed. The strawberry-blond curls were now straight and brown. Just like Dana's.

Dana took hold of the girl's wrist with both of her hands and tried to break her grip. But despite the girl's slight frame, her hand wouldn't budge. Maybe the girl was stronger than she looked, or maybe those finger spines had sunk too deeply into her neck. Given how numb Dana's throat was, she could be doing all kinds of damage to herself by trying to pull the spines free, and she wouldn't know it. She let go of the girl's wrist and started hitting her. Her arms felt heavy as lead now, and it took an effort of will to raise them after each blow and strike again. She wasn't able to hit with any real force, and the girl ignored the blows as if she didn't even feel them.

The girl seemed taller now, and had to crouch to stay level with Dana. Her clothing had changed too. She was now wearing the same denim jacket and pullover Dana was, her jeans no longer had holes in the knees, and her once bare feet were now covered by a pair of boots identical to Dana's. Her body remained that of a female, but now she looked like an adult. And not just any adult— she looked exactly like Dana.

Dana could no longer raise her leaden hands to strike at the girl. No, it wasn't a girl, was it? It was some kind of *thing*. She was so weary, so empty, as if she had been hollowed out inside. It wasn't just her energy that was gone. Her mind had become a complete void. She no longer remembered where she lived. No longer remembered her husband's name. She couldn't even remember her own name, nor was she aware of ever having had one. Her body fell limp, and she would've collapsed to the sidewalk if the creature who now resembled her in every detail didn't have its finger spines embedded in her throat.

The creature stood up, and as it rose, it lifted her into a standing position. Dana's body hung slack in the creature's grasp, and there was no longer anything she could do to try to free herself. She couldn't think, let alone move. She was still conscious, still aware, at least on some primitive level, but that was all.

"Don't worry, honey," the creature said in her voice, its

tone gentle, almost loving. "It's almost over. But I need one last thing from you."

It… *she* reached out with her free hand, slipped Dana's purse off her shoulder, and slid it over her own.

Dana, or at least the last remnant of what had once been Dana, opened her mouth to scream, but no sound came out. She experienced a sensation of release, or letting go, and then she felt like she was falling, falling forever.

The darkness rushed upward to take her and she felt no more.

The Wechselbalg retracted its finger spines and examined its hands. *Her* hands. It was female again. It—*she* had to remember that. She was old, *very* old, and she became confused far too easily and often these days.

She, she, she, she, she.

She gazed down at the body on the sidewalk. She didn't regret what she'd done to the original Dana; soon the dead woman would be nothing but a viscous puddle of dissolved flesh and bone. She was Wechselbalg, and this was how she survived. She felt no more remorse for what she'd done to the woman than a wolf felt for preying on a doe. Still, something wasn't right, but she couldn't put her finger on it—then it came to her. She had approached the woman in the open, but her kind were supposed to be careful to take their victims where they couldn't be seen, deep in forests and valleys, places where the residue could be easily disposed of. If any humans discovered it, they wouldn't know what to make of it. But if any other Wesen found it…

She shrugged. So what if they did? Her kind was rare enough that they might not recognize the residue for what it was. And even if they did understand, they wouldn't be able to track her. Her scent was long gone, along with the original Dana. That was her kind's great strength: to change, to hide, to disappear. And that's precisely what she intended to do now.

She sidestepped the prone figure, picked up Dana's groceries, then closed her eyes and began searching the woman's memories. She found an image of Dana's house, and a man polishing a Chevy out front.

Rich, she thought, *my husband's name is Rich.*

She opened her eyes and started walking.

CHAPTER TWO

"Come on, guys. Why don't we step outside and talk about this?"

Nick Burkhardt flicked his gaze from one man's face to the other as they squared up to each other, trying to gauge their reactions to his words. But as near as he could tell, neither had heard him. The two men were in their early twenties, both brown-haired, with similar stocky builds. One had a full beard, while the other was clean-shaven. The bearded one wore a brown sweater, while the clean-shaven one wore a blue long-sleeved shirt with the cuffs rolled up to his forearms. They both wore jeans and sneakers. The two looked enough alike to be brothers, although from what Nick could gather, they were cousins. And to make matters worse, they were both *Jagerbaren*: bear-like Wesen capable of great strength and savagery.

"I think you may need to turn up the volume a little." Hank Griffin flanked Nick, his voice calm. But Nick could detect the tension in his partner's words, telling him that Hank was ready to go into action any second, if necessary. And it was looking more necessary with each passing second. Hank was a tall African American man with a neatly trimmed mustache and goatee. He had what Nick thought of as a quarterback's build—broad-shouldered and thick-bodied, all of it muscle. He could present an intimidating figure when he wanted to, which came in handy when questioning a suspect, but most of the time he had a twinkle in his eye and an easy smile. Right now he was in full-on intimidation mode.

In contrast to his partner, Nick was lean, with short black hair and stubble to match. His eyes were his most striking feature, or so he'd been told. Juliette said there was an intensity in his gaze, and that his eyes were always moving, taking in everything around him. Except when he interacted with people. Then all of his attention was centered on them. He now focused that intensity on the two Wesen, but he hadn't been able to get a response from them. So far neither of the cousins had thrown the first punch, but Nick didn't know how much longer that would last.

Blind Bill's was a small bar, not far from Lewis and Clark Law School. It had a deliberately grungy vibe, the kind of place that looks like it tries a little too hard to be a dive, but the microbrews listed on the chalkboard hanging behind the bar told a different story. The clientele were all college students, and while they had a tendency to dress down, their almost conspicuous lack of obvious tattoos and piercings told Nick these were classic Type As—future doctors, lawyers, and MBAs—who didn't want to risk their future employment opportunities just for the sake of fashion.

"They've been like that for the last fifteen minutes."

Beverly Burello—the server who'd called Nick out to deal with this problem—stood next to him. She was a thin, almost sleek woman in her late twenties, with long, full, reddish-brown hair that hung to her waist. She wore a black T-shirt with the Blind Bill's logo on the front, and skinny jeans so tight they looked as if they'd been painted on.

She went on. "They just stand there, trash-talking each other. I was hoping they'd either cool off or take it outside. As you can see, my hopes were *not* fulfilled. I tried talking to them, but I'm not exactly the most intimidating person, you know?"

Her features shifted, and for a moment her face was covered with glossy reddish-brown fur, her nose had receded and turned black, and long delicate whiskers protruded from her cheeks. But the moment passed and her features became those of a woman once more.

Hank caught Nick's eye and raised a questioning eyebrow. Hank couldn't see Wesen when they involuntarily woged, not unless they were so overcome with emotion that they lost control of their ability to shield their true nature from the eyes of humans. But over the last few months, Hank had gotten good at noticing when Nick got what he called "That Look," which meant he'd seen a Wesen.

Nick gave Hank a quick nod to indicate Beverly was indeed Wesen, followed by an equally quick shake of the head to indicate she wasn't one of the more dangerous varieties. She was a Luisant-Pêcheur, an otter-like being more at home in the water than on land, and gentle for the most part.

Blind Bill's had a good-sized crowd for a Thursday night. Three-quarters of the seats were taken, and while a few people had open textbooks or laptops in front of them, most had come here to hang out, have a good time, and decompress from the pressures of academic life. Right now, though, everyone was paying attention to the drama playing out in their midst. Some were talking and laughing about it, others were taking pictures or filming videos with their phones, while a few looked as if they would've preferred to get out of there before the situation took a violent turn, only they were too afraid to do anything other than sit still and stay quiet.

Nick absorbed all of these details in an instant, almost on an unconscious level, and he processed them just as swiftly. His attention was then drawn to a young woman sitting alone at a table—a table with two empty chairs. Like everyone else in the bar, her gaze was fixed on the two angry cousins, but her eyes shone with amusement mixed with a healthy dose of shrewd calculation, and her mouth formed a small smile. Thick auburn hair spilled over her shoulders, and she was pretty in a cold, severe way. She wore a white sweater and jeans, and expensive-looking cowboy boots that were highly polished and didn't have a mark on them. The woman's smile and the two empty chairs at her table told Nick everything he needed to know. She was playing the two men against each other, and odds were she was also a Jagerbar. While he wasn't sure, based on his first encounter with this type of Wesen it seemed the females of her kind were stronger-willed than the males. If that was true, a show of strength and aggression to impress a female might be normal for Jagerbaren. But normal or not, he couldn't allow them to conduct their mating rituals in public.

Nick raised his hands, palms forward, fingers spread apart to appear the least threatening he could, and took a step toward the two Jagerbaren.

"Take it easy, guys. This isn't the kind of thing you want to do in front of an audience, is it?"

Neither of the men looked at him, but the one with the beard said, "We don't have to do it at all. He just needs to walk out of this place and never come back."

The unshaven cousin made a noise deep in his throat that sounded too much like a growl. He woged, and his features took on an ursine aspect. His eyes blazed with anger, and he opened his mouth to display his fangs. His cousin woged in response, and now two bear-like creatures stood facing each other. Nick could feel the angry energy radiating off them in waves, and he knew he had only a few seconds to act before they started fighting in earnest. So far none of the humans in the bar could see the two Jagerbaren's true appearance. If they could, they'd be shouting, screaming, and trying to get the hell out of there as fast as they could. But once the Jagerbaren started fighting, they could lose control of their illusion of humanity and innocents could get seriously hurt in the brawl, or in their panic to escape it.

So far, he'd tried to handle this like a cop. Time to try handling it like a Grimm.

He stepped between the two Jagerbaren, placed his hands on their chests and shoved them back a few inches. They were strong in their Wesen forms, but Nick was stronger than a normal human, and although the Jagerbaren struggled to move toward each other again, Nick held them where they were.

Nick glanced back and forth between the two men. This close, their animal scent was almost overpowering to his enhanced sense of smell, and he felt their combined fury as a physical force. As if in answer, anger welled up within him, and he felt an urge to grab the Jagerbaren by the backs of their heads and smash their faces together. It was his Grimm nature—which wasn't so different from that of the Wesen—urging him to act. These two beasts were a threat, and they had to be put down—*now*.

Nick gritted his teeth and fought the anger down. He was still a cop and couldn't let his emotions get out of control in a tense situation.

Hank caught his eye and gave him a questioning look. They'd been partners for so long that Nick had no trouble interpreting it. Hank was asking if Nick needed him to step in and help. Nick shook his head slightly, the gesture a reply which meant, *Not yet, but stay ready.* Hank acknowledged it with a brief nod.

"You guys know who I am?" Nick asked the cousins. "Or, more importantly, *what* I am?" He kept his voice low, so only the two Jagerbaren could hear him.

Neither replied, but both took a second to glance at him, and while he didn't see fear in their gazes, he did see acknowledgment.

"I'll take that as a yes. Tell me your names."

The cousins returned to glaring at each other, but the clean-shaven one growled, "Josef," and his bearded cousin growled, "Thorsten."

"Now we're getting somewhere." Nick jerked his head toward the girl at the table. She didn't seem distressed at seeing her two suitors confronted by a Grimm. If anything, she looked even more amused by the development. "And what's her name?'

"Sylvia," Josef said.

"Okay. So you two are trying to put on a good show for her, right? You each want her to see you as the strongest and meanest."

Thorsten's gaze flicked to Nick for an instant.

"That's the general idea."

"So how impressive is it that you're standing in the middle of a bar with a Grimm between you, holding you back like you're a couple of little boys caught fighting on the playground?"

Nick watched both of their faces to gauge their reaction to his words. Thorsten looked uncertain, and Nick could tell he'd scored some points with him. Josef, however, narrowed his eyes at Nick and bared his fangs.

"Nice try," Josef said. "My cousin might fall for that crap, but I won't. There's only one way this ends, and that's with one of us on the ground. Preferably *him*." He turned back to glare at Thorsten.

Despite their bestial nature, Jagerbaren—modern ones, at least—tended to be peaceful enough. They reserved their aggressive tendencies for their work, choosing professions in law and politics. But under the influence of alcohol, Jagerbaren could be incredibly dangerous, and Nick could smell that these two had been drinking. And even if he couldn't, the empty mugs on their table would've tipped him off. Nick wasn't sure exactly how alcohol affected them, but he knew one thing: these two were determined to fight, and it didn't look like there was any way to talk them out of it.

Time for Plan B.

"You know, it seems to me that there isn't anything particularly special about one Jagerbar fighting another. If I were you two, I'd be thinking about how much more impressed Sylvia would be if I knocked a Grimm onto his ass. How many Jagerbaren can say they did that?"

Josef and Thorsten exchanged looks, and then their features shifted as they assumed human guises. For the first time since Nick had entered Blind Bill's, he could see the cousins' anger ebbing, replaced by thoughtful calculation.

"I don't like where this is headed," Hank said.

"Me neither," Beverly added.

Up to this point, Sylvia hadn't said a word, but now she leaned back in her chair, crossed her legs, and said, "Well *I* love it."

And just like that, the Jagerbaren's minds were made up for them.

Josef looked at Thorsten, and the two nodded in silent agreement. Josef turned to Nick and said, "You're on."

"Let's step into my office."

Nick removed his hands from the Jagerbaren's chests and started walking toward the door without another glance at them. Nick knew he was taking a gamble by turning his back on the cousins. Without him standing between them, one or both might decide this was an opportunity to catch the other off guard. Or they might decide to attack him inside the bar, hoping to gain an advantage by surprise. But Nick had something going for him that the Jagerbaren didn't. He had a partner. He knew Hank would watch the Jagerbaren for any sign that they intended to renege on their agreement. And even though Nick knew the last thing Hank would do was draw his Glock in here—not with so many bystanders—the cousins didn't know that. And while Jagerbaren might be tough, they weren't bulletproof.

Nick also had a personal reason for wanting to take the fight outside. Not long ago, he'd encountered a Wesen who called himself Baron Samedhi, after the legendary voodoo priest. Samedhi had been a Cracher-Mortel, a puffer-fish-like creature that could spit a type of venom that put its victims into a deathlike state. But the venom had a different effect on Nick due to his Grimm physiology, and he'd become an enraged, near-mindless madman, wandering through the city at random and committing acts of violence. His memories of that time were hazy at best, but he knew that he'd gone into a bar and, predictably enough, a fight had broken out. One of the patrons there that night had pulled a knife on him, and Nick—unable to exert any sort of self-control—had hit the man with all his strength. The strength of a Grimm. The man had died, and even though Nick knew that it was a terrible accident, the incident still weighed heavily on him. If he had to fight tonight, he wasn't going to do it inside a bar. No way.

Nick pushed open the bar door and stepped out into the night. The cool air came as a relief after the stuffiness inside. He looked up, hoping to see stars, but the cloud cover was heavy. Typical for this time of year. He smiled. All in all, not a bad night to fight a couple of monsters.

He continued into the parking lot. He heard the door open again, and he glanced over his shoulder to see Josef and Thorsten following. Hank came after them, followed by Beverly and then Sylvia. No one else came outside, and Nick was glad. The last thing he wanted was an audience who didn't understand what was really going on. He could see the headline in tomorrow's *Tribune*: PORTLAND POLICE OFFICER IN BAR BRAWL! Captain Renard would just *love* that.

Nick picked a spot where there was enough empty space to give him room to maneuver, and sufficient illumination from a nearby streetlight to see clearly. In a fight, every little advantage mattered. He turned around, and as if that was signal, the two cousins started running toward him, hands curled into fists, features contorted into masks of rage.

At least they're working together, Nick thought.

They woged as they came, and although it might have been his imagination, he thought they appeared even more bestial than before. He'd once seen a female Jagerbar transform all the way into a bear, and he had no idea if she was a special case or if all Jagerbaren could do that. He hoped for the former. Fighting a pair of enraged alcohol-fueled Jagerbaren was bad enough. He'd rather not have to deal with a couple of full-grown, pissed-off bears.

His senses, normally heightened, sharpened even further, and a deep calm settled over him. At the same time he felt a surge of energy rush through him, as if somewhere inside him a switch had been thrown. Rather than clashing, these two sensations complemented one another in a strange way he didn't fully understand. All he knew was that it was moments like these, just before battle, that he felt truly himself.

Hank ran behind the Jagerbaren, drawing his Glock in case things got out of hand. Beverly jogged behind him, looking scared as hell. Sylvia walked at a measured pace, as if she were in no hurry. *Too cool for school,* Nick thought.

Nick watched the Jagerbaren approach and tried to get a quick read on them. Would one reach him before the other? Would they attack in unison or take turns? They spread apart as they drew near, and Nick knew they intended to strike at the same time. He doubted they'd planned it that way. At this point they were acting on instinct rather than thought. He'd have to use that to his advantage.

Jagerbaren were fast, but not agile, and as the first one reached him—Thorsten, as it turned out—Nick grabbed hold of the man's wrist with both hands, spun him around, and let go. Off-balance, Thorsten stumbled several stops and then fell, hitting the asphalt hard. Nick didn't wait to see if he got up. He turned to meet Josef's charge. When the Jagerbar was within several feet of Nick, he leaped toward him with a deep bellow, clawed hands outstretched and ready to rend flesh.

Nick started to sidestep to avoid the Jagerbar's claws, but as fast as his reflexes were, they weren't quite quick enough this time. The claws on Josef's right hand clipped his shoulder. The blow would've knocked down a normal man and probably broken his shoulder, too. But Nick managed to stay on his feet, and although he could feel sharp pain where the claws had scratched him, he was otherwise uninjured.

Josef landed on all fours, spun around, and straightened into a standing position. He bellowed a challenge, the sound as much human as it was animal, and came at Nick again. Nick felt a tingling on the back of his neck, and he jumped to the side just as Thorsten made a leap at him from behind. The cousins slammed into each other with a sound like two sides of beef colliding. They staggered backward, stunned, but neither went down.

Of course it couldn't be that easy.

He took advantage of the cousins' momentary confusion and hit Josef with a hard right cross, then advanced on Thorsten and hit him with a left. He didn't pull either punch, for the Wesen were far tougher than ordinary humans and could withstand a great deal more punishment. The impact of the first punch knocked Josef onto his behind, but Thorsten managed to stay on his feet.

Got to work on that left, Nick thought.

Thorsten bellowed and charged, all anger and no finesse. Nick easily avoided the man's attack and caught him on the back of the neck with a savage chop. Thorsten grunted in pain and fell face-first to the ground. Just then Nick's instincts screamed at him to turn around, but before he could do so, Josef wrapped his powerful arms around Nick's chest and squeezed.

Bear hug, Nick thought, and he might've smiled if his ribs hadn't been on the verge of being snapped like toothpicks. Josef had grabbed him from behind, and his arms were pinned to his sides. To make matters worse, Josef leaned back and lifted Nick off the ground, depriving him of the leverage he'd need to fight back.

"Need some help?" Hank called out, sounding more than a little worried.

Nick shook his head once, and although he could barely breathe, he managed to choke out, "Thanks, but I got this."

He dipped his chin to his chest and then threw his head backward with as much force as he could muster. The back of his head slammed into Josef's face, and Nick felt as much as heard the Wesen's nose break. Josef moaned in pain, but while his hold on Nick slackened, he maintained his grip. Nick had to slam his head into Josef's face twice more before he finally released him and slumped to the asphalt semiconscious, his features shifting to human once more.

Nick's ears were ringing and gray nibbled at the corner of his vision, but he wasn't concerned. He knew he'd recover soon. Right now he had more important things to worry about. Like Thorsten.

Nick spun around to face the other Jagerbar, but the man—who like his brother had reassumed his human aspect—was standing still and looking straight past Nick. Nick turned to look in the same direction, and he saw Sylvia walking away. She pulled keys from her purse, thumbed the remote, and the locks on a Lexus clicked open. She got in, turned on the engine, flicked on the headlights, backed out of her space, hit the gas, and roared onto the street without so much as a backward glance.

Hank joined Nick.

"I think it's safe to say that lady wasn't impressed by either of her would-be suitors," he said.

"Yeah." Nick looked at Thorsten once more. He expected the man to take out his frustration and disappointment on the Grimm who'd embarrassed him in front of Sylvia. But the man seemed subdued, all the fight drained out of him. He walked over to his cousin, who'd risen to one knee but didn't look ready to stand up yet. Thorsten held out his hand, and after a moment Josef took it and allowed his cousin to help him to his feet. His nose was swollen and crooked, and blood had spilled over his mouth and chin, and onto his shirt. Thorsten's face looked equally as bad, scraped and bruised from where he'd struck the asphalt.

The two regarded each other for several seconds.

"Buy you a drink?" Josef said.

Thorsten shrugged. "I guess. After you get yourself cleaned up, that is."

Josef nodded and the two men started walking back toward the bar, their bruises, cuts, and scrapes already in the process of healing.

"Hey," Nick called.

The cousins stopped and turned to look at him.

"Stick to club soda this time, okay?"

The men nodded and resumed walking back to Blind Bill's.

Beverly had hung back during the fight, but now she joined Nick and Hank.

"Thank you *so* much for coming, both of you! You're real lifesavers!"

Nick smiled. "You're welcome, but all we did was break up a bar fight."

"Between two guys with fangs and claws," Hank pointed out.

"There is that," Nick agreed.

"Well. I really appreciate it," Beverly said. "And you won't have to worry about those two. Not for the rest of the night, anyway. They'll stick around and have a couple sodas to save as much face as they can, then they'll go home and lick their wounds. Metaphorically speaking." She grinned, thanked them again, and started back toward the bar. Halfway across the parking lot, she stopped and turned back around to face them. "You know something? You're not what I expected from a Grimm."

She gave them a last wave and continued toward the bar.

"Yeah," Nick said. "I get that a lot."

Hank pulled the Dodge Charger out of Blind Bill's parking lot, Nick riding shotgun. Even though it was cool out,

Hank lowered the driver's side window a couple of inches.

"Do I offend?" Nick asked jokingly.

"Are you kidding? You barely broke a sweat with those two. I just like the smell of fall, you know? How's your shoulder?"

"Fine. The scratches weren't deep. I'll need to get the rip sewn, though."

Luckily for Beverly, Nick and Hank had been working the late shift. There had been a robbery at a liquor store the night before, and the clerk behind the counter had tried to stop it and got himself killed for his attempt at heroism. Nick and Hank had been canvassing the neighborhood, showing around a photo of the robber that had been captured by the store's security camera. They'd been at it an hour or so without any luck when Beverly called, and they'd rushed to Blind Bill's.

The liquor-store robbery had taken place on the other side of town, and Hank headed back in that direction. They had a couple more hours of showing photos and asking questions ahead of them until their shift was over.

"Ready to go back to pounding the pavement?" Hank said.

"That's where real police work gets done, right?" Nick said.

"That's what they told us at the academy, anyway." Hank paused before going on. "Tell me something, do you ever get bored with regular police work?"

Nick glanced over at his partner. "I'm not sure what you mean."

"Well, one minute you're walking the street, asking people 'Have you seen this man?' and the next you're fighting a pair of drunk bear-creatures mano-a-mano-a-mano. Waving blurry photos around in front of people seems pretty dull compared to that."

"I don't know. I guess I haven't really thought about it. In a way, it's all the same thing to me, you know?"

"To serve and protect," Hank said.

Nick smiled. "Something like that. When it first started happening—all the Grimm stuff, I mean—I would've loved for all of it to have gone away so I could have my normal life back. Most of all, I hated lying to you and Juliette about it."

Nick still felt guilty whenever he thought about how long he'd concealed the truth from both his partner and fiancée: that the world was filled with creatures called Wesen who appeared human but could change into bestial forms when they wished. These creatures were responsible for many of humanity's myths and legends, and a special breed of humans called Grimms hunted them—Nick was descended from this ancient line of monster killers. He'd told himself that he was hiding his identity as a Grimm to protect them, and while that was true, a small part of the reason was so he could hold onto a remnant of his normal life. Hank and Juliette had been like refuges from the craziness, even though they'd both got caught up in it eventually, despite his best efforts. But they knew the whole truth now, and they'd understood why he'd lied to them and, more importantly, they'd forgiven him. He was glad. He didn't think he could do this without their love and support.

His ancestors—the Grimms of old—had been known and feared as merciless slayers of Wesen. They were supposed to hunt only "bad" Wesen, but from the accounts Nick had read in his Aunt Marie's books, some of his ancestors had a pretty loose interpretation of the word "bad." He sometimes wondered if those Grimms had been that way because they lacked the kind of support he was lucky enough to have. Not just from Juliette and Hank, but from Monroe and Rosalee, too, and he supposed even from Captain Renard—although he wasn't completely sure about him—and even Wesen like Bud Wurstner. Without all of them in his life, would he become a hard-hearted killing machine like the Grimms of legend? He thought of the man he'd killed while in the grip of the Cracher-Mortel venom. *Maybe,* he thought. He just hoped he'd never have to find out.

With effort, he turned his mind away from this dark train of thought.

"How about you?" he asked Hank. "I was born to this kind of thing. In a way, I'm like the Wesen, just following my true nature. I'm sure I could stop if I wanted to. Do you ever wish I hadn't dragged you into my weird world?'

"You may be my partner, but you didn't drag me into anything. I may be a garden-variety *Homo sapiens*, but once I learned what the world was really like… well, I just couldn't turn a blind eye to it, you know?'

Nick knew very well indeed.

Hank continued. "Sometimes I wonder just how many Wesen there are. There's something like seven billion people in the world, right? How many of those do you think are Wesen? A fifth? A quarter? More? There's no way to know. They can see each other for what they are, and you can see them, but ordinary humans like me can't. When I first leaned about Wesen, I was pretty paranoid. I kept looking at people and wondering, 'Is he one? Is she?' It started driving me crazy after a while."

"Why didn't you ever say anything to me about it?"

Hank shrugged. "You adjusted. I figured I would, too. And I did. You know what helped? I realized the reason Wesen hide from humans isn't so that they can prey on us more effectively—although admittedly that's what some do. It's because they know how humans would react and what they would do if they ever learned the truth."

Nick thought about his ancestors' attitude toward Wesen. They'd lived in very different times, when prejudice, racism and classism were far more prevalent than they were today. But however enlightened the modern world might be, Nick knew the majority of the human race wasn't ready to accept the existence of Wesen. Maybe one day it would be different, but for now, it was a good thing they could hide so effectively.

They drove in silence after that for a time, Nick gazing out the passenger window and watching the city go by. Eventually Hank broke the silence.

"Something's bugging you. I can tell."

Nick smiled. Sometimes he wondered how he'd ever managed to keep his being a Grimm secret from Hank.

"It's just a little strange to get a call like that, you know? From Beverly, I mean."

"You talking about getting asked to break up a bar fight? I admit, it's not the usual sort of thing highly skilled and devastatingly handsome homicide detectives like us do."

"That's not it. I'm a Grimm. The Wesen think of my kind as cold-hearted killers, almost monsters. You've seen how they react when they realize what I am."

"Yeah. Some of them are pretty damned scared."

Nick nodded. "I was never comfortable with that, but it proved useful sometimes. But I've been, for lack of a better word, 'out' as a Grimm for a while now, and some of the Wesen in town—like Beverly—are starting to treat me differently. Like a… I don't know exactly."

"A protector," Hank said. "Someone they can turn to when they're in trouble."

"Yeah. I mean, that's a good thing, right? But for some reason, it makes me a little uncomfortable."

"That's because you're too modest. You need to accept

the whole hero thing, maybe get yourself a tricked-out Grimm-mobile."

"It's not modesty. I don't know what it is."

"Maybe it's a Grimm thing. You know, like with cats and dogs."

Nick frowned. "I'm afraid you lost me there."

"Dogs and cats don't get along in general, right? It's an instinct thing. In the wild they're competing predators. Maybe you're not comfortable with Wesen reacting positively to you because deep down, the Grimm part of you expects them to be afraid. Who knows? Maybe it even *wants* them to be."

"Great. So you're saying I *am* a monster."

"I'm saying that whatever else is going on, you're a man named Nick Burkhardt, and you get to make your own choices about who you want to be." He smiled. "Besides, my family had both cats and dogs when I was growing up, and they got along well enough. It just takes some adjustment."

"I suppose. But what if—"

Nick's phone rang then, and he removed it from his pocket and answered it.

"Burkhardt."

"Wu here. I know you guys are working that liquor-store homicide, but I've got something strange over by the community college. And since you and Hank kind of specialize in strange, I figured you'd want to come check it out."

Nick glanced at Hank.

"Give me the details."

CHAPTER THREE

"Maybe you should slow down, honey. You don't want to make yourself sick."

Rich Webber stood in the kitchen, leaning against the counter, a bottle of beer in his hand. He hadn't opened it yet, and in truth, he'd forgotten he was holding it. He was too concerned about his wife.

Dana sat at the small table—there was only the two of them, and they didn't need anything larger—hunched over an open carton of ice cream. Butter pecan, to be exact. She was shoveling huge spoonfuls into her mouth and swallowing them down without bothering to chew. Rich was afraid she might choke, but if she was aware of the danger, she didn't seem to care. The lower half of her face was smeared with ice cream and blobs of it were melting on the table around her. When she'd arrived home, Rich had been in the front room watching pro wrestling on TV. He knew it was fake, but he loved it anyway. The colorfully named characters, the heroes and villains… It was like watching a comic book come to life. Dana hated wrestling, though. No, *hate* wasn't a strong enough word for it. She *loathed* it, so he only watched it when she wasn't home.

When she arrived tonight, carrying a bag of groceries, he'd been so caught up in the match—a showdown between two archrivals—that at first he didn't hear her come in. When he finally noticed her standing there, front door still open and staring at the TV screen, he'd expected her to make some sort of disparaging remark, something along the lines of, "Aren't you too old to be watching this junk?" or, "Glad to see you're making yourself useful while I'm out." But she hadn't said anything. She'd just closed the door—without locking it, which was weird because she was almost OCD when it came to locking doors—and then headed to the kitchen without saying a word.

He'd tried returning his attention to the match, but he couldn't get back into it, not after Dana's strange entrance. So he turned off the TV, got off the living room couch, and went into the kitchen. He'd found the groceries sitting out in the hallway, as if she'd been too impatient, or maybe just absent-minded, to put them on the kitchen counter. She was sitting at the table, just starting to dig into the ice cream. That had been only a few minutes ago, and in that time he'd taken a beer out of the fridge and held it while Dana devoured butter pecan. As near as he could tell, she'd managed to polish off three-quarters of the container so far, and she showed no signs of stopping before she'd eaten the entire thing.

Something was wrong, that much was obvious, but he was hesitant to ask her what it might be. She wasn't the type of person who ate when she was upset or depressed. She was more the hold-me-while-I-cry type. So whatever had happened to make her want to go on an ice-cream binge, he figured it had to be pretty bad.

He raised the beer bottle to his mouth, intending to take a sip and stall for another moment, but he'd forgotten he hadn't opened it, and he hit one of his eyeteeth on the cap.

"Ow! Damn it!"

Dana was usually so attentive to her husband that she hurried toward him whenever he hurt himself, even if only in the smallest of ways. But she didn't even look up, just continued gorging herself, oblivious.

Rich put the bottle on the counter, stepped over to the table, pulled out a chair, and sat.

"Did something happen in class tonight?" he asked. "Or on the way home? Maybe when you stopped for groceries?"

She kept eating, one heaped spoonful after another. He could hear the spoon scrape the bottom of the container now, and he knew she'd almost polished it off. He wanted to reach out and take her hand, but he couldn't bring himself to. For the first time since they'd been married, hell, in the entire time that he'd known her, he was scared of her.

"Dana, please talk to me."

She lifted the last spoonful of ice cream, swallowed it, and then licked the spoon clean. She examined the inside of the empty container, and her lower lip protruded in a pouty expression that made her look like a disappointed child. Then finally, Dana looked up at Rich.

"I like ice cream," she said.

"Yeah, I can see that."

And now that her face wasn't lowered over an ice-cream container, Rich could see something else as well. She looked sick. Her skin was pale, the flesh around her eyes so dark it almost looked bruised. The eyes seemed to have receded into their sockets, too, and her cheeks were sunken in. Her hair looked dry and stiff, like straw. As he watched, several strands detached from her head and fell to the tabletop, where they became mired in melting smears of butter pecan.

"I like ice cream," she repeated. She smiled this time, revealing yellowed teeth and sore, bleeding gums.

Equal parts fear and revulsion swept through him. "Oh my God, Dana, what happened to you?"

He rose and hurried to her side. He took her hand now, and found it sticky with ice cream, but beneath that, it felt frail and fragile as a baby bird. He was afraid the bones would break if he grasped it too tightly.

Rich was on the verge of panic now. "We need to get you to a hospital, honey. Can you stand? Here, let me help—"

That was as far as he got before Dana's elbow slammed into his chin. Despite her sickly appearance, there was no weakness in the strike, and Rich's teeth clacked together hard, shearing off the tip of his tongue. His head snapped back, and he staggered to the side. His shoulder hit the refrigerator door, and he slumped into a sitting position. His vision was blurry, pain throbbed in his skull, and his tongue felt as if it were on fire. His mouth was filled with something warm and wet, and he spit it out. At first he didn't recognize the crimson fluid that splattered onto the kitchen floor, but then his vision cleared and he realized he was looking at blood. *His* blood. And lying in the middle of it was a tiny hunk of meat that used to be attached to his tongue.

He was still staring at the blood when he heard Dana's chair slide on the floor. He glanced toward her and saw her rise and walk past him to the kitchen counter.

"I can't go to the hospital, Rich," she said. Her voice sounded thick and wet, almost as if she were trying to speak while gargling.

She reached across the counter and removed a large knife from the butcher block. She gripped it tightly as she turned around to face him.

"I'm going to stay right here," she said. "After all, this is my home." She paused and then added, "Now."

Rich pressed his palm to the refrigerator's surface and

used its mass to support him as he stood. He knew he should be afraid. Something had happened to Dana to turn her crazy and violent. She'd already hurt him, and now she was gripping a knife and staring at him with cold, dead calm. And he *was* scared, sure, but mostly he was worried. The woman he loved needed help, and he had to convince her to let him get her that help before she did something—

The expression on Dana's face didn't change as she raised the knife and swung it in a vicious backhanded strike. Rich's throat opened as easily as if it were made of paper, and blood gushed onto his chest like a waterfall. He took two steps backward, his mouth opening and closing as if he were trying to speak, but no sound emerged. His legs collapsed beneath him, and he fell to the floor. He didn't feel it when he hit. He lay there, head turned to the side, blood pouring from his wound, pooling on the floor in front of his face. He felt himself slipping away into nothingness, and the last thing he heard was the sound of the freezer opening. He realized that Dana was searching for more ice cream.

And then he was gone.

The creature that now thought of itself as Dana Webber closed the freezer door in disgust. Nothing but bags of vegetables and boxes of microwaveable meals. What a disappointment.

She noticed the body lying on the floor and realized she was holding a knife. The blade was slick with blood, and there was more blood—a lot of it—on the floor around the man's head.

"Rich," she said. "He's my husband."

She remembered what she had done. Had it really been only a few minutes earlier? She knew it was happening again, and much faster this time. She was already losing her grasp on this new identity. Her thoughts were as hard to hold onto as mist, and her body was burning itself out at a rapid rate. She felt lightheaded, feverish, weak. She looked at Rich's corpse and regretted her impulsiveness in killing him. She could only assume the identity of the living; she should've left him alive and saved him for when she needed him. But he'd threatened to take her somewhere. She couldn't remember exactly where, but it was somewhere she hadn't wanted to go, she knew that much. So she'd had no choice but to kill him—hadn't she?

If only she could think straight...

One thing was certain. She needed a new identity, and she needed it fast. If she didn't manage to change before this body burnt itself out completely, then that would be the end of the road for her. She'd lived a very long time, so long she couldn't number the years. But she wasn't ready to die yet. She'd do anything, *become* anything, in order to survive. It was the way of her kind.

Whatever she was going to do, she had to do it quickly, before—

Her thoughts, scattered and desperate, were interrupted by a knocking at the front door. She grinned. It seemed as if her dilemma was about to be resolved.

"Just a minute!" she called out.

She looked down at her clothing, and was relieved to see she'd managed to escape getting bloodstains on it. She caught her reflection in the toaster and grabbed a handful of paper towels from the counter, quickly cleaning the ice cream off her face. She tossed the used towels in the sink and then concentrated. Her physical appearance shifted as she once more assumed a guise of health and strength. She had to draw on this body's dwindling energy reserves to effect the transformation, but she could hardly answer the door looking half-dead. The last thing she wanted to do was make her visitor suspicious.

The knocking came again, louder this time.

"Coming!" she shouted, and hurried to the door, grinning in excitement. She wondered who she was going to be next.

But when she opened the door to find a man in a police uniform standing there, her hopes died away. A police officer meant trouble. Perhaps someone had seen her duplicate Dana Webber and had called in a report. She knew better than to take someone out in the open like that, but she'd been so desperate... Her instincts for self-preservation kicked in, and she decided to hide in this identity for the time being rather than risk taking the officer. She'd already made a couple of serious mistakes by being impulsive tonight. She didn't want to risk making another.

"Good evening, ma'am," the officer said. "My name's Sergeant Wu, and I'm with the Portland Police Department. Do you mind if I ask you a few questions?"

She forced a smile.

"Not at all."

"That's supposed to be a body?" Nick said.

Nick, Hank, and Sergeant Wu stood on the sidewalk, looking down at a colorless, viscous mass containing bits of solid material that Nick had to admit looked uncomfortably like pieces of bone.

Sergeant Wu was an Asian American man, lean and athletically built, dressed in a police uniform. He had a permanently wry expression on his face that made him look equal parts cynical and amused.

"According to the man who called in the report, yes." Wu referred to his notebook. "A Mr. Ernest Delgado called 911 at 8:27 p.m. to report that he was taking out the trash when he saw a woman lying face-down on the sidewalk in this exact spot. According to Mr. Delgado, she was unconscious and wasn't breathing. He went inside to call an ambulance, but by the time he'd hung up, she was gone."

"Anyone else see anything?" Hank asked.

"I spoke with the neighbors. One Mrs. Dana Webber was of the opinion that Mr. Delgado is, and I quote: 'A crazy old bastard who needs to mind his own business.' So no."

"But diligent law officer that you are, you decided to check the sidewalk," Nick said.

"I *am* known for my thoroughness," Wu said. "And I found this." He nodded to the liquid mass and grimaced. "Reminds me of something a cat would yak up. A very big cat." He flipped his notebook closed and looked at Nick. "That's when I called you two."

Wu didn't know about Wesen or Nick's identity as a Grimm, but he was highly intelligent and one hell of a cop. He might not suspect there was a possibility that something unnatural had occurred here, but he knew better than to completely dismiss Mr. Delgado's story when there was some kind of physical evidence at the scene.

"Did you call in CSU yet?" Hank asked.

"Honestly, I was waiting for you guys to make that call," Wu said. "Do you really think there's a chance that glop is human remains? Acid couldn't dissolve a body in the timeframe we're talking about, right?"

"I don't know," Nick said. "Let's let the crime lab figure it out. And have the Coroner's office send someone out, too. Just in case."

"You got it." Wu took out his phone and stepped off to the side to make the calls.

When Wu was out of earshot, Hank said, "You know anything that can do this to a person?"

Hank didn't speak the word *Wesen*, but Nick knew what his partner meant.

"No. This is a new one on me."

"But you think it *is* something," Hank pressed.

"Maybe."

Wu finished his calls and rejoined them.

"CSU's on the way, along with the Deputy Coroner."

"Good," Nick said. "Do you mind staying here to keep an eye on this… stuff until they get here? Hank and I need to talk to Mr. Delgado."

"And Mrs. Webber," Hank added.

"Sure," Wu said, a sarcastic edge to his voice. "There's nothing I'd love more than to babysit a giant puddle of phlegm."

"Then this is your lucky night." Nick clapped Wu on the shoulder, then he turned to Hank. "Which do you want?"

"I'll take Mr. Delgado. It sounds like he'll have the better story."

Nick smiled. "I'll take Mrs. Webber then."

Wu directed Hank across the street toward Mr. Delgado's house, and Nick headed to the Webbers'. He walked up the driveway, past the car and up the front steps to the door. He knocked, waited for a response, and when he didn't get one, knocked again.

This time the door opened, but only a crack.

"Yes?" said a woman's voice.

Nick could only see one eye and part of her face.

"I'm Detective Burkhardt." He took hold of the badge her wore around his neck and held it up so she could get a better look at it. "Are you Dana Webber?"

The woman didn't bother looking at his badge. Instead, she kept her gaze fixed on his eyes. There was an unsettling intensity in the way she looked at him, almost as if she were sizing him up somehow. Judging him.

She opened the door the rest of the way and smiled. "That's me."

Nick let his badge drop.

"You spoke with Sergeant Wu earlier. I'm just here to follow up. One of your neighbors reported seeing something out of the ordinary outside earlier tonight, and I was hoping you might be able to answer a few questions for me."

He watched the woman closely to gauge her reaction to his request. A person's response to a cop showing up at their door could tell you a lot about them. She didn't appear nervous; if anything, she seemed happy to see him. Maybe too happy.

Her smile widened until it was almost a grin, and she opened the door the rest of the way and stepped aside.

"Come in, please."

As he entered, a snatch of nursery rhyme drifted into his mind. *Come into my parlor...*

He told himself that he was being paranoid. Suspicion was an occupational hazard for a cop, and it had only gotten worse since he'd become aware of his identity as a Grimm. He had a tendency to think that, until proven otherwise, everyone he met was Wesen and potentially dangerous. He didn't want to think like this, though. It wasn't a healthy way to live, let alone do his job properly. "Innocent until proven guilty" wasn't just a legal maxim when you were a cop. It was an important reminder, and he did his best to live by those words as both a cop *and* as a Grimm. Maybe if his ancestors had done the same, they wouldn't have the bloodthirsty reputation that they did.

So there'd been a report of something weird happening in the neighborhood tonight, and there was a strange puddle of goo on the sidewalk. That didn't necessarily mean Wesen were involved. Then again, it didn't mean they weren't, either.

Dana closed the door and locked it. Nick found that odd. In his experience, most people didn't lock the door after letting the police inside. It might just be a habit, though, especially if she was security-conscious. But this wasn't a dangerous neighborhood. He mentally shrugged. Who said he was the only one allowed to be a little paranoid?

The Webbers' front door led to an open hallway, to the left of which was a small living space consisting of a couch, chair, chrome-and-glass coffee table, and a medium-sized flat-screen TV sitting on top of a wooden stand.

Dana gestured toward the couch. "Would you like to sit down?"

"Sure."

He took a seat on the couch, and she sat in the chair next to it.

"According to Sergeant Wu's notes, you're married," Nick said. "Is your husband here?"

She hesitated. Not long, only a split second, but enough for him to notice.

"He went to the store."

"Really? Because there's a sack of groceries out in the hall."

Another hesitation, a bit longer this time.

"We needed more ice cream."

There was something off about her reply. Not the words themselves, although they were strange enough, but rather the way they sounded. They sounded slurred, as if her mouth had trouble forming them.

"All you all right?" he asked.

"Fine. Never better." It sound like she said *"Ffffine. Neffer bedder."*

Her voice was lower now, the words garbled and drawn out, as if it were a recording that was slowing down. Her facial features slacked, the skin sagging as if she were

47

aging before his eyes. No, not aging. More like *melting*. He thought of the goo puddle on the sidewalk that Wu was guarding.

He stood. "Mrs. Webber, I think you should—"

"Sorry," she said. "I tried to keep myself together. I'm so glad I restrained myself and left the other officer alone. You're a strong one. Stronger than anyone I've ever met before. I could sense it when I opened the door. You'll do just fine."

Her head tilted to one side and then the other in a gesture Nick had become very familiar with over the last few years. Her hair withdrew into her skull and her sagging features disappeared as her flesh became a silvery liquid mass. She no longer had eyes, ears, nose, or mouth—just a rippling quicksilver surface that was unlike anything he had ever seen before. If she was Wesen, she was a type new to him. All of her skin had taken on a silvery cast, and she—if she even *was* a she anymore—raised her silver hands and flexed all ten of her fingers in a single spastic motion. Needle-like spines extended from her fingertips, and she leaped out of the chair and came at him.

Nick had no idea what those finger spines could do, but he didn't want to find out. Moving with inhuman speed, he grabbed hold of the metal-and-glass coffee table and swung it toward the faceless creature. Glass shattered as the table struck the creature's outstretched hands, and the impact knocked her to the side. She stumbled and hit the TV, knocking it off the stand. Only the metal frame of the coffee table remained in Nick's hands, and he threw it aside and reached for his Glock.

The creature recovered quickly and lunged toward him again, hands outstretched once more. The impact of the coffee table had broken off several of her finger spines, but most remained intact. Nick had barely freed his gun from its holster when the creature hit him. It grabbed hold of his neck with both hands, and he felt piercing pain as the black spines sank into his flesh.

The creature knocked him back onto the couch, and their momentum caused the entire thing to fall over backward. As they fell, Nick grabbed hold of the creature by the upper arm, raised his knee to its stomach, and as they rolled, he thrust it away from him. The creature flew through the air, and Nick grunted as the finger-spines tore free from his neck. The pain ebbed as soon as he felt it, though, as if the creature had injected him with some sort of anesthetic.

The creature hit the far wall, bounced off, and landed face-first on the hardwood floor. Nick rolled to his feet, Glock still in hand, and as he spun around, he flicked off the safety and drew a bead on the creature.

"Don't move or I'll…"

A sudden wave of weariness washed over him, so intense that it was almost crippling. His weapon seemed to increase in weight until it was too heavy to hold. It slipped from his fingers and dropped to the floor. His legs could no longer support his body, and he fell onto his side, his head thudding against the wood. A not altogether unpleasant sensation of numbness spread throughout his body, and it became a struggle to keep his eyes open. He wanted to sleep so badly, just for a little bit, until he could get his strength back. He almost did, but at that moment the creature—which had lain still after hitting the floor—bucked violently, as if a high voltage current surged though its body. It flipped onto its back and with a single motion, rose to a sitting position.

Can't sleep, Nick thought. *Have to… stop it.*

He got his hands beneath him and struggled to push himself up. He couldn't remember ever feeling so weak before, but he kept at it, and he began to feel a measure of his strength return.

The creature had been wearing what Nick presumed were Dana Webber's clothes, but now the sweater and pants took on the same silvery color as its flesh. The clothes seemed to sink into the creature's body, to merge with it, until it became a single smooth surface. There was no hint of gender to the form, and it no longer had separate fingers or toes. Spines still jutted from its hand, but they retracted now, and the creature turned its featureless face toward Nick. Despite the fact that it had no eyes, Nick had the sense that the creature was regarding him somehow. As he watched, features began to emerge from the silvery substance, but before it could resolve into an actual face, the creature looked away from him, stood, and started toward the door.

It gripped the knob and tried to open it, but the door was locked. It tried the knob again, as if it had forgotten it had locked it earlier. As Nick rose to his feet, he saw the creature's hands had grown fingers again, and its silver skin was changing color. Black hair emerged from its scalp, and it grew taller, its shoulder broadening. A jacket, shirt, jeans, and shoes formed—or at least the appearance of them. The creature's back was to him, so Nick couldn't see its face, assuming it had one yet. The creature finally remembered to unlock the door, then it opened it and stepped out into the night.

Nick was feeling stronger by the second, and he quickly retrieved his Glock from where it had fallen and hurried out the door after the creature. He still felt a trifle lightheaded and unsteady on his feet, but the cold night air drove away the last of the weariness, and his mind felt sharp and alert once more. The puncture wounds on his neck stung like crazy now, but he didn't bother to check to see if he was bleeding, and if so, how badly. He had work to do.

As he ran onto the Webbers' small lawn, he swung his

head back and forth, searching for the creature—or rather, the person the creature had become. He didn't see anyone except Wu, who was still standing next to the goo puddle, waiting for the Crime Scene Unit and the Deputy Coroner to arrive. Nick jogged over to him, gun in hand, and Wu immediately drew his weapon.

"Everything okay?" Wu asked.

Nick didn't bother to explain. Besides, how could he?

"Did you see anyone run out of the Webbers' home?"

Wu shook his head. "Only person I've seen is you. Who was it? Mrs. Webber?"

Nick started to answer, but he realized he had no idea what to say.

"I… don't think so."

Wu frowned.

"What do you mean, didn't you see who it was?"

"It was a man." Nick was confident of that much, at least. "Dark hair, about my height."

"That narrows it down to several thousand people in Portland," Wu said. "Should be easy enough to find."

Wu holstered his gun, and Nick did the same. Whatever appearance the creature had assumed, the thing was long gone by now. There was no telling which direction it had taken, and since Nick hadn't gotten a good look at its new face, he probably wouldn't recognize it if he saw it again. And he had no idea how often it could change appearance. Even if he managed to track it down, it might look like someone else entirely by then.

Wu frowned again and stepped closer to Nick.

"What happened to your neck?"

CHAPTER FOUR

By the time Hank had finished with Mr. Delgado and rejoined Nick and Wu, both CSU and the Deputy Coroner had arrived, and Nick took Hank aside as the men and women began their work. Wu looked a little put out not to be invited to join them, but he didn't say anything. Nick didn't like excluding Wu. He was a good cop, and he deserved to know the truth about the bizarre cases he sometimes found himself on the periphery of. But Nick had placed both Hank and Juliette in danger by introducing them to the world of Wesen and Grimms, and while he knew they wouldn't have had it any other way, he wanted to keep Wu out of it if he could. For the man's own safety, if nothing else. Besides, it was nice to have one friend he didn't have to worry about all the time.

"What's up?" Hank asked.

"I don't know for sure, but whatever it is, it's not good," Nick said. "Something was in the Webbers' house. It looked like Dana Webber, but it wasn't her. It started to... to lose its shape, almost like it couldn't hold onto it anymore. It attacked me. That's how I got these." He pointed to his neck.

Hank made a face. "Looks like a bunch of bug bites. You okay?"

"Yeah. I was weak at first, almost like I'd been drugged or something. But I feel all right now. A little fuzzyheaded, maybe, like when you're coming down with a cold, but that's all."

Hank frowned. "You say the thing stuck you?"

"Yeah. It grew needles on its fingers, kind of like hypodermics."

"Ouch. I hate needles." Hank shuddered before continuing. "So what does it look like now?"

"I don't know, as it left it started to take on a new shape. A man's. I didn't get a good look at it, though."

"You think this thing is responsible for the pile of goo over there?"

"Could be. I know one thing, though. When I asked the creature where Dana's husband was, it told me that he'd gone to the store, even though she'd just gotten home with groceries."

"There's a car in the driveway. You think the Webbers have another?"

"I don't know, I'll ask Wu to run a search."

"I think we'd better go back into their house and find out what happened to Mr. Webber," Hank said. "How much do you want to bet that whatever it was, it wasn't pretty?"

"No bet."

Together the partners headed for the Webbers' house, guns drawn.

The Wechselbalg ran through the night, cutting across backyards, hurdling short fences and climbing the higher ones with almost ridiculous ease. The creature had worn many faces during the course of its long life, and it had possessed many bodies. But it had never experienced such strength and energy before. It was almost intoxicating, and it—no, *he*—couldn't help laughing with exuberance as he ran.

Normally after a transformation, the Wechselbalg's mind was a jumble of information as the new memories he had acquired from his latest host settled. But his current confusion was far worse than usual. A riot of sights, sounds, thoughts, and emotions swirled inside the creature's brain, and no matter how hard he tried, he couldn't make sense of the deluge. He wasn't even sure why he was running, only that it was really important that he do so. Eventually he found himself jogging down a sidewalk, and he slowed to a walk. He didn't feel tired in the slightest, and he wasn't breathing hard either. Extraordinary!

He maintained a brisk pace as he walked, and was soon out of the residential area and entering a business district. Nothing fancy, just gas stations, fast-food restaurants, and convenience stores. The street was busier here—more pedestrians and vehicles—and the Wechselbalg felt more relaxed. Camouflage was the creature's primary defense, and his kind always felt more comfortable when lost in a crowd.

He wasn't sure how long he continued walking, but eventually his mind began to clear and he was able to start making sense of the newfound data crammed into his skull. The first thing he realized was that something had gone wrong this time. The information he possessed was fragmentary and incomplete. Was something wrong with the man he'd duplicated? Was he ill, or worse, insane? But as the Wechselbalg continued sifting through the imperfect memories, he realized what had happened. The man he'd copied—a police detective, as it turned out—was a Grimm. The realization came as such a shock that he stopped walking. People gave him strange looks as they moved around him, but he paid them no attention.

A Grimm... He knew about them, of course. What Wesen didn't? But he'd never see one before, let alone interacted with one. And he'd done much more than that, hadn't he? He'd *joined* with one, taken on his shape and copied his memories. Some of them, at any rate.

Although he hadn't witnessed it, he assumed the Grimm had undergone the *Auflösen*, the dissolving process, just as all his other victims had. But the Wechselbalg's new memories told him the Grimm hadn't worked alone. He had friends, allies, some of them quite powerful. He experienced a surge of fear accompanied by a powerful urge to shed this form and don another so the Grimm's companions wouldn't recognize him. Without thinking, he flexed his hands and black spines began to emerge. He would grab hold of the next person who came within reach—man, woman, young, old, it didn't matter—and he would assume their identity right here in the open, regardless of who might see.

A tall, redheaded woman wearing a tight, long-sleeved black dress came toward him, and he started to raise his hands. But then he hesitated. The bodies he took these days didn't last long at all, but so far this one was showing no signs of wear. It was strong, far stronger than any he'd ever had before. Did he really want to give it up so soon?

The redheaded woman passed by, giving him a glance and a smile as she did. He watched her go, his finger spines retracting.

The Grimm's allies didn't matter, he decided, for the simple reason that *he* was the Grimm now. He could fool them into thinking he was their friend. After all, he'd had many years of experience at pretending to be something he wasn't. All he had to do was get to know who the

Grimm was and become him. Simple as that.

A memory came to him then, the sound of a woman's voice, so strong and clear it was almost as if she were present and speaking right next to him.

You have to hunt down the bad ones.

He remembered the woman's name. It was Aunt Marie. *His* Aunt Marie. And with her name came his own. He was Nick Burkhardt. He was a Grimm. And he had work to do.

The Wechselbalg started walking down the sidewalk again, humming happily to himself.

"At least this one's still solid," Wu said.

Nick and Hank looked at him.

"I'm just saying it's a lot easier to work with an actual body."

Wu was one of those cops who sometimes took the whole professional detachment thing a bit too far, Nick thought. Then again, he had to admit that practically speaking, Wu had a point.

Crime-scene technicians were processing the kitchen, while the Deputy Coroner knelt next to Rich Webber's corpse. One of the CSU techs had remained outside with what Nick was fairly certain were the liquefied remains of Dana Webber. Everyone else had relocated to the Webbers' kitchen after Nick and Hank had discovered Rich's body.

"I know that look," Hank said.

"What?" Nick asked.

"You're thinking that if you'd known Mr. Webber was in the kitchen when you were talking with—" he paused "—*Mrs. Webber*, you might've been able to get to him before he died, maybe even save his life."

"Yeah."

"Don't beat yourself up," the Deputy Coroner said. He

was a stocky man in his mid-thirties, with curly black hair, glasses, and a thin mustache. He wore a coroner's jacket, slacks, rubber gloves on his hands and blue cloth booties over his shoes. "Even if you'd been standing in the kitchen when he was attacked, you couldn't have saved him. The way he was cut, he was basically dead before he hit the floor."

Nick had seen enough murder victims to know the man spoke the truth, but it didn't make him feel any better.

Nick turned to Hank. "Now that this is officially a homicide investigation, I think we should have another chat with Mr. Delgado. If nothing else, I'd like to get a look at him."

Wu raised a questioning eyebrow at that comment, but Hank nodded in understanding. Nick wanted to meet Mr. Delgado and see if he might be Wesen. If so, they'd be able to talk to him openly about what he witnessed.

Nick looked at Wu. "Can you hold down the fort here?"

"Consider it held," Wu said.

Nick thanked him, and he and Hank left the kitchen, walked down a short hallway to the living room, then out the open front door. As they made their way to the sidewalk, Nick glanced toward the lone CSU tech and saw she was collecting samples from the goo puddle.

"So we're dealing with some kind of shapeshifting Wesen that kills people by turning them into tapioca," Hank said.

"Looks like."

The partners stepped into the street and continued walking as they talked.

"The creature seems to have trouble maintaining a stable form," Nick said. "It was starting to fall apart, almost melting as if it was made of wax or something."

"But it managed to assume a new body before it left," Hank said.

"Maybe it just needed some time," Nick said. "What I can't figure out is why it cut Mr. Webber's throat instead of dissolving him."

"You got me," Hank said.

"You know, the creature didn't make a lot of sense when it talked. It seemed off somehow, like it wasn't thinking straight."

"You think maybe its brain was melting, too?" Hank asked.

"Something like that. It could explain why it killed Rich Webber instead of dissolving him. It just acted on impulse instead of thinking the situation through."

"Could be," Hank agreed. They reached the other side of the street, and he nodded toward a simple house with a black shingled roof and red-brick walls. "This is it."

Nick looked at it for a moment, then turned to gauge the distance to the Webbers' house and to the spot on the sidewalk where the CSU tech was working.

"It's a fair distance," he said.

"Not to worry. Our man tells me he has eyes like a hawk."

Nick smiled. "Then I wouldn't trust a thing he says."

They headed for the house.

The CSU techs were still processing the scene at the Webbers' house when Nick and Hank climbed in the Charger and pulled away from the curb. Mr. Delgado hadn't given them any information that he hadn't already passed on to Wu and Hank, and he hadn't woged in Nick's presence. That didn't necessarily mean he wasn't Wesen, but Nick's instincts told him the man was human.

"Now what?" Hank asked.

"I suppose we should let the Captain know what's going on." Nick took his phone out of his pocket and called

Captain Renard. The man answered on the second ring.

"Renard."

"It's Nick. Hank and I ran into a case that looks like it's Wesen-related. It's a messy one."

"I'm listening."

Nick gave him a quick rundown of what had happened at the Webbers'. When he was finished, Renard said, "Messy *and* weird. Any idea who—or what—might be responsible?"

"Not yet. I was hoping you might have some thoughts on that."

"Sorry. Nothing you've told me rings any bells. See what sort of leads you can turn up and keep me informed."

Renard disconnected and Nick returned his phone to his pocket. He filled in Hank on what the Captain said, and then he sat back and thought.

As usual, Nick had felt uncomfortable talking with Renard. They'd had a decent working relationship during Nick's time with the department, but the revelation that Renard was Wesen—technically half-Wesen and half-human—and a member of the Royal Family to boot had changed things between them. On the one hand, it made working together easier, since they could openly discuss Wesen-related cases. But Renard liked to play things close to the vest, and while Nick knew the man was embroiled in political intrigue with the Wesen royals, he didn't know much beyond the basics. It was hard to fully trust someone that kept his agenda as well hidden as Renard, and for this reason, Nick tended to view him as an uneasy ally rather than a friend.

Nick turned his thoughts to the mysterious shapeshifting Wesen. It seemed as if the shapeshifter had "copied" Dana Webber, killing her in the process and reducing her body to a puddle of slime. But after attacking him, the creature had assumed a man's form. Although she'd killed Rich Webber, she hadn't copied him. His body was still intact. Maybe there had been another man in the house that the creature had copied, and they simply hadn't located his liquefied remains yet. The creature seemed to change form fairly often, but whether that was by choice or out of need, he didn't know. Whichever the case was, it might not remain in its current shape for long. And if it changed again, the physical description they had of their suspect—vague as it was—would be useless. They needed information, and they needed it fast. He knew of only one place they might find it.

"Let's head for the trailer," he said. "Better stop for coffee on the way, too. We might have a long night ahead of us."

Hank sighed. "When don't we?"

On the way to Forest Hills Storage, the facility where Aunt Marie's trailer was parked, Nick called Monroe to tell him what had happened and to ask if he and Rosalee had ever heard of a shapeshifting Wesen like the one he'd encountered. Monroe said he hadn't, but he and Rosalee would head to the spice shop and go through her reference books on Wesen anatomy and physiology to see what they could find. Nick then called Juliette to let him know what was going on, and she told him she'd go to the spice shop to give Monroe and Rosalee a hand. Nick was grateful for their help. He didn't have an ego when it came to solving these kinds of problems. All that mattered to him was stopping the shapeshifter before it killed again.

It had been Nick's Aunt Marie who'd first revealed the family legacy to him. She'd been a Grimm herself, and tough as nails, even when she'd been dying from cancer. She'd given Nick her trailer, which was filled with books of lore, weapons, and chemicals that she'd used throughout her years battling evil Wesen, and after her death, it not only became an invaluable treasure trove of resources for Nick, the trailer kept Aunt Marie close in his memory. Whenever he was in it, researching a new type of Wesen or adding his own accounts to the accumulated lore of his ancestors, it was like he could feel her presence, as if she were still watching over him.

Nick and Hank spent the better part of an hour searching through Aunt Marie's books without any luck. Juliette called to tell them that they'd found something in Rosalee's books, so Nick and Hank got back in the Charger and drove to the Exotic Spice & Tea Shop. Rosalee Calvert had inherited the shop from her brother, and while all the substances she sold were legal and unregulated, in the right proportions and combinations, they acted like medicine for Wesen. In a sense, Rosalee was like a medical doctor to the Wesen community in Portland, and she'd been a big help to Nick on a number of cases.

Nick parked on the street, and he and Hank walked to the shop. The sign on the door was turned to CLOSED, but the lights were on inside. Nick tried the knob, found the door unlocked, and he and Hank entered. As always, the first thing that hit him was the smell, a thick miasma formed from hundreds of different substances: spices, roots, dried flowers, incense, seeds, desiccated insects, acrid liquids, and aromatic powders. It was almost overwhelming to his Grimm sense of smell, and not for the first time he wondered how Rosalee and Monroe, with their enhanced Wesen senses, could stand it.

The shop walls were covered with shelves from floor to ceiling, filled with canisters, bottles, and vials, all covered with typed or handwritten labels, some yellowed from having been on display for years. Nick always felt as if he were stepping back in time a century or more whenever he came in here, and that sensation, coupled with the intense smell, was a little disorienting.

Rosalee stood behind the counter, Monroe at her side. Juliette stood in front of the counter, and they were all looking at a large leather-bound book lying open between them.

The three looked up as Nick and Hank entered, and Monroe and Rosalee smiled a greeting. Juliette's hello was a bit more demonstrative. She walked forward to meet Nick, put her hands on his shoulders, and leaned in for a kiss. Nick slipped his arms around her waist and when their kiss was finished, they hugged. Juliette Silverton was a veterinarian, and her work schedule and Nick's rarely coincided, so each time they saw each other, they made sure to make their moments together, however brief they might be, count.

Juliette possessed an almost ethereal beauty that took Nick's breath away every time he saw her. She was an elegantly thin woman with long auburn hair, whose intelligence and good humor showed in both her gaze and her smile. She exuded an aura of caring and concern that served her well as a vet, and which made her a sympathetic friend and a supportive partner. She was Nick's rock, his safe harbor, and he didn't think he'd be able to keep doing what he did—both as a cop and as a Grimm—without her.

"Break it up, you two," Monroe said in mock irritation. "We have some serious Grimm-type work to do."

Nick smiled at him as he and Juliette separated. The two of them went to the counter, Hank close behind.

Monroe had curly brown hair, a thin beard, and thick eyebrows. He was of medium height and build, and tended to wear plaid shirts or sweaters with jeans. Nick thought he looked like a college professor or maybe a professional artist. These impressions were reinforced by Monroe's seemingly inexhaustible supply of offbeat trivia.

"Thanks for coming down here so late," Nick said.

"No problem," Rosalee said. "It's not even ten thirty yet."

"And you know Blutbaden," Monroe said. "We do our best work at night." He frowned. "That didn't come out the way I meant it."

In German, *Blutbad* meant *blood bath*, and the name was more than appropriate. Blutbaden were a wolf-type Wesen infamous for their savagery and bloodlust. Monroe was, in his own words, a "reformed" Blutbad, who maintained a tightly controlled regimen of diet, exercise, meditation, and medication designed to help him suppress the violent tendencies of his kind. He was neat in his habits and dress, a sign of the control he exerted over every aspect of his life to keep the wilder aspects of his Blutbad nature in check. But from time to time, Nick could see the wolf in Monroe peering out through his friend's eyes: a calculating feral intelligence combined with barely restrained urges. In these moments, Nick felt very glad that Monroe worked as hard as he did to keep the beast inside him contained.

Rosalee was a Fuchsbau, a fox-type Wesen, and while on the surface, a Fuchsbau and a Blutbad might seem an odd combination for a couple, she and Monroe made it work. She was a gentle-natured woman with brownish-red hair, large eyes, and full lips. She was extremely pretty, but Nick thought her most attractive feature was the way her face mirrored her emotions. Whatever Rosalee felt, good or bad, was displayed for the world to see. Given his job, he often had to keep his own feelings hidden, and he admired such openness. He found Rosalee's apparent lack of guile to be ironic, though, as Fuchsbau had a reputation for being manipulative, scheming, and shady. Rosalee didn't seem to possess any of these traits, but every once and a while, a sly look came into her gaze, and Nick knew there was more to her than met the eye.

Nick nodded to the book on the counter. "So what have you got?"

Rosalee placed an index finger on one of the entries.

"Read this and tell me if it sounds like the Wesen you encountered tonight," she said.

Nick turned the book around so he could see it better and read aloud.

"'Wechselbalg. German for changeling. These Wesen are born without identities of their own and exist by periodically assuming the identity of others. They take on their victim's appearance, personality, and memories, reducing the victim into basic proteins in the process.'" He paused and looked up at Hank. "Sounds a lot nicer than 'puddle of goo,' doesn't it?"

"Sure does."

"Wechselbalgen are where the legends of doppelgangers came from," Monroe said. "You know, evil spirits that duplicate their victims' bodies and replace them? I've never met one before."

"Me neither," Rosalee said. "From what I understand, they keep to themselves for the most part."

Nick continued reading. "'The Wechselbalg is known to duplicate only humans. It is unclear if this is a biological restriction or a preference. While the Wechselbalg has no true appearance of its own, it does have a transitional form that resembles fluid quicksilver. It uses retractable needle-like spines to absorb a victim's identity, and while the specifics of how the process functions remain unclear, it is believed that duplication is accomplished in a relatively short time. Wechselbalgen are generally healthy and are immune to disease even while in human form. Their borrowed bodies do tend to show signs of wear and decay after a time, signaling the need for the Wechselbalg to seek out a new victim. The length of time a Wechselbalg can retain a specific form is uncertain, but it's believed that five years is the average, with ten years being the upper limit. As long as the Wechselbalg can find new forms to duplicate, it can conceivably live far longer than a normal lifespan. Health concerns for Wechselbalgen include infection of digital spines if they are not cleaned regularly, loss of dermal elasticity—especially as the time to seek a new host approaches—and in their later years… *Verfallserscheinung*.'" Nick hesitated as he stumbled over the pronunciation of the word. He looked up from the book. "What does that mean?"

Monroe was fluent in German, and he translated. "It means symptom of decline. Kind of like dementia."

Nick nodded and returned his attention to the book, skimming the rest of the entry. Treatments were listed for spine infection and dermal non-elasticity, but for *verfallgerscheinung*, the entry had only three words to offer. "No treatment known."

"If this Wesen is suffering from some kind of dementia," Juliette said, "that would explain its erratic behavior. In the animal kingdom, creatures who use camouflage as a means of defense do so by staying hidden."

"And cutting the throat of your victim's husband isn't exactly keeping a low profile," Monroe said.

Juliette nodded. "Exactly."

"The entry says that a Wechsel… a shapeshifter can keep a stolen form for years," Hank said. "But we think this one killed Dana Webber and copied her, and then it turned around and changed form a short time later. No idea who it copied that time, though."

"There might have been someone else in the house," Nick said. "Someone we don't know about."

"Maybe that last change was a defense mechanism," Rosalee said. "A reaction to being threatened by a Grimm."

Nick shook his head. "The creature's body started falling apart in front of my eyes before it attacked. It was like it was melting or something. It definitely *needed* a new body."

"It could be part of the creature's decline," Juliette said. "There could be a physical component to it as well as a cognitive one."

"Great," Hank said. "So we not only have a crazy shapeshifter on our hands, we've got one that needs to find new victims to copy every hour or so. That's going to add up to a lot of dead people."

"And if the Wechselbalg keeps assuming new forms, how will we ever be able to find it?" Nick asked.

"The Wechselbalg stuck you with its finger spines, right?" Rosalee asked.

Nick touched the pinprick wounds on his throat. "Yeah, but it must not have had them in me long enough to affect me."

"You're hardly an ordinary human," she said. "Maybe you're immune to the duplication process."

"Yeah," Monroe put in. "You *are* looking distinctly ungooified."

Juliette turned to Nick. "Are you *really* sure you're okay? I mean, if the duplication process normally *kills* people…"

He gave her a reassuring smile and took hold of her hand. "I'm fine. Seriously."

Hank stepped in. "You told me that you felt cotton-headed after the attack, like you were coming down with a cold."

Juliette scowled at that.

"Okay, so I feel a little off," Nick admitted. "But *just* a little. I'm not going to collapse into a puddle of protein slime any time soon. I promise."

Monroe made a face. "Now *there's* an image I could've done without."

"We have to find him before he needs to kill again," Nick said. "Somehow."

"In the meantime, I'll keep looking for more information on Wechselbagen," Rosalee said. "Maybe I can find some kind of treatment for *verfallserscheinung*."

"I know what kind of treatment I'd give him," Hank muttered.

Rosalee gave him a dark look. She was a healer, and a naturally gentle and empathetic soul. She preferred to help rogue Wesen whenever possible instead of killing them. Nick felt the same way, but he knew that it was all too often easier said than done.

"I don't want to sit around and wait for the thing to kill someone else," Hank said. "There's got to be some way to track it down."

Rosalee turned to Monroe. "Do you think you could follow its trail?"

He thought about it for a moment. "I could try. But if the Wechselbalg's scent changes every time it shifts form…" He trailed off and shrugged.

"Then we should get started," Nick said. "The fresher the trail, the better, right?"

Before Monroe could respond the door opened, and Bud Wurstner entered. He was carrying a basket, the contents of which were covered by a red-and-white checkered cloth. Bud was a short, stout, middle-aged man with thinning gray hair, a mustache and a short beard. He gave off so much nervous energy that at times he almost seemed to vibrate. Nick feared that part of the reason for Bud's nervousness—maybe even the majority of it—was that Bud still hadn't adjusted to being in the presence of a Grimm. Nick tried to make him feel comfortable whenever they were together, but Bud's anxiety ended up putting Nick on edge, which in turn only made Bud more anxious. Juliette said that Bud just needed more time to get to know Nick, but he wasn't sure that any amount of time could help Bud relax around him.

"I saw the lights were on, so I thought I'd stop and see if you were here. And you are. Well, you *all* are, but I was coming to see Rosalee specifically. Not that it isn't great to see all of you, and I apologize if I'm interrupting anything. I'm interrupting *something*, but I hope whatever it is isn't too important. Not to say that it's *un*important, because you wouldn't be here this time of night if it wasn't important on some level, right? Which is why I'm glad I drove by on my way to drop this off at Monroe and Rosalee's house. Because if I hadn't, you two wouldn't have been there because you're here."

As usual, Bud's words came tumbling out of his mouth in a nervous rush, and no one could get a word in until he paused for breath. And he could say a lot on a single breath of air. Nick wondered if that was because he was an Eisbiber. Didn't beavers have to be good at holding their breath when they were working underwater?

Bud bustled over to the counter, Nick, Juliette, and Hank moving aside to make room for him. He deposited the basket on the counter next to the book.

"My wife's been baking thank-you gifts for people all day, and I've been delivering them all night. She made a spice cake for you, Rosalee, to thank you for the toothache remedy you made for our daughter." He turned to the others. "Believe me, when an Eisbiber gets a toothache, it's a *big* deal."

"That's so sweet," Rosalee said. "Thank her for me, Bud, okay?"

"Sure thing." He glanced down at the open book.

"Grimm trouble? Not to say that Grimms *are* trouble, you understand, but that you might have trouble to deal with. But then, that's what Grimms do, right? Not that it's my place to tell you what a Grimm's job is, Nick. You'd know better than anyone, right?"

Nick jumped in before Bud could go any further.

"We think we may have a Wechselbalg in town. Do you know anything about them?"

Bud frowned as he thought. "Wechselbalg? That's some kind of shapeshifter, isn't it? I mean, technically all Wesen are shapechangers. But this one changes shapes the same way most people change clothes. I've never met one— that I know of. Unless one introduces him or herself as a Wechselbalg, how would you know? One of my cousins said she heard there was one in the town where she lived as a kid, but that might've just been a rumor." He paused. "Now that I think of it, isn't there a legend of some kind involving a Wechselbalg? I think I remember hearing one once, but I can't remember the details." He gave Nick an apologetic look. "Wesen have a lot of legends. It's hard to remember them all."

"It's the whole oral history thing," Monroe said. "With some exceptions—" he tapped the volume open on the counter "—we don't write a lot of stuff down. Easier to stay hidden that way."

"How about you two?" Nick said to Monroe and Rosalee. "You ever hear of this legend?'

"I haven't," Rosalee said. "But I can keep looking through my brother's books and see what turns up, if anything."

"Sorry, man," Monroe said. "If I ever heard anything about this legend, I forgot it."

Juliette turned to Nick. "While you guys go see if you can track down the Wechselbalg, I can go to the trailer and research the legend."

"Hank and I already tried that," Nick said.

"But you didn't know the shapeshifter's name," Juliette pointed out. "Now we do. That might make a difference."

He smiled. "It might. But—"

"Some of the books are written in German. I know. If any of those mention Wechselbalgen, I'll bring them back here for Monroe to translate."

"And if we get lucky, we may have the shapeshifter captured before then," Hank said.

"We don't need luck," Monroe said. He tapped the side of his nose. "Not when we have this baby on our side."

"I've got a couple more deliveries to make," Bud said. "I'll ask if anyone knows anything about Wechselbalgen and if they can remember anything about the legend." He drew the back of his hand across his forehead. "Is it hot in here, or is it just me?"

Rosalee frowned. "Now that you mention it, it *is* a little warm."

"I hadn't noticed, but yeah, you're right," Monroe said. "Maybe the heat's turned up too high."

Nick exchanged looks with Juliette and Hank. He felt fine, and from their expressions, so did they. He shrugged. Maybe it was a Wesen thing.

"Well, I'll let you good people get on with your work," Bud said. "Hope you like the cake, Rosalee. And keep the basket. We've got a ton of them. Nick, I'll call you if I learn anything about the Wechselbalg legend. Good look and take care."

He headed for the door, wiping his forehead one more time as he went. He turned to give a final wave before stepping back out into the night.

Monroe clapped his hands together and rubbed them. "Let's get to work. That scent trail isn't getting any fresher while we stand here gabbing. Besides, it'll be nice to get out into the cool air."

"Yeah," Rosalee said. "Maybe I'll open up a window while I work."

Monroe gave her a quick kiss and then came out from behind the counter. Nick wasn't sure, but he thought his friend's face looked a little flushed. Rosalee's too, for that matter. And hadn't Bud looked a bit red as he departed? Maybe.

"You feeling all right?" Nick asked Monroe.

Monroe frowned. "Who me? Never better. Why?"

"It's nothing." Nick turned to Juliette and gave her a kiss.

"Be careful," she cautioned.

He smiled. "Always."

"Hank?" she said.

"I'll watch out for him." He smiled, amused.

"Me too," Monroe added.

"I'm relieved to know I'm in good hands," Nick said. "Let's go."

Juliette left with them, and as they went through the doorway, Rosalee said, "I'll call if I find out anything, Nick."

He turned to wave goodbye and saw Rosalee looking down at the open book and pulling her sweater collar away from her throat as it were stifling her.

CHAPTER FIVE

The Wechselbalg—who increasingly thought of itself as Nick Burkhardt—was walking down the sidewalk when a sound came to his ears. His senses were much sharper than he was used to, especially his hearing, and over the sounds of vehicles passing by on the street, he detected a hissing noise that sounded like escaping air. His instincts told him it was out of place, so he turned in its direction—an alley he'd just passed—and walked back toward it.

In the alley, a couple of teenagers—one male, one female—held cans of spray paint and were hard at work defacing a brick wall. They'd evidently been at it a while, for several empty cans lay on the ground around their feet. Light from the street filtered into the alley, providing enough illumination for the Wechselbalg to make out the graffiti artists' features. They looked to be in their mid-teens, fifteen, maybe sixteen. The male had shoulder-length hair and wore a leather jacket and jeans. The female had shorter hair, most of which was concealed beneath a stocking cap. She wore a gray sweater, the sleeves a bit too long for her arms, and jeans.

The Wechselbalg approached them, moving silently as a

cat. While he was within six feet of them—a distance his new memories told him was close enough to get their attention, but not so close he was within their reach—he spoke.

"What's wrong? Run out of canvas?"

The two whirled toward him, shocked, and in their surprise they let their guard down for an instant and involuntarily woged. Their human features gave way to lizard-like countenances. Mouths stretched into savage grins and revealed pointed teeth, and forked tongues emerged and flicked the air, as if tasting it.

The Wechselbalg recognized them. Or rather, Nick's memories did. Skalengeck.

Aunt Marie's voice whispered in his mind.

Hunt down the bad ones.

The female spoke in a rough voice, like two rocks grinding together. "If you know what's good for you, you'll turn around and walk away right now."

The male hissed and held up clawed hands, his grin widening. "What she said."

The Wechselbalg ignored them and glanced at what they'd been painting. It was a green lizard, roughly ten feet long, with bright red eyes, a mouthful of wickedly sharp teeth, and a coiled tail.

"Not bad," the Wechselbalg said. "You two have talent. Shame you couldn't have applied it to something more constructive."

The Skalengeck female's eyes narrowed. "You can see us, right? *Really* see us. So why aren't you afraid?"

The male lowered his head and extended it forward, as if examining the Wechselbalg more closely. He made a choking noise deep in his throat and withdrew his head so fast there was an audible click as his neck vertebrae snapped back into place.

"He's a *Grimm*!" He practically spat the word.

"The one that's supposed to be living here in town?" the female said.

"How many Grimms do you think there are in Portland?" the male said.

The Wechselbalg could feel the fear rolling off of them. He could smell it, too. The Skalengecken were exuding an acrid odor of some kind, probably a defense mechanism designed to discourage an attacker. Too bad it had no effect on him.

He was surprised to find that he was rather enjoying this. Throughout his long existence, the Wechselbalg had been forced to hide, to conceal his true nature from all around him, including his fellow Wesen. He'd always done his best to fit in with whatever family or community he'd found himself in, but even when he'd come to believe his stolen memories were actually his, he'd never felt he'd truly belonged anywhere. Plus, there was always this feeling, as if he were a consummate actor who, no matter how spectacular a performance he gave, never got to hear the audience's applause. But now here he was, standing before these two Skalengeck teens, feeling their fear... no, their absolute *terror*, and it was delicious. They were his audience tonight, and he was determined to give them a hell of a show.

"You know tagging is illegal, right?" He took a step toward them, just to see how they'd react. The male took a step backward, but the female held her ground. Interesting.

She resumed her human aspect once more, perhaps in an attempt to appear less threatening, the Wechselbalg thought. Even so, she tried to maintain a tough façade. She held the can to the wall and defiantly sprayed GRIMM. "You may be a Grimm, but you're not a cop."

When a Wechselbalg took on a new identity, it shed its outer layer of skin, which transformed into duplicates of its victim's clothes. So perfect were these copies that they'd pass all but the most sophisticated of scientific scrutiny. But there was a limit to what the Wechselbalgen could create from their shed skin. They couldn't replicate the contents of pockets—wallets, keys, phones, and the like—and thus the Wechselbalg that had duplicated Nick Burkhardt hadn't been able to copy his badge, or his gun, for that matter. Since he had nothing to prove he was a cop, he supposed he'd have to let attitude do the work for him.

"Who says I can't be both?" the Weschselbalg said, smiling.

The male Skalengeck remained in Wesen form the entire time, and although he'd retreated when the Wechselbalg had first advanced, he found his courage now. He hissed loudly and hurled the can of spray paint he'd been holding at the Wechselbalg. Skalengecken were stronger than humans, and the can was a blur as it hurtled toward the Wechselbalg. Without being consciously aware of it, the Wechselbalg's hand reached out and plucked the can out of the air as easily as taking low-hanging fruit from a tree. He held the can for a moment, enjoying the expressions of disbelief on the teens' faces. Then he drew his arm back and with a single swift motion, hurled the can back at the male Skalengeck. It flew through the air and struck the boy directly between the eyes. Nick's memories informed the Wechselbalg that Skalengecken were highly resistant to pain, but that didn't make them invulnerable. They could still be hurt, regardless of whether or not they felt it.

The can made a satisfyingly solid *thunk* as it connected with the Skalengeck's lizardish hide. The impact knocked the boy off his feet, and he hit the ground hard. The spray can bounced off his head, ricocheted off the wall, and clattered to the ground, spinning several times before coming to a stop. The male Skalengeck resumed his human form and groaned, but he made no move to get up.

The female looked horrified at seeing her companion brought down so easily, and the Wechselbalg sensed that she was fighting an inner battle as she tried to decide between fight or flight. In the end, it wouldn't matter which she chose because the Wechselbalg had no intention of allowing her to escape. But he was curious to see which way she would jump.

Fight won out. She spun to face the Wechselbalg, returning to her Skalengeck aspect as she did so. She still held onto her can of paint, and she raised it, stepped forward, aimed at his face, and pressed the nozzle. The Wechselbalg was impressed by the way the girl was using the only weapon available to her. But he was a Grimm— more or less—and he wasn't about to let himself fall for such a simple trick. Just as paint began to shoot from the nozzle, he slapped the girl's hand aside, and the blow caused her to lose her grip on the can. It hit the wall and bounced to the ground.

The girl didn't wait for the Wechselbalg to make the next move. Snarling, she slashed at him with one of her clawed hands. The Wechselbalg pulled in his stomach just in time to avoid getting gutted. When the Skalengeck was off balance, he stepped forward, grabbed hold of her shoulders, and slammed her against the wall as hard as he could. Her back struck the brick where she and the male had been painting, and her head hit the spot where they'd rendered the lizard's head. Breath gusted out of her lungs and she went limp. If the Wechselbalg hadn't still been holding her against the wall, she would've slumped to the ground. She returned to her human appearance, the change occurring more slowly than normal, as if her body wasn't functioning properly. He noticed a dark smear in the middle of the painted lizard's green head. At first he thought the girl's hair had smeared the paint, but then he realized that what he was looking at was blood.

It gave him a wonderful idea.

He placed his hand over her face, gripped her with his fingers, and then began pounding the back of her head against the brick. When he finally let go of the girl, her Grimm graffiti was almost completely obscured by blood and brain matter. The female Skalengeck's body fell to the ground, and the Wechselbalg immediately forgot about her. She was no longer a threat, and therefore no longer important.

He turned his attention to the male. While the Wechselbalg had been dealing with his companion, he'd gotten to his feet, but he just stood there, staring in horror at the female's corpse. The Wechselbalg decided to take advantage of the male's distraction. He stepped forward and struck the male with an open-handed blow to the chest. The Wechselbalg felt bone crunch beneath his hand, but although the male Skalengeck staggered backward, this time he didn't go down. The Skalengeck resistance to pain no doubt helped him remain on his feet. As much fun as the Wechselbalg was having, he needed to wrap this up. He could hardly stay here in the alley all night. He had an entire city to protect.

He rushed forward, grabbed hold of the male, and spun him around until he had him in a headlock from behind. He applied pressure to the boy's neck, gritted his teeth, and gave a single hard twist. There was a harsh *crack*, and then the teen's body went slack. The Wechselbalg held onto him for several more moments before releasing his grip and letting the corpse fall to the ground. The boy lay near the girl, their hands almost touching. The Wecheselbalg found it a rather poetic sight, in its own way.

The Wechselbalg turned away from the two dead teens and began walking toward the mouth of the alley. He'd made a good start at his work, but he had more to do.

A lot more. And while he'd been capable of dealing with these two with only his bare hands, they were just kids with no combat experience. If he planned to continue with this work, he was going to need to equip himself.

He needed weapons.

"I'm sorry, but I'm getting nothing. And I mean *nothing*."

Monroe stood in the middle of the Webbers' living room while Nick and Hank stood off to the side to keep their scents from interfering with Monroe's sense of smell. But some reason, it seemed as if it wasn't working.

"Don't get me wrong," Monroe said. He tilted his head back and sniffed the air. "I can smell a lot of things—blood, mostly." His stomach chose that moment to growl, and he looked suddenly embarrassed. "Sorry. Reflex action."

They were the only people in the house. The CSU techs had finished, and the Deputy Coroner had removed Rich Webber's body. No one had found anymore "goo puddles," which indicated to Nick that there hadn't been a third person present in the house. The place now had the empty, uneasy atmosphere that Nick had become all too familiar with during his time working homicide. This was a place where violence and death had occurred, and that dark energy seemed to linger in the air, like the aftereffect of a turbulent storm.

Monroe walked slowly around the small living room, picking his way around the remains of the smashed TV. He continued to sniff the air as he spoke. "I can smell the couple who lived here. The man's scent is fresher than the woman's. He was here a couple hours ago. The woman—her scent is real faint. I'd say the last time she was in this room was sometime this morning."

Nick frowned. "But she sat in that chair when I questioned

her earlier. I mean, when I questioned the Wechselbalg."

Monroe stepped over the chair and leaned close to it. He breathed in and out several times, then straightened and faced Nick.

"I don't know what to tell you. I don't smell *anything*. It's like no one's sat in this chair for at least twelve hours, maybe longer."

"You mean the shapeshifter doesn't have *any* scent?" Hank asked.

"It would make sense," Monroe said. "A Wechselbalg can protect itself by taking on different shapes, but it would need another form of defense to protect it from predators who can track it by smell. Can't find what you can't smell." He looked around the room. "Where did you say the Wechselbalg attacked you?'

Nick pointed to the area where he'd battled the Wechselbalg. Monroe nodded, went over to it, got down on his hands and knees, and sniffed.

"There's definitely plenty of you here, Nick, but that's all. You might think about switching deodorants. The one you're using isn't doing its job."

"Thanks for the tip," Nick muttered.

Monroe stood. "Don't get defensive. Friends tell each other these things. Once my cousin Albrecht came down with *haarlos*. It's a kind of mange Blutbaden get sometimes. But he got it in a certain area of the body that you can't see yourself, if you know what I mean. No one wanted to tell him. I mean, how do you tell a guy that he's got *haarlos* on his—"

Hank interrupted him, and none too soon, Nick thought.

"How is it possible for the Wechselbalg to have no scent at all? Wouldn't its clothes have some kind of scent? And wouldn't the things it touched leave some kind of residue on its skin? Couldn't you smell that?"

"Look, I don't understand how it works. But it does. I can tell by the *amount* of scent. There's only enough here for one person. Second, Nick's scent is fresh enough that I can not only smell him here, I can *see* what he did. Well, s*ee* isn't the right word, of course, but I know which movements he made and what sequence they were in. From what I can smell, it's like he was the only one here—except based on his movements, it's clear that he was fighting someone. I'd say that pretty strong evidence that our Wechselbalg doesn't have a scent, no matter what form it's in. But let's go outside and I'll have a sniff around to make sure."

As Monroe started toward the door, he drew the back of his hand across his forehead, just as Nick had seen Bud do at the spice shop.

"Something wrong?" he asked as he and Hank followed after Monroe.

"It's just warm in here, that's all," Monroe said. "I'll be glad to get back outside in the cool air."

Nick exchanged a look with Hank. It didn't seem particularly warm inside to Nick, and from Hank's expression, he felt the same. Weird. But then again, Wesen were all about the weird, weren't they?

The three men stepped out into the night once more, ducking beneath the yellow crime-scene tape affixed to the outer door frame. Nick closed the door behind them, and once they were in the yard, he and Hank stepped a dozen feet away from Monroe to give him room to work. As he'd done inside the home, Monroe walked slowly around the Webbers' front yard, scenting the air, at times getting down on his hands and knees and lowering his face to the glass. He woged only once, fur sprouting on the backs of his hands, the sides of his face and neck. The hair on the top of his head became thicker, and his mustache and beard became wild and tangled. His facial features sharpened, his brow became more pronounced, his eyes bestial. His teeth sharpened, and he inhaled deeply, exhaling with a soft growl.

For a moment, Nick felt hope that Monroe had been wrong, that the Wechselbalg did have some kind of scent, and he'd found a trace of it. But then Monroe returned to his human form and stood.

"Sorry about that. I thought I had something, but it turned out to be a squirrel."

Nick and Hank looked at him.

"What? It was a really *big* squirrel." He wiped his hand across his forehead again, and this time when he finished, he removed his jacket and draped it over his arm. "Man, you wouldn't know it's November, as warm as it is tonight."

Nick and Hank walked over to join him.

"You sure you're okay?" Nick asked.

Monroe looked puzzled. "Why do you keep asking? It's not like *I'm* the one who went a couple rounds with a psychotic shapeshifter tonight."

"Touché," Nick said.

"So now what?" Hank asked. "We know what we're dealing with, but we don't have any way of finding it."

"Sorry I couldn't help you out," Monroe said. "I'm going to head back to the shop and see if I can help Rosalee with her research. Maybe we'll turn up something that'll help us locate the Wechselbalg."

Monroe gave them a parting wave and headed toward his beloved 1973 yellow Volkswagen Super Beetle. It wasn't the kind of car Nick would drive, but it suited Monroe's personality. A little offbeat and old-fashioned at the same time.

"Well, we need to do *something*," Hank said. "Or else we're going to be stuck twiddling our thumbs until the shapeshifter kills someone else."

Nick's phone vibrated in his pocket. He took it out and checked the display to see who was calling. He was hoping it was either Juliette or Rosalee with a new lead on the Wechselbalg. Instead, he saw that it was Sergeant Wu.

"I think we can stop twiddling our thumbs," Nick said.

The Wechselbalg continued walking through the streets of Portland, with only a vague notion of where he was going. There was a place—a special place—where Nick Burkhardt kept the weapons of his trade, and since *he* was Nick Burkhardt, he should remember where it was. And he did… after a fashion. He could see the trailer—a 1963 Airstream Globetrotter—sitting in a lot with various other vehicles. He had memories of being there before, of spending hours looking through old volumes with dry yellowed pages. Of taking medieval-looking weapons from a cabinet, holding them, running his hands over them, trying to guess what they had been designed to do, wondering how many Wesen lives they'd taken. But despite having these memories, which were so strong and clear it was as if he'd experienced them only a few hours ago, he could not for the life of him access any memories that told him where the damned trailer was. It was beyond frustrating.

So… where else could he get his hands on weapons? He considered stealing some from a gun shop, but he immediately discarded this idea. Not because he was against stealing, per se. Sure, he was a cop and sworn to uphold the law, but that didn't mean he had to be fanatical about it. Besides, the way he saw it, his duties as a Grimm took precedence over everything else. He was part of an ancient lineage, a protector of humanity, and his people pre-dated modern notions of law and justice. Grimms were born with the ability to see Wesen for what they truly were, and that meant they had a responsibility to stop them, regardless of the cost. What was a little theft compared to that?

No, the main reason he decided against trying to break into a gun shop was because they were too well protected. Alarm systems, security cameras... His mission was too important to risk being arrested for attempting to arm himself. So if gun shops were out, what was left?

He turned a corner, and as he did, he saw a police cruiser and a red pickup truck sitting in the parking lot of a strip mall. The cruiser's emergency lights were on, and a uniformed officer stood next to the pickup's driver's side window, talking with the vehicle's operator. The businesses in the strip mall—a short-term loan place, a Thai take-out restaurant, and a thrift store—were all closed, but the parking lot was well lit, which, the Wechselbalg's stolen memories told him, made it a good location for a traffic stop—which in turn presented a good opportunity for him.

The strip mall was across the street from him, so he waited for a break in the traffic and then jogged over. The officer was too busy dealing with the motorist to notice his approach, which was just the way he wanted it. As he drew closer, he saw that the officer was female, medium height, with short blond hair. Her gender didn't make any difference to him. An officer was an officer as far as he was concerned. Besides, he wasn't here for her, but rather for what she carried on her person—and what was stored in the cruiser.

The officer was in the process of writing a ticket, and the driver—a greasy-haired, pimple-faced kid who appeared as if he'd gotten his license yesterday—looked on the verge of tears.

Probably figures he's going to get in a heap of trouble when his parents find out, the Wechselbalg thought. They might even take his license away for a time as punishment. Sitting next to the kid was a teenage girl with curly black hair. To add insult to injury, it looked as if the kid was also being embarrassed in front of his date. The Wechselbalg almost felt sorry for him.

The Wechselbalg drew nearer the officer as she tore the completed ticket from her pad and handed it through the window to the kid behind the wheel, along with his license. The kid took them, looking absolutely miserable.

"Can't you just let me off with a warning? Please?" He sounded scared, and his voice had a wheedling tone.

"Afraid not," the officer said. "You were doing thirty miles an hour over the speed limit. Five I could let go. Ten, even. But not thirty. I should arrest you."

The Wechselbalg knew she was bluffing about this last part as an attempt to scare the kid into driving more safely. He doubted it would work.

"Try to take it easy from now on, okay?"

"Yeah. Sure," the kid mumbled. "Can I go now?" He seemed nervous, and the Wechselbalg guessed that the girl had a curfew and he'd been rushing to get her home before it was too late. *If he hadn't gotten pulled over, he might've made it,* the Wechselbalg thought. *Too bad.*

"You can go," the officer said. "Have a good evening."

The Wechselbalg had reached her now, and just as she was turning to head back to her cruiser, he rushed forward, grabbed the side of her head, and slammed it into the side of the pickup's cab. The officer went limp and fell to the ground, out cold.

The Wechselbalg had moved so fast, he'd doubted she'd been aware of his presence, let alone realized what he'd intended to do. And because of that, he'd taken her out easily.

The kid in the pickup gaped at the downed officer while his girlfriend stared at the Wechselbalg with wide, frightened eyes. The kid then turned his gaze on the Wechselbalg.

"What the hell did you do *that* for?" He sounded more incredulous than scared.

"Secret sting operation for Internal Affairs," the Wechselbalg said. He held out his hand. "Let me see that ticket she gave you."

The kid hesitated, then passed the slip of paper through the open window. The Wechselbalg pretended to read it, then tore the ticket into shreds and allowed the bits of paper to fall from his hands. The Wechselbalg's eyes narrowed as he peered closely at the kid. He *looked* human, but that didn't mean he *was*. Same for the girl.

"How do I know you're not Wesen?"

The kid looked blankly at the Wechselbalg for a moment before turning to his girlfriend.

"You know what he's talking about, Mandy?"

She didn't respond. She continued starting at the Wechselbalg, eyes glistening with the beginnings of tears. The kid faced the Wechselbalg once more.

"I— I'm sorry, sir, but we don't know—"

The kid's words were cut off as the Wechselbalg reached through the pickup's open window, grabbed hold of the kid's shirt, and pulled him halfway out of the vehicle.

"Woge," the Wechselbalg ordered.

The kid paled, and although he opened his mouth to reply no sound emerged. Mandy more than made up for his silence by screaming. The Wechselbalg ignored her and leaned his face close to the kid's until they were only a couple inches apart.

"Woge," he repeated, low and dangerous. "*Change.*"

Mandy kept screaming, and the kid's mouth opened and closed, as if he were desperately trying to form words, but still he made no sound.

The Wechselbalg waited several more seconds, but

still the kid didn't woge. Maybe he wasn't Wesen, the Wechselbalg thought. But he couldn't be sure. Same with the girl. They were both under obvious emotional stress, and most Wesen woged during such times, if only for a moment or two. But the teenagers maintained human appearance. This could mean two things. Either they *were* human, or they were Wesen who possessed an uncommon degree of control over their transformations.

Maybe he should kill them both, just to be sure.

He almost did it, but then something—not a memory, precisely, but rather a strong, almost overpowering instinct—told him that wasn't what Nick Burkhardt would do. That meant it wasn't something that he would do, either. The Wechselbalg wasn't happy at the prospect of releasing the teens, but he could see no help for it. Besides, he had to deal with the police officer. She wouldn't remain unconscious forever.

"Go on," he said. "Get out of here."

The kid lost no time in complying. He fired up the pickup's engine and roared into the street, already breaking the speed limit again.

Shaking his head, the Wechselbalg turned his attention to the downed officer. She stirred a little, but she made no move to stand, and while her eyelids fluttered, she didn't open them. Working swiftly—and drawing on Nick's memories for help—the Wechselbalg removed the officer's Glock and a pair of handcuffs. He considered taking her cruiser, too, but decided against it. A police cruiser would be too conspicuous, too easy to trace. He laid the officer in the cruiser's backseat, cuffed her hands behind her back, and then closed the door. He didn't consider killing her. As long as she was unconscious, there was no way to tell if she was Wesen. Besides, she was an officer of the law. A fellow cop. No way would he kill her.

Sufficiently armed, he walked off into the night's shadows, ready to get back to work. He needed a vehicle, one that wasn't as noticeable as a police cruiser, and after that... well, he was a cop, wasn't he? He'd stop by the station and fill out a report on the Skalengeck graffiti artists he'd dealt with earlier. He didn't look forward to doing paperwork, but Nick Burkhardt always made sure to do his, so that's what the Wechselbalg would do, too.

Right after he found himself a car to steal.

"Somebody in this town seriously hates street art," Wu said.

Nick and Hank stood at Wu's side, all three of them shining flashlights to illuminate the scene. Nick focused his beam on the two bodies—a couple of teenage taggers—before raising the beam to the image they'd presumably painted: a large stylized lizard.

"Kids had some talent," Hank said.

"The operative word in that sentence is *had*," Nick said. He looked at the lizard more closely.

The lizard's body was green, but part of the wall was daubed with red. Then Nick realized the red wasn't paint. Hank must've come to the same realization, for he too was looking at the red smear. Together, Nick and Hank turned their flashlight beams to the bodies. The back of the girl's head was tacky with blood.

"Nasty way to go," Hank said.

The girl's head was lumpy and malformed, and Nick didn't need a coroner to tell him her skull had been crushed—and how. The blood on the alley wall told the story.

There was no blood on the male, but his head canted at an odd angle, and the skin on his neck was bruised.

"Broken neck," Nick said.

Hank nodded. "That'd be my guess."

"He probably died faster than the girl," Nick said.

"That's something," Hank said.

"Maybe," Wu said. "But it's not much."

Nick couldn't disagree with the man.

He swept his flashlight beam across the ground near the bodies, saw some cans of spray paint scattered around, but that was it. There wasn't even any trash—no discarded fast-food wrappers, empty coffee cups, or items of a less savory nature, like used condoms or hypodermics. Only a few cigarette butts. As alleys went, it was remarkably clean. Or had been until someone had decided to leave a couple of dead bodies in it.

"Let's bag those cigarettes for the crime lab." Nick's gut told him the butts had been here before the murders had taken place and most likely didn't belong to the killer. But as important as hunches were in police work, being thorough and making sure were even more important.

Wu nodded. Nick knew he'd make sure CSU took care of it once they were at the scene.

"So what are we looking at here?" Hank said. "Some kind of gang thing?'

"You're thinking the lizard might be some kind of new gang symbol?" Nick asked.

"Yeah."

"It's a possibility," Nick acknowledged. "I've never heard of a lizard gang in Portland, though."

"Hence the word *new*," Hank said.

While Nick thought his partner had a point, nothing about this scene said "gang-related" to him. The kids didn't have any obvious gang signs on their bodies or clothing, and the lizard painting didn't look especially menacing. But the biggest indication to Nick that the taggers' deaths had nothing to do with gangs was the way they'd died. Gang members' weapons of choice were knives and guns—weapons they could use for intimidation first and for violence second. Whoever killed the teens had done so barehanded and had possessed enough strength to kill quickly—witness the boy with the broken neck—but had also possessed the sadism to make a victim suffer first, as the girl had. From the way her blood was smeared on the wall, Nick was pretty sure she'd endured multiple blows before dying. And while he supposed there could've been more than one assailant, that didn't feel right to him. The alley was narrow, which meant not a lot of room for more than three people to fight, plus both murders had been committed by hand, and both had required a significant amount of strength to accomplish. All that, plus the animalistic savagery of the killings, told him that there was an excellent chance that a Wesen was responsible. Was this the work of the Wechselbalg?

Nick pointed his flashlight at the graffiti and examined it more closely. He made out a word, partially obscured by the drying blood, that sent a chill rippling down his spine. *Grimm.*

At once Nick knew what form the Wechselbalg was wearing: his. He didn't know how it was possible—he hadn't died during the duplication process—but he knew it was true nevertheless. He could *feel* it.

"Anything?" Hank asked.

"Nope." He couldn't tell the truth in front of Wu, but he gave Hank a look that said, *I'll explain later*, and Hank nodded.

Nick looked at the two dead taggers again and wondered what sort of Wesen they were. They had to be Wesen, or at the least one of them did, or else they wouldn't have known what a Grimm was. Based on the wall painting, he'd guess Skalengecken, but he supposed it didn't matter.

They were dead, and their killer needed to be stopped.

He wondered what they'd thought when they saw a being they took to be the city's Grimm approaching them. Had they been scared? Probably, out of reflex, if nothing else. And what had they thought when the "Grimm" attacked them? Had they thought that Nick Burkhardt had gone insane? Or had they thought he'd finally dropped the pretense of wanting to help Wesen and reverted to the monster he'd always been inside? Nick had worked hard the last few years to gain some measure of trust from Portland's Wesen community. And that trust, tentative and fragile as it was, was in danger of being destroyed, perhaps forever, by this demented shapeshifter.

As before at the Webbers' home, CSU and the Deputy Coroner arrived, and because the alley was so cramped, Nick and Hank stepped onto the sidewalk to give them room to work. Wu remained with the bodies to supervise evidence collection. But Nick didn't need any more evidence. He was contemplating his next move when his phone rang. He took it from his pocket and saw that Juliette was calling.

"Hey," he answered in a soft voice.

"You need to come to the trailer, Nick. Fast. I found an entry about a Wechselbalg in one of Marie's books." She paused. "You're not going to like what it says."

CHAPTER SIX

Rosalee looked up as Monroe entered the shop.

"How did it go?" she asked.

A number of books were piled on the counter, and Monroe noticed that she'd removed her sweater and was now wearing a Portland Fire T-shirt. A light sheen of sweat coated her skin. The perspiration intensified her natural scent, and he found himself responding to it. *Down boy,* he told himself. *We have work to do.*

As he headed for the counter, he slipped off his jacket. It was still too warm in here, almost sweltering, really.

"No luck," he said.

He went into the back room, tossed his jacket onto a chair, and then joined Rosalee at the counter.

"Turns out Wechselbalgen don't have a scent," he said.

Unlike you, he thought. He sidled closer to her without being fully aware he was doing so.

"Don't stand so close!" she snapped. She was immediately apologetic. "Sorry. It's just so hot in here."

Monroe did as Rosalee requested and moved a couple feet away from her. Something inside him bristled at having to give up the territory he'd claimed, even if it was only a handful of inches.

"What's up with that anyway?" he said. "Did you turn the heat up full blast while I was gone?'

Rosalee gave him a withering look. "Now why would I do something stupid like that? I actually turned the heat off. And it's *still* hot in here."

"Maybe you only *thought* you turned it off. Maybe you really turned it up higher."

"Seriously? Are you saying you think I'm too dumb to read a thermostat?"

What's her problem? he thought. Aloud, he said, "I'm saying that anyone can make a mistake."

Without waiting for her to reply, he went into the back room to check the thermostat. The heat *was* off, and the readout said the temperature in the building was currently sixty-two degrees. He stared at it for several moments. He felt an urge to slam his fist into the damned thing and knock it off the wall, but instead he turned away and walked back out to the front.

"Maybe there's something wrong with it," Monroe said. "Maybe it just looks like the heat's turned off, but it's really still going."

Rosalee looked down at one of the books open on the counter. "Maybe there's something wrong with *you*," she breathed. The words were almost inaudible, but Monroe heard them clearly.

He scowled. "What's *that* supposed to mean?"

She didn't look up from the book as she replied. "What's *what* supposed to mean?"

Monroe heard a low rumbling sound then. At first he had no idea where it was coming from, but he realized with a start that it came from his throat. He was growling. At Rosalee. *His* Rosalee.

She looked up at him then, and he saw anger flash across her face. Her eyes narrowed and her upper lip curled. He wouldn't have been surprised if she'd growled back. But she didn't. After a moment her anger drained away, and she looked shocked.

"I'm... sorry. I didn't mean to snap at you. Again. It's the heat. It's put me on edge."

The irritation that had built inside him vanished when he saw the regret in Rosalee's eyes and heard the upset tone in her voice.

He stepped toward her once more, not thinking about territory, thinking only of being close to her, to give and seek comfort in equal measure.

"I'm sorry, too. I don't know why I growled. Maybe I'm just frustrated that I couldn't help Nick."

She reached out and squeezed his hand. "The full moon is less than a week off. You usually get a big more growly around that time."

He gave her a sheepish smile. "I suppose. So, you find anything new while I was gone?"

She shook her head. "Nope. Want to help?"

"Of course. Which books haven't you looked through yet?"

Rosalee slid a stack toward him. "Here you go."

She smiled at him, he smiled in return, and they started reading. But despite their apologies, tension still lingered in the air between them, and Monroe felt sweat began to bead on this forehead. Why was it so damned *hot* in here?

Juliette sat at the table in Aunt Marie's trailer, a small volume the size of an address book sitting before her.

"I'm not surprised you missed this one earlier," she said. "Not only is it small, it was tucked beneath one of the bookcases. I think Marie used it to keep the case level."

Nick and Hank stood on either side of Juliette, looking down at the small book.

"Aunt Marie had her own way of organizing things, that's for sure," Nick said.

"You told Nick we weren't going to like what you found," Hank said. "On a scale of one to ten, with one being a minor irritation and ten being complete disaster, this is…?"

"It depends," Juliette said. "If what's recorded in this book is just a legend, we have nothing to worry about. If it's an historical account, we're looking at a ten-plus."

"Great," Nick said. "Okay, give us the bad news."

She opened the book and flipped to a page that she'd bookmarked with one of her business cards. She removed it and set it to the side. Nick gazed down at the open pages, and although the text was written in cramped handwriting, the ink faded by the years' passage, he was relieved to see that it was written in English.

"This account tells the story of a Grimm named Soffya who encountered a Wechselbalg in a small village in Hungary in the late 1800s. Soffya tried to kill the Wechselbalg, but the creature attempted to duplicate her to protect itself. Soffya didn't die, but she was weakened long enough for the Wechselbalg to get away. The Wechselbalg survived, but it ended up duplicating Soffya's form."

"That's pretty much what happened to you," Hank said.

Nick had informed both Hank and Juliette of the word he'd found in the Skalengeck graffiti, and what he believed it meant.

"Yeah," Nick said. "But bad as that is, it doesn't sound like a ten-plus yet."

"Here's where it gets bad," Juliette said. "The Wechselbalg, acting as if it were a distorted version of a Grimm, became an indiscriminant killer of Wesen. Good, bad, it didn't matter. And it gets worse. Something else happened to *both* the Wechselbalg and Soffya. Some sort of weird side effect of their very powerful but very different physiologies coming into contact. They both became carriers of a disease—or at least what the people of the time thought of as a disease."

Nick tensed. "What sort of disease?" Was he in danger of infecting Juliette and Hank? Should he get away from them? Without thinking about it, he took a step backward.

As if sensing his unease, Juliette said, "Don't worry. It only affects Wesen."

Nick let out a relieved breath. If he did have this disease, or whatever it was, it sounded like Juliette and Hank were in the clear.

"What are the symptoms?" Hank asked.

"Wesen are normally able to control their transformations, but this condition caused them to woge uncontrollably, and eventually they became stuck in their Wesen forms, unable to change back. What's more, they were unable to conceal their Wesen appearance from humans. Anyone could see what they truly were."

"That's bad," Nick said. "*Really* bad."

"I can see how not being able to hide their Wesen identities would be a problem," Hank said, "but couldn't they have just left the village and gone into hiding? I'm not saying it's a perfect solution, but it would've gotten them away from humans. And more importantly, from the kill-crazy shapeshifter."

"Some tried," Juliette said. "But they soon realized they could spread the condition to other Wesen. That meant they couldn't go anywhere, because if they did, they risked breaking the Wesen's highest law."

Nick nodded. "The Wesen's book of law, the *Gesetzbuch Ehrenkodex*, states that Wesen must keep their true nature a secret from humanity at all costs."

"Right," Juliette said. "And the Wesen Council enforces those laws."

"With an iron hand," Nick said. "Or maybe that should be with an iron claw."

"The Wesen Council feared the Woge Plague, as they called it, would spread out of control if they didn't act swiftly. So they sent an agent to stop the disease."

Nick had a sinking feeling he knew where this was leading. "This *agent* was really an assassin, right? He or she was sent to kill the Wechselbalg and Soffya."

"Yes," Juliette said. "As well as all the infected Wesen. And after that, this assassin—who'd also become infected—committed suicide. The incident became known as *die Zeit Totzuschlagen*: the Killing Time."

The phrase sent a chill through Nick. "Do you think it's happened again? Am I carrying this… whatever it's called?"

"*Ewig Woge*," Juliette said. "According to the entry, it's German for 'perpetual wave.' And there's no way to know until Wesen you've come into contact with start to show signs of being affected."

"You were around Monroe and Rosalee," Hank said. "Bud, too."

"And Bud was going to visit more Wesen to drop off his wife's thank-you gifts," Nick said. "If he had the *Ewig Woge*, he might've given it to all of them."

He thought of how Monroe, Rosalee, and Bud had all complained about how hot it was in the spice shop, even though none of the humans had been uncomfortable with the temperature.

"They've got it," he said.

Juliette's eyes widened. "They kept talking about the heat."

"That's right," Hank said. "And Monroe mentioned

being bothered by how warm it was when we were trying to find the shapeshifter's trail. I didn't think much about it at the time, but ..."

Nick took out his phone and called Monroe. As it rang on the other end, he waited impatiently for his friend to answer, but eventually it sent him to voicemail.

"I don't want you to panic," Nick said, "but there's a chance that you and Rosalee were exposed to a disease that makes Wesen lose control of their ability to woge. Sit tight. I'm on my way."

He disconnected and put his phone away.

"Maybe he and Rosalee are busy researching and he didn't notice you were calling," Juliette said.

"Maybe." But he doubted it. Monroe would've kept his phone close by since he and Rosalee were helping him with a case. The fact that he hadn't answered was more than a little troubling. "Come on. Let's get back to the spice shop and check on them."

Juliette grabbed the book that contained the account of the Killing Time, and the three of them left the trailer. Juliette decided to ride with Nick and Hank. She'd come back for her car later.

As they left Forest Hills Storage and pulled onto the street, Nick prayed that another Killing Time wasn't beginning in Portland, but if the *Ewig Woge* was already spreading, what could they possibly do to contain it before the Wesen Council got wind of what was happening? And once that occurred, would any of the city's Wesen survive? And if the disease spread outside the city limits, would it eventually affect Wesen worldwide?

They had to do whatever they could to prevent that from happening—if it wasn't already too late.

* * *

"Want some tea?" Rosalee asked.

Monroe didn't look up from the book currently open in front of him. "Better make it coffee—and strong. We might be at this for a while."

But as Rosalee started for the back room, Monroe looked up from the page he had been reading—an entry on Siegbarste foot fungus—which was precisely as interesting as it sounded—and gestured to catch her attention.

"On second thought, skip the coffee. It's too hot in here for coffee. Same for tea."

Rosalee frowned at him. Actually, it was closer to a scowl. But then her brow smoothed and she smiled.

"I think we have some regular soda in the back. Chock full of sugar and caffeine."

"*And* calories," Monroe said, patting his stomach. "How about energy drinks?"

Now she did scowl. "I said we have *soda*. If you want an energy drink, maybe you should go get in your car, drive to a convenience store, and get one."

Normally, Monroe would've been shocked by Rosalee's attitude, which was so unlike her usual easygoing, gentle personality. But all he felt at that moment was a surge of anger that rapidly built to all-out fury. A part of him that was still calm, still in control, warned him not to give in to the turbulent emotions roiling inside him.

"What did you say?" he said, almost growling.

"I thought Blutbaden had strong hearing," Rosalee said, also through gritted teeth. "Or is that just a bit of exaggerated folklore?"

A snarl escaped Monroe's lips, and he felt a woge coming. He didn't try to resist it, but even if he had, it came upon him so fast and strong that he couldn't have stopped it. He changed so swiftly he was barely aware of it, and his snarl—which had already sounded bestial while he was in his human form—became deeper and more menacing.

As if in response to his transformation, Rosalee woged as well. Her features became a cross between human and vulpine, and reddish-brown hair with hints of white covered her skin. Normally when she changed, her large dark eyes remained gentle, and her expression one of calm watchfulness. But now her lips curled away from sharp teeth, and she returned his snarl. Although hers was higher-pitched and not as loud as his, it contained an equal amount of anger. Fuchsbau might not be Blutbaden, but they were still predators, and Rosalee showed no signs of submitting to him.

Blutbaden were not wolves any more than they were humans, but one of the traits that they shared with their canine cousins was a pack hierarchy based on dominance and submission. As a modern and, more importantly, reformed Blutbad, Monroe didn't take part in such rituals, but that didn't mean he didn't feel the drive to indulge in them at times. And this was definitely one of those times.

Rosalee's defiance was what set him off. When a Blutbad snarled and displayed his or her teeth, that was a sign for another to back down or risk getting into a fight. And the last thing most Wesen wanted to do was go claw-to-claw with a pissed-off Blutbad—unless they were Blutbaden themselves, of course.

Monroe's instincts told him that a Fuchsbau might put up a brave front for a moment or two, but in the end, he or she would always stand down rather than risk getting torn to bits. Monroe's kind hadn't been named 'blood bath' for nothing.

But Rosalee continued snarling, her voice rising in pitch and volume. He could sense the fury emanating from her, could smell it, could almost *feel* it roll over him like psychic waves of force. His snarl became a deep-throated growl, and he flexed his hands, his claws growing longer and sharper. He could feel his features taking on an even wilder aspect, fur growing thicker, eyes more feral, nose sharper, teeth longer... This had never happened to him before. Until now, when he changed, he changed. He didn't get more Blutbady the angrier he got. It wasn't like he was some kind of Wesen version of the Incredible Hulk. But that was exactly what it felt like was happening, including the increasing rage that threatened to sweep away the last vestiges of his reason and turn him completely into a beast.

The same thing was happening to Rosalee, too. Her fur grew thicker, its colors more intense, her snout lengthened, and her teeth became more pronounced. Her claws normally weren't very sharp in her Wesen form, and while they were nothing compared to his, they were larger and sharper than he'd ever seen them before.

It was Rosalee who made the first move. In this situation, she should've turned to flee, for a Fuchsbau— no matter how skilled a fighter—simply wasn't a match for an enraged Blutbad. But she raised her claws and came rushing toward him. Monroe responded as if a switch had been thrown inside him. He released a roar and ran forward to meet Rosalee's challenge.

"I'm still not getting an answer," Juliette said. "From either of their phones."

She sounded worried, and Nick didn't blame her. He was plenty worried, too.

He drove this time, Juliette in the passenger seat, Hank in the back.

"We'll be there in a couple minutes," he said, although he knew it wouldn't make her feel better. He was glad for his police training. It allowed him to put aside his fear for his friends and concentrate on the task at hand. Mostly.

"So how does this woge sickness work?" Hank asked.

Juliette thought for a moment before answering. "Without blood samples from Nick, the Wechselbalg, and affected Wesen—along with a few weeks in a specially equipped lab with the help of a geneticist or two—I can only speculate. Nick described the Wechselbalg's true form as looking like a semi-solid silvery mass. All Wesen change shape, but none do so as completely as Wechselbalgen. None that we know of, anyway. I suspect Wechselbalgen possess an enormous amount of the hormone that allows all Wesen to woge. In fact, its entire being might be comprised of a highly evolved form of the chemical." She thought for a moment. "It's even possible that this creature is the ancestor of all Wesen. If it can sample DNA and replicate bodies, it might've done so with animals as well as humans in the past. And then the two types of DNA become combined, and hybrid creatures developed, which eventually became the Wesen we know today."

"So how does the *Ewig Woge* work?" Nick asked.

"When the Wechselbalg tried to duplicate you, it caused a chain reaction in both your bodies. You received an infusion of Wechselbalg super-woge hormone, which your body is working to expel, probably in both breath and sweat. Wesen are so sensitive to this hormone that when they're in the presence of a carrier—in this case you, Nick—their bodies go into overdrive and produce too much of it. Then *their* bodies try to shed the excess—"

"And the condition spreads like a disease," Nick said.

"Right. Technically, it's not a disease but a severe hormone imbalance. But people in the past wouldn't have been able to tell the difference. By this point, you've probably expelled all traces of the hormone, and it's safe for Wesen to be around you. But the damage has been done. The hormone imbalance will keep spreading, like a row of falling dominoes, until all but the most reclusive Wesen in town are affected."

"But why is the shapeshifter a carrier, too?" Hank asked.

"Because it copied Nick's form down to the cellular level," Juliette said. "So now its own body is trying to expel its own woge hormone just like Nick's. But because it has so much more of the hormone inside, it will remain a carrier for much longer than Nick.

"And if all that wasn't bad enough," Juliette continued, "the Wechselbalg's version of the hormone is much stronger than the normal Wesen version, and it overwhelms their systems. They can no longer control their woge and remain stuck in their Wesen forms. I'm afraid that the longer they stay changed, the more they'll exhibit the behaviors of their particular type. If that's true, then Mauzhertzen would become more meek than usual, and Blutbaden—"

"Would become more aggressive," Nick said.

She nodded.

"But how can the Wechselbalg dissolve its victims like that?" Nick asked.

"And it's not just flesh and bone that gets dissolved," Hank added. "The victim's clothes do, too."

Juliette thought for a moment before answering. "A lot of creatures in nature produce powerful chemicals that liquefy their prey, especially in the insect kingdom. The hormone that allows Wesen to woge could act the same way. A substance like that, which promotes change in Wesen, could totally destabilize the structure of a human body. And once the biological material starts to break down, it could in turn become acidic enough to dissolve clothing."

At first it didn't seem possible that a victim's clothes might be dissolved by a biologically produced chemical, but as a homicide detective, Nick had seen bodies in all sorts of conditions, and he knew it didn't take long for a corpse to basically become toxic waste. He'd seen some horrific crime scenes where the bodies weren't discovered for some time, and the things that happened to their clothes or any cloth, upholstery, or carpet the corpses were in contact with... When he thought of those scenes, he had no trouble believing the Wechselbalg's super-woge hormone could dissolve an entire victim, clothing and all.

He recalled his encounter with a type of Wesen called a Fuchsteufelwild. That creature had two bone-like fingers which released a type of acid. He wondered if the Wechselbalg was related to Fuchsteufelwilden in some way. He supposed it was possible.

"If the victims' remains are acidic enough to dissolve clothing, are the CSU techs in danger from them?" Hank asked.

"I doubt it," Juliette said. "It would be difficult for the residue to remain that volatile for any length of time. My guess is that it becomes safe to handle after a few minutes."

"Sounds like Mrs. Webber's remains might've dissolved some of the sidewalk before they cooled off," Hank said. "CSU's going to be scratching their heads over that one."

"So why didn't I dissolve?' Nick asked. "Not that I'm complaining about it."

Juliette smiled. "Grimms must have some kind of immunity—or at least resistance—to the hormone the Wechselbalg injects. Speaking in purely biological terms, you wouldn't make a very effective predator of Wesen if you didn't possess resistance to a wide range of Wesen-based chemical attacks. Even a substance as powerful as the Cracher-Mortel toxin didn't affect you the same way as it did others."

Nick grinned. "You are *so* sexy when you talk all sciencey."

She grinned back. But her grin quickly fell away.

"I just hope Monroe and Rosalee are all right," she said.

"Even if they are woged, and stuck in their Wesen forms, that doesn't mean they'll become aggressive," Hank said. "After all, this is Monroe and Rosalee we're talking about."

"If they're affected, and I believe they are," Juliette said, "then their animal natures have been intensified. So we're not talking about Monroe and Rosalee. We're talking about a Blutbad and a Fuchsbau."

After that, she fell silent and continued trying to call Rosalee and Monroe without any more luck than she had before.

Nick pulled into the spice shop's neighborhood, found a nearby parking space, and moments later the three of them were running down the sidewalk toward the shop, Nick in the lead. As he ran, he drew his Glock from its holster. He didn't want to hurt either of his friends, but he couldn't let them hurt each other, either.

When he reached the shop's front door, he was relieved to find it unlocked. He threw it open and rushed inside. He swept his gaze around the shop, searching for Monroe and Rosalee. He didn't see them, but he heard snuffling and snarling coming from behind the counter. He headed for it as Juliette and Hank entered the shop. The snarls grew louder, and now they were accompanied by yipping noises. Keeping his weapon low, Nick moved around the side of the counter.

He paused and blinked several times, not quite able to believe what he was seeing. Then he lowered his gun, stepped back, turned, and walked slowly toward Juliette and Hank.

Juliette stopped when she saw the look on Nick's face. "What's wrong?" she said. "Are they all right?"

"They're more than all right," he said softly. "They're, uh... well..."

At that precise moment Monroe let out a long, loud howl.

"Oh," Juliette said. And then her eyes widened in understanding. "Oh!" she repeated, her cheeks reddening.

Hank grinned. "I guess the side effects of this woge disease aren't *all* bad."

The Wechselbalg pulled into the parking lot of the Justice Center, where the Central Precinct was housed. He was relieved to have finally found the place. He'd spent much of the last hour driving around the area, knowing he was close but unable to recall the building's precise location. This little victory encouraged him. With any luck, he'd be able to access more of his new memories as time went on. And even if he couldn't, that was okay. He'd make do with what he had.

Humming to himself, he pulled his recently acquired vehicle into an empty parking spot. He'd picked up his new ride—a red Jeep Cherokee—outside of a twenty-four-hour diner. The vehicle had been locked, but the Wechselbalg ran his fingers beneath the wheel rims until he found a small magnetic box with a spare key in it affixed to the metal. Couldn't have been easier if the vehicle had been delivered to him. It wasn't bad as SUVs went, but he would've preferred a Toyota.

He turned off the engine, got out of the vehicle, locked it, then pocketed the key. He carried his "borrowed" Glock tucked into his pants against the small of his back. He started toward the building's entrance, enjoying the dual sensation of seeing it for the first time and returning to a familiar, even comforting place. He felt as if he belonged here, a feeling that wasn't easy for his kind to come by and was all the more precious because of it. Wechselbalgen changed forms and identities often during the course of their long lives, and the feeling of stability—of being *home*—was difficult, if not almost impossible, to come by. But seeing the Justice Center gave him the feeling now, and it was almost enough to make him weep.

As he walked into the building's lobby, he was hit by a combination of smells, some of which were the same as any workplace. Coffee, body wash, shampoo, deodorant… But there were other smells unique to a police department: metal and gun oil, and the sour tang of suspects' sweat, desperation, and fear. In and of themselves the smells weren't strong, and he doubted most of the men and women who worked here were aware of them. As he reached the top of the lobby steps, he stood, eyes closed, savoring the mingled scents.

I am Nick Burkhardt, and this is what my workplace smells like.

"Falling asleep on your feet?"

The Wechselbalg opened his eyes and found himself looking at a uniformed officer.

He struggled to recall the man's name and was glad when it came to him.

"Hey, *Wu*. I *am* a little tired, I guess. Been a long night."

"Tell me about it," Wu said. "Sometimes I feel like I'm the only officer in the precinct on duty, you know? Good thing I have tomorrow off. So what brings you in so late—and without your trusty partner?"

Why *was* he here? The Wechselbalgen had originally headed for the Justice Center out of instinct. But now that he was here, he needed a reason. Especially this time of night. He wasn't sure how late it was. It hadn't occurred to him to check. He guessed it might be close to midnight, or even later. He saw the manila folder filled with paper—

yellow sticky notes attached to some of the pages—that Wu held, and Nick's fragmented memories supplied the answer for him.

"Figured I'd get the paperwork out of the way while everything's still fresh in my mind." He searched his memories for the name of Nick's partner. "I told *Hank* I'd take care of it. I'm too wired to sleep anyway."

"Same here. I need to start cutting back on the coffee, especially when I'm working late. Mr. Caffeine isn't always kind to me."

The Wechselbalg frowned. "Do you want me to have a talk with this man? Does he work here?" The Wechselbalg swept his gaze around the lobby, searching for the person who'd been treating Wu badly.

Wu looked at him for a long moment without expression before breaking out in laughter.

"Thanks for the offer, but I think I can handle him." He clapped the Wechselbalg on the shoulder and then walked away, grinning.

The Wechselbalg watched Wu go, puzzled by the man's response to his words. Finally he shrugged. Humans could be so strange sometimes.

He dismissed the encounter with Wu from his mind and started walking. He entered the Central Precinct's main office area and paused for a moment as he worked on identifying which desk was Nick's. No, which desk was *his*. About a third of the desks had people sitting at them, typing on computer keyboards, filling out forms by hand, or talking on the phone. Nick's memories told him that the office was quieter and less busy than during the day, and that was fine with the Wechselbalg. This was, in a sense, his first day on the job, and he wanted to ease into it. Just because Wechselbalgen could duplicate their victims' memories didn't mean they were automatically perfect at all aspects of their new identity. In some ways, they were like actors who'd been instantly programmed with all the information they needed to play their roles effectively, but who hadn't had a chance to run through their lines yet. They needed a bit of time to settle into their new roles, and coming here this late, when the precinct was less crowded, would give him a chance to familiarize himself with his new workplace. The less pressure on him right now, the better. It was taking longer than usual for his new memories to settle, and he could use a bit of peace and quiet to help the process along.

Then he saw his desk. At least, he *thought* it was his desk. He started toward it, doing his best to look relaxed and unconcerned. Several of the men and women on duty looked up as he passed, nodded in greeting, sometimes adding a smile or a "Hey, Nick." The Wechselbalg smiled back and returned their nods. He wondered who they all were, but his memories gave him no answers.

He reached the desk that he was almost positive was Nick's, and he only hesitated a few seconds before pulling out the chair and sitting. He glanced around, but no one was looking at him curiously, and he felt relieved.

Nailed it, he thought.

He took a couple moments to absorb the feel of the space. Aside from a computer monitor, keyboard, and phone, the top of the desk was clean. Nick was a man who liked to get his work done and off his desk before the end of the day. Good to know. He opened the desk drawers one at a time and sifted through their contents, occasionally picked up an object—a stapler, a quarter, a small stuffed dog with a heart in its mouth with the words "Happy Valentine's Day!" stitched on it. He held each object for a time, turning it this way and that, before putting it away. Eventually, he found a blank incident-report form and a pen, and he got to work.

He was concentrating so thoroughly that he was only partially aware of the sound of approaching footsteps. He didn't worry, though. He recognized them.

"Burning the midnight oil, I see," Captain Renard said.

The Wechselbalg looked up from the partially completed report.

Renard was a tall, slender man with neatly trimmed black hair and an intense, penetrating gaze. Everything about him—suit and tie, facial expression, voice, stance— spoke of controlled strength and power.

"Do you know how to spell *Skalengeck*?" the Wechselbalg asked.

Renard didn't answer right away. When he did, he simply said, "My office," then turned and walked away.

The Wechselbalg put down the pen, pushed the chair back from the desk, stood, and followed after the Captain.

CHAPTER SEVEN

The Wechselbalg was glad Renard led the way. It meant he didn't have to search his new memories for the route, which allowed him to concentrate on other matters. Nick's feelings about Sean Renard were complicated, to say the least, and the Wechselbalg was having difficulty sorting through memories regarding the Captain. Some of the memory fragments indicated that Renard was an ally, if not exactly a friend, while others whispered that the man should not be trusted, at least not fully. But there was one memory—more of an image, really—of Renard's face, the skin ravaged by what looked like raw, red wounds. But the Wechselbalg knew those marks weren't injuries. They were signs that Renard was more than he appeared to be. He was Wesen. A... The Wechselbalg scowled. The name wouldn't come to him, but he supposed it didn't matter what type of Wesen the Captain was. All that mattered was what the Wechselbalg should do about him. Was he a good Wesen or a bad Wesen?

Renard made a perfect target right then. His back was to the Wechselbalg, and he had no idea he might be in danger. And why should he? Nick Burkhardt was one of his people, wasn't he? Renard had nothing to fear from one of his own. It would be so easy. All the Wechselbalg had to do was draw his Glock, take aim at the back of the Captain's head, and fire.

His right hand twitched, and he almost reached around to draw his weapon. But a couple things prevented him. If he killed the Captain—especially here in the Justice Center—that would end the Wechselbalg's police career before it had properly started. And while the Wechselbalg wouldn't have minded that, for it would give him more time to devote to killing bad Wesen, he could do without the extra burden of being a fugitive from "justice." Plus, he supposed he really should give Renard the benefit of the doubt. For a little longer, anyway. His hand relaxed, and he followed the Captain into his office.

Renard shut the door behind them. He didn't sit, nor did he ask the Wechselbalg to, so he remained standing. He took a moment to glance around the office. The lighting was a bit on the dim side in here, and he wondered if there was something about the Captain's Wesen nature that caused him to avoid bright light, or if it was simply a personal choice. If so, it was just about the only personal touch. There were a couple framed diplomas and certificates hanging on the walls, and a small picture or two sitting atop cabinets. But there was nothing about the office that gave a solid sense of the man who occupied it. Which, the Wechselbalg supposed, told him something about Renard after all. This office said Renard was a man who kept his true self—and his agenda—well hidden from others. And regardless of whether the Captain was ultimately "good" or "bad," that made him dangerous.

"What the hell is going on?" Renard snapped.

"I don't know what you mean." The Wechselbalg frowned. "Is this because I forgot how to spell *Skalengeck*?"

"Quit joking around. This situation isn't the least bit funny. I want to know what you were thinking killing a couple teenagers for the unspeakable crime of spraypainting a lizard on an alley wall."

The Wechselbalg wasn't certain, but he thought Renard was being sarcastic. Renard went on.

"I know you did it. I read Wu's report. I came into the office this late in case you discovered something about the shapeshifter and needed help dealing with it. Little did I know I'd end up reading about you killing two *different* Wesen. One of the kids sprayed a word on the wall before they died. Can you remember what that word was?"

The Wechselbalg remained silent. It was a tactic that had served him well over the long years. But not this night.

"It was *Grimm*," Renard said, his voice rising. "I can make sure that tidbit doesn't go in the final report, but I want to know what's gotten into you. Because unless there's something I missed, it doesn't look like there's any evidence these two kids were anything other than the taggers they appeared to be."

Renard stopped talking and let out a long breath, and with it, much of the tension drained out of him.

"We've worked together a long time, Nick. Even before either of us knew who and what the other was. I'm going to give you the opportunity to explain yourself, but right now I have to tell you—this doesn't look good."

Renard moved behind his desk, pulled out his chair, and sat. He folded his hands on the desk before him, and looked at the Wechselbalg, waiting for him to start talking.

The Wechselbalg understood that the protocol in this situation would be for him to also sit. There was a chair in front of the Captain's desk for this very purpose. Sitting would've been the smart thing to do. It would be a sign that he recognized the Captain as his superior and was willing to submit to his authority. But the Wechselbalg didn't want to do that. Renard might not know what the Wechselbalg was, but he clearly knew too much. And that made him even more dangerous than he already was. Instead of sitting, the Wechselbalg paced as he spoke.

"I came across the Skalengeck teens when they were in the process of defacing private property. At first I only intended to talk to them, maybe scare them into thinking twice about going out and tagging again. But they became belligerent."

"So you decided to kill them?"

"That's not how it happened. They woged in an attempt to frighten me off. When it didn't work, they became aggressive."

The Wechselbalg walked in a circular pattern around Renard's desk as they talked. He wanted the Captain to become accustomed to having him standing behind him in order to make sure he kept his guard down. Until it was too late.

"I didn't have to tell them I was a Grimm. They sensed it. And while that initially gave them some pause, they came at me, claws and teeth bared. I tried to defend myself without hurting them, but you know how resistant to pain Skalengecken are. No matter what I did, they just shrugged it off. So I had to get tougher with them. I guess things just… got out of hand."

The Wechselbalg had continued his slow circuit of Renard's desk, and the Captain continually turned his head to keep his gaze focused on "Nick" as he spoke.

"You slammed the girl's head into the wall at least a half dozen times. And if you were attempting to exercise restraint, I'd say you did a pretty lousy job. And if the Skalengecken attacked you as you said, how come your clothes aren't torn or your face scratched? You may be fast, but so are Skalengecken, and there were two of them. And where was Hank during all this? Was he in the alley, too?"

At this point, the Wechselbalg was once again standing behind Renard, and as the Captain began to swivel in his chair to keep his gaze trained on the Wechselbalg, the shapeshifter grabbed hold of the man's head with both hands and slammed his head down onto the desk. Since the Wechselbalg wasn't sure what kind of Wesen Renard was, he slammed his head against the desk several more times until the man's body fell limp. The Wechselbalg placed his fingers against Renard's neck to check for a pulse. He found it, and although it was a bit uneven at the moment, it was steady enough. Renard might be unconscious, but he didn't appear to be in any danger of dying soon. But that was easily remedied.

The Wechselbalg lifted Renard off the desk and pushed him back in his chair. He then wrapped his hands around the man's throat and began to squeeze. The Captain might fall into the "good' category of Wesen, but the Wechselbalg couldn't let him live. As the saying went, he knew too much.

The Wechselbalg squeezed harder, but as Renard's face reddened, he began having second thoughts. Nick Burkhardt might not consider the Captain a friend, but he didn't think of him as an enemy, either. The man had done a lot of good as a police captain—*and* as a Wesen in a position of authority. Nick couldn't have accomplished as much as he had without Renard's support.

The Wechselbalg's grip began to loosen until he removed his hands from the man's throat. He watched as the Captain's face—which had been edging toward dark purple—slowly returned to its normal color. Reassured that the Captain would recover, the Wechselbalg left his office. But instead of returning to Nick's—to *his*—desk, he headed for the lobby. In time, maybe he could come up with some kind of explanation for why he'd assaulted his superior officer. But right now he needed to get out of the building and away from Renard. When the man returned to consciousness, he was *not* going to be happy, and the Wechselbalg didn't want to be around when Renard woke up pissed and started looking for him.

As the Wechselbalg headed for the lobby, Wu crossed his path once more. The officer was holding another manila folder containing papers, but this time the sticky notes affixed to the pages were purple.

"Leaving? Good thing I caught you. We just got the Coroner's preliminary findings on the tapioca we recovered near the Webbers' house. You want to take a look at the report, or do you want me to give you the Cliff Notes version?"

The Wechselbalg frowned. This man spoke too fast, and he had trouble understanding the words he used. The Wechselbalg had no time to stand here and listen to the man's prattling. He was tempted to punch the man in his throat and crush his trachea, but he restrained himself. Wu was a fellow cop and a friend. The part of the Wechselbalg that was Nick Burkhardt wouldn't allow him to hurt Wu any more than he'd been able to hurt Renard.

"Neither," the Wechselbalg said, then turned and continued toward the lobby.

He didn't look back, but he heard Wu mutter to himself. "Looks like someone gets cranky when he stays up past his bedtime."

The Wechselbalg went outside and into the parking lot. He headed for the Cherokee and pulled the key out of his pocket. He wasn't sure where he would go, but he'd figure that out once he was on the road. Right now he just wanted to get out of there.

"I see you got a new ride," Renard said.

The Cherokee was less than ten yards from where the Wechselbalg stood. He debated whether he could reach the vehicle before Renard attacked. He didn't think much of his chances, so he turned around to face the Captain. Renard's forehead was swollen and already in the process of bruising, but otherwise, he didn't seem much the worse for wear.

"What happened to your Toyota?" Renard asked. He glanced around the deserted lot. "For that matter, what happened to the Charger you and Hank took out?'

The Wechselbalg strugged to think of a reply, but the questions came at him too fast. Renard didn't let up on the pressure. He took a step closer and said, "You didn't tell me how the investigation into the shapeshifter murders was going. How about it, *Nick*? Do you have any idea where the shapeshifter might be—or *who* it might be?"

The Wechselbalg's instincts—both Wesen and Grimm—told him that the Captain's true intent wasn't to talk, but rather to keep his opponent off-balance and stall for time to get close enough to attack. But the Wechselbalg wasn't going to continue playing this game. Renard had just proved himself to be a clear and persistent threat, and whether or not the Nick part of the Wechselbalg liked it, the man had to be eliminated.

He reached around to draw his Glock from where it was tucked against his back. But before he could bring the weapon around and train it on Renard, the Captain twisted his head from one side to another, and patches of ravaged crimson skin erupted on his face. Renard lunged forward, moving far more swiftly than a human, and as he came, he let out a sound that was a cross between a shout of fury and an animalistic roar.

The Wechselbalg was just raising the Glock for a shot when Renard slammed into him, grabbed him by the shoulders, and drove him backward against the Cherokee.

The impact crumpled metal and drove the Wechselbalg's breath from his lungs. It also caused him to lose his grip on his weapon. He heard the sound of the Glock clattering to the ground, but he didn't see where it landed.

Before the Wechselbalg could do anything else, Renard pulled him away from the vehicle and then slammed him back into it again. The Captain had hold of his arms, so since the Wechselbalg couldn't strike the man with his fists, he was forced to improvise. He drove his forehead into Renard's, and although he'd never attempted such a blow in his life, his new body knew what it was doing. The blow hurt far less than he expected, and it had the desired effect on Renard. The man's head snapped back and he released his grip on the Wechselbalg's shoulders. He staggered backward a couple steps, shaking his head as if to clear it. The Wechselbalg wasn't about to give him that chance. He stepped forward, curled his right hand into a fist, and struck Renard on the jaw. Once more Renard's head snapped back and he took another couple stagger-steps backward.

The Wechselbalg pressed his advantage, stepping forward and following up his first punch with a hard left. This time Renard went down on one knee, and the Wechselbalg grinned. Whatever type of Wesen Renard was, he didn't seem to be all that tough. The Wechselbalg took a quick look around for his Glock, but didn't see it. He realized then that he'd lost the Cherokee's key as well. He'd been holding it when Renard had first attacked. He must have dropped it the same time he'd lost his grip on the Glock. He looked for the key, but couldn't see that either. To hell with it. He'd finish Renard off with his bare hands, just as he'd done with the two Skalengeck teens.

He turned to Renard and saw that the Captain stood upright. And he'd drawn his own Glock. His facial features had returned to full humanity, and he fixed the Wechselbalg with a deadly serious look.

"Let's try this again," Renard said.

The Wechselbalg didn't take his gaze off Renard's eyes. Looking into them, he saw no doubt, no wavering. If the Wechselbalg so much as twitched a finger, the man would start firing. Renard had the upper hand, and the Wechselbalg knew it. There was no way he would be able to beat the man in a physical confrontation now. If he hoped to defeat Renard and escape, he would have to find another way.

He rapidly searched through Nick's memories, but he couldn't find anything in the Grimm's repertoire that would serve him now. But he had other skills to draw on, honed from a long lifetime of pretending to be something he wasn't.

He lowered his head and reached up slowly with trembling fingers and ran them through his hair.

"I'm sorry, Captain. I… Something's not right with me. The shapeshifter attacked me. Injected me with some sort of chemical. I think it was trying to copy me, but something went wrong."

He ran his hand down his face and rubbed his stubbled chin.

The Wechselbalg snuck a quick glance at Renard. The man hadn't lowered his Glock so much as an inch. But his gaze no longer seemed quite so certain.

"Nick told me that," he said evenly.

These words shocked the Wechselbalg. Nick *couldn't* have spoken with Renard. He'd died when the Wechselbalg duplicated his form, just as all the Wechselbalg's victims had over the years. Hadn't he?

Did you see Nick die? Did you stay to watch his body liquefy?

No, he hadn't.

The Wechselbalg would worry about that later. Right now he had a performance to finish. He rubbed the back of his neck, then curled his shoulders forward and drew in his abdomen to make himself look weaker, less of a threat.

"I think the process, whatever it is, goes both ways. At least it did this time. The shapeshifter took something from me, but it also gave me something of itself. It…"

The Wechselbalg allowed his knees to buckle, and slumped to the ground. He put out a hand to catch himself and fell into a sitting position.

Renard lowered his weapon. Not much, but it was a start.

The Wechselbalg raised his eyes, looked directly at Renard, and spoke in a near whisper. "I'm having trouble remembering who I am."

Renard lowered his Glock a bit more.

"If you really are Nick Burkhardt, then you'll come with me peacefully, and you'll let me put you into a holding cell until we can figure this out."

The Wechselbalg nodded.

"Yeah. Sure."

Since collapsing to the ground, the Wechselbalg had been slowly edging his hand beneath the Cherokee—toward his Glock, which had slid underneath the vehicle when he'd dropped it.

"Okay," Renard said. "Get on your feet. Slowly."

The Wechselbalg took hold of the Glock and brought it up with him as he rose unsteadily. He angled his body slightly to hide the weapon from Renard. He had hold of the gun by its barrel, and he doubted he'd be able to maneuver it into firing position before Renard could shoot his.

Time to improvise again.

As he stood he hurled the Glock toward Renard as if it were a shuriken and immediately dove to the side. Renard managed to squeeze off a single round which exploded through both the Cherokee's driver and passenger side windows. The butt of the Wechselbalg's Glock struck Renard dead center between the eyes. He staggered for a couple seconds before finally going down.

Smiling, the Wechselbalg walked over and retrieved the Glock from where it had fallen. Renard had managed to hold onto his weapon when he fell, and the Wechselbalg removed it from his limp fingers. He briefly considered using Renard's own weapon to kill him, and he even went so far as to aim the gun at the man's head and put his finger on the trigger. But now that the Captain was unconscious and no longer an immediate threat, the Wechselbalg didn't feel the same pressure to kill him. Knowing it was probably a mistake, he took his finger off the trigger and lowered the weapon to his side. He turned away from the Captain and there—lying on the ground several yards from the Cherokee—he saw the vehicle's key.

Time to go. Good thing it wasn't too cold out tonight. Thanks to Renard's bullet, the Cherokee now had permanent air-conditioning.

Nick drove, while Hank rode shotgun.

"What do you think we'll find when we get there?" Hank asked.

As they approached an intersection, the light turned yellow. Nick checked to see if any cars were coming, and when he saw the way was clear, he hit the gas and the Charger passed through the intersection just as the light turned red.

"I don't know," Nick said. "Bud sounded pretty upset when he called, but—"

"He sounds kind of upset all the time," Hank said.

"Yeah."

While Monroe and Rosalee had been getting dressed—a process that required their hunting around in the back of the shop for replacements for clothing that had been shredded by claws—Bud had called Nick. The man had been so upset that Nick could barely understand what he was saying. Something had happened to his wife and children, that much was clear, and he wanted Nick to come over to his house right away. He'd ended the call before Nick could get anything more out of him. Juliette had assured Nick that she'd be all right staying at the shop with Monroe and Rosalee, and she'd insisted that he and Hank go help Bud and his family. Nick hadn't been so sure it was a good idea. Monroe and Rosalee were his friends, and he'd trusted his life—and Juliette's—to them on more than one occasion. But he had no idea how the *Ewig Woge* would affect them. They were both predator-type Wesen. What if they weren't able to control their bestial impulses? Juliette could be in real danger.

But once Monroe and Rosalee were dressed, Rosalee told him she'd prepare a calming elixir and mix it with some tea. She and Monroe would take it, and it should take the edge off the *Ewig Woge*'s symptoms.

Should, Nick had thought at the time. Not *would*.

But Juliette had insisted, and in the end he'd decided to trust her and their friends. He just hoped that in this case his trust wouldn't be misplaced. After being affected by the Cracher-Mortel toxin, he knew it was possible for someone's personality to be overwhelmed by the compulsion to enact violence.

Now, driving as fast as he could toward Bud's neighborhood, Nick once more saw the security video footage that Captain Renard had shown him. In his mind, he watched a black-and-white image of himself spin around and hit a knife-wielding man with all his strength.

Watched the man go down and not get up again.

"Nick? Hey, Nick!"

Shaken out of his thoughts, Nick said, "Yeah?"

"Isn't this Bud's neighborhood?"

He'd been driving on automatic pilot for the last several minutes and wasn't sure exactly where they were. He took a quick glance around and saw that Hank was right. This was the section of town where Bud lived.

Bud, like most of the Eisbiber in Portland, worked in construction. Their type of Wesen had a strong talent for building things, and from what Bud had told him, that talent extended to engineering, architecture, and even certain branches of the fine arts.

But most of us like being able to get our hands on our work, you know?

Bud wasn't a rich man, but he was highly skilled in his profession and did more than all right for himself and his family. He lived in a solidly middle-class neighborhood— nice two-story houses with large, well-landscaped lawns. A homey, quiet neighborhood, exactly the sort of place where Nick would've expected Bud to live. As they pulled onto Bud's street, everything looked peaceful enough, but Nick had been a cop long enough to know that appearances almost never told the whole story. Anything could be happening behind those closed doors and drawn curtains. Anything at all.

At least Bud's porch light was on. Nick knew that didn't necessarily mean anything, but he took it as a good sign anyway. He pulled the Charger into the driveway, and he and Hank got out and hurried to the door. Before Nick could knock, Bud opened it.

"Thank God you're here! Come in, come in!"

Nick tried not to stare. He'd seen Bud in his Wesen aspect many times before, but Bud didn't often stay woged for long, maybe a few seconds at the most. That wasn't particularly unusual, though. Most Wesen remained in their human aspects a majority of the time. But over the years Nick had noticed that some of the more timid varieties of Wesen—non-predators such as Mauzhertzen, Seelenguter, and Eisbiber—tended to return to human form as swiftly as they could after they woged. He'd mentioned this to Juliette once, and she'd theorized that this tendency was a defensive reflex on their part. Not only did it benefit them to keep their true natures hidden, when confronted by other Wesen—or by a Grimm, for that matter—reassuming human form was a sign of non-aggression.

Whatever the reason, up to now Nick had only gotten brief glances of Bud in Wesen form. So seeing him fully woged and remaining that way came as something of a mild shock. Bud's round face was covered with short bristly brown fur that edged to gray around his mouth and chin. His nose was black like a beaver's and whiskers extended from either side beneath it. His two front teeth were larger and protruded from his mouth, giving him a bit of a lisp when he spoke. His eyes remained more human than those of some Wesen, and they were filled with fear.

Bud stepped aside and Nick and Hank entered. As soon as they were in, Bud closed and looked the door. He then turned to face them, wringing his fur-covered hands nervously.

"Something's wrong with us, Nick. *Really* wrong! We can't woge. Well, as you can see, we *can*. I mean, look at me, right? But what I'm trying to say is we can't change back. We're stuck like this, as Eisbiber. It's not so bad if only other Wesen can see us like this, although I have to say, I'm not comfortable with certain Wesen knowing me and my family are Eisbiber. Better not to tempt predators like Blutbaden, you know? No offense to Monroe. But if *everyone* can see us like this, humans included, it'll be a disaster! We won't be able to leave the house. And if the Wesen Council finds out…" He shuddered, his fur rippling as if he were trying to shake water off himself. "You have to help us, Nick! Please! For the sake of my wife and kids!"

"Speaking of which," Hank said, looking around. "Where are they?"

Bud looked at him as if he'd asked an extremely stupid question.

"Hiding, of course."

Nick raised an eyebrow. "From us?" he asked.

"No, of course not. They love you. We all do. I mean, yeah, you're a Grimm, but you're *our* Grimm, you know? They're hiding because that's what Eisbiber do in bad situations. And when things are *really* bad, we hide *really* well. My family are geniuses at it." He let out a nervous laugh. "*I* don't even know where they're at!"

Nick remembered something Juliette had said about the *Ewig Woge.*

I'm afraid that the longer they stay changed, the more they'll exhibit the behaviors of their particular type.

Eisbiber were already timid by nature, but it appeared the *Ewig Woge* had made them downright terrified.

"But you're not hiding," Hank said.

"Believe me, I would be if I hadn't needed to call you guys. My wife's so worried, she even suggested we go to the Hafen. That was before she hid wherever she hid. I'd be worried she took the kids to the Hafen, but her car's still here, so I figure she's in the house somewhere. I hope."

"What's a Hafen?" Nick asked. "I don't think I've ever heard of it before."

"It's a German word," Bud said. "It means Haven. I suppose a better translation, at least the way Wesen use the word, is s*afe place.* Every Wesen community has one. It's a place where we can go in times of emergency, a secret place that humans don't know about. We even keep it a secret from Kehrseite-Schlich-Kennen. No offense."

Kehrseite-Schlich-Kennen was a Wesen word for humans that knew the truth about them, and it also held a connotation of someone who was a friend.

"But you're telling us about it now," Hank pointed out.

"I am?" Bud looked suddenly horrified. "Oh God, I am, aren't I? Please don't tell anyone I told you. I'll get in *so* much trouble."

"So a Hafen is like a hiding place?' Nick asked.

"Yeah. They're different for each town, not that every town has a lot of Wesen, of course. A place like Portland, which is tolerant of different lifestyles—Keep Portland Weird, right?—has a ton of us, so we need a *big* place where we can gather."

"Forest Park," Nick said.

"Yeah," Hank agreed. "That would be perfect. Close to the city, yet large enough for a significant amount of people to hide in, at least in the short-term."

"I'm not saying if you guys are right," Bud said, "but you didn't hear about the Hafen in the park from me."

Hank smiled. "Your secret is safe with us, Bud."

"So do you have any idea what's happened to us?" Bud asked. "And more importantly, do you know how to fix it?"

Nick frowned. "Juliette was supposed to call and explain it to you. Didn't she get through?"

Bud fished his phone out of his pants pocket and checked the display.

"Yeah, she called four times. I had my ringer off, I guess. My bad." He put the phone back in his pocket. "So what's going on?"

Nick started to tell him, but Bud insisted that he and Hank follow him into the kitchen so he could make them some coffee. By the time Nick was done talking, he and

Hank were sipping from mugs of warm coffee.

"So it's important that you call every Wesen you had contact with since you left the spice shop," Nick said. "You need to tell them what's happening and make sure they know to avoid spreading the condition further. Tell them to sit tight until we can figure out what to do."

Bud looked suddenly uncomfortable. Even more uncomfortable than usual, that is.

Nick frowned. "What?"

"I told you I had some more stops to make after I left Rosalee's shop. Most of them were at people's houses. But my last stop was at the Blue Monkey."

"Isn't that a bar?" Hank asked.

Bud nodded. "Yeah. It caters mostly to Wesen. The owner's a friend of mine. His brother's a mechanic, and he gave my wife a really good deal when her car needed some transmission work. I can give you his number if you want. He does great work and his rates are really reasonable." He let out another nervous laugh. "He'll probably give you a special Grimm discount."

"Let me guess," Nick said. "The bar was packed when you got there. So crowded, in fact, that you had to push and shove to make your way through the crowd."

"Yeah," Bud said. "How did you know?"

Hank sighed. "It's been that kind of night."

Despite the seriousness of the situation, Juliette couldn't help being fascinated. While she'd gotten somewhat used to being around Wesen over the last few months, most of the time she couldn't see their true appearances, even when they were in full woge—not unless they were so emotionally disturbed that they lost control of their ability to cloak their appearance from ordinary humans. Or if they chose to let her see them woged, of course. But now here she was, in the presence of two good friends while they were in their Wesen forms—and she could *see* them. Yes, they were still Monroe and Rosalee, but not only did they look different in their Wesen aspects, they moved, sounded, and even acted differently. It only made sense given the large amounts of woge hormone constantly flowing through their bodies, a hormone altered and made stronger by exposure to the Wechselbalg's "disease." She thought of how the Cracher-Mortel toxin had altered Nick's personality not long ago, and how the Hexenbiest potion had nearly killed her and resulted in her losing her memories of Nick for the better part of a year. As a scientist, she understood that biological entities could be seriously affected by chemical substances of all kinds, including those produced naturally by their own bodies. But as a person, she found the thought profoundly disturbing. *What are we if we can be changed so easily?* she thought. *Who are we?*

And what did that mean for a being like the Wechselbalg, who changed shape and identity periodically, never truly having a self of its own? The creature was a murderer who knew how many times over, but right then she couldn't help feeling sorry for it, at least a little.

Rosalee and Monroe stood behind the counter, looking through more old books. Juliette stood in front of the counter, doing the same. The main difference between their earlier research efforts and now was that they were attempting to find some kind of treatment for the *Ewig Woge*. Juliette had hoped that since they now had a name for the condition, they'd be able to find references to it more easily in Rosalee's collection of Wesen lore. But so far, they hadn't had any luck.

"Too bad the Wesen Council doesn't have a database

of lore we could access," Juliette said. "It might make our job easier."

"They do," Rosalee said, "but it's for their own personal use. It's supposed to be protected by some of the best security software on the planet."

"Besides," Monroe said, "even if we could access it, the moment we searched for *Ewig Woge*, you can bet it would set off all sorts of alarms. They'd have a squad of agents on a plane to Portland in minutes to *deal* with the outbreak—not to mention everyone who's infected."

Juliette still hadn't gotten used to her friends' more guttural Wesen voices, but Monroe's was especially disturbing to her for some reason. Maybe it was an instinctive reaction to being in the presence of a predator, even if he was a friend. It didn't help that he seemed constantly on the verge of snapping at either one of them if they said anything to him. Juliette knew he was doing his best to keep a rein on his temper, and she knew he wasn't angry with either one of them specifically. The overabundance of woge hormone in his system was acting like an overdose of caffeine, making him jittery and irritable. But she could feel the tension radiating from him, and that made her uneasy. A pissed-off Blutbad, even if he was a friend, was an intimidating creature.

Several more minutes went by as they worked, the only sound the occasional turning of a page. But the silence was broken when Monroe let out a roar, grabbed the book he'd been looking through, and hurled it across the room. The volume struck a shelf filled with bottles and vials, causing glass to shatter and sending liquids and powders spilling onto the floor.

"This is hopeless!" The words were as much growled as spoken. Monroe dug his claws into the countertop and began to draw them toward him, digging furrows into the wood.

Rosalee stepped closer to him and reached out to take hold of his hands in an attempt to calm him—and to keep him from further damaging the counter. Monroe's head snapped to the side to face her. His eyes blazed with anger and his lips curled back to display his fangs. Juliette was so startled that she took several steps away from the counter without realizing she'd done so. Rosalee, however, showed no sign of fear. She kept one hand on Monroe's, but with the other she reached up and scratched behind his left ear. If Juliette hadn't been so frightened by Monroe's outburst, she might have found the scene amusing. But as it was, she was just glad that Rosalee's soothing gesture seemed to do the trick.

Monroe's brow smoothed and his lips relaxed and once more covered his teeth. His gaze still held a hint of menace, but it was subdued, distant. In her veterinary practice, Juliette had a great deal of experience calming scared and aggressive animals, but she doubted she'd be able to work up the courage to calm an enraged Blutbad. But then Rosalee had a huge advantage: she was, after all, Monroe's mate.

When she pulled her hand away from Monroe's ear, he gently took hold of it and kissed her palm.

"Thanks," he said.

Rosalee smiled as Monroe continued to hold her hand. "I take it my special tea isn't doing its job," she said.

He sighed deeply. "The sad thing is, it *is* working. Without it, I'd be even worse." He turned to look at Juliette, his eyes filled with shame. "I'm so sorry, Juliette. I didn't mean to scare you."

"I know," she said. Mentally, she added, *And that scares me even more.* How much worse would it be if he completely lost control? And if he did, how far would he go before Rosalee could stop him—if she could?

She'd assured Nick that she'd be fine with Monroe and Rosalee, and at the time, she'd believed it. But now she was beginning to wish she'd made a different choice.

She was debating whether it would be safer for her to leave—and maybe easier for Monroe if she wasn't around to irritate him unnecessarily—when the door to the shop opened.

Everyone froze. Juliette felt so stupid. With Monroe and Rosalee woged, they should've locked the door to make certain no one came in and saw them. But with everything that had been going on tonight, they'd all forgotten. When Juliette saw who entered, she felt an equal mixture of relief and surprise.

Sean Renard stepped into the shop and immediately turned and locked the door behind him. That was Renard, she thought. Intelligent and secretive.

Renard was a Zauberbiest—the male equivalent of a Hexenbiest—and his ravaged face spoke of his heritage. He might be half-Wesen technically, but he looked all Wesen now. Juliette's stomach flipped when she saw Renard's Zauberbiest features. It was like seeing the Phantom of the Opera without his mask. It didn't help that when Renard had used an elixir to wake her from a coma induced by Adalind Schade, they'd become physically and emotionally bonded somehow. It had taken some time for that condition to run its course, but no matter how strong the attraction had become, Renard had fought to keep from taking advantage of her. She deeply appreciated that and respected him for it. But she still wasn't comfortable around him, and she doubted she'd ever be, at least not entirely.

Before he said anything, he stopped and sniffed the air. Then he looked over at the shattered glass and powdery-liquid mess on the floor, next to the book Monroe had thrown. His upper lip curled in distaste, and while Juliette could smell nothing from where she stood, she knew Renard—although farther away from the mess—could smell it far more intensely. And from his reaction, he didn't appreciate the odor. From what she understood, Hexenbiester and Zauberbiester were incredibly sensitive to chemical substances. This ability allowed them to create potions and elixirs that could dramatically alter a person's biochemistry. They were also sensitive to various forms of energy, which allowed them to influence magnetic and electrical fields to achieve feats that seemed almost supernatural. Of course, these abilities were honed with training and practice, and while Juliette had no idea if Renard had ever received such training, she wasn't about to ask him any time soon. But given his sensitivity—especially now that he was affected by the *Ewig Woge*—being in the spice shop surrounded by hundreds of different substances and their smells must have been almost intolerable for him.

Renard shook his head as if to clear it, and looked at Monroe and Rosalee.

"I'm relieved to see I'm not the only one having trouble changing back," he said.

Before Juliette or Rosalee could speak, Monroe began growling deep in his throat, gaze locked on Renard, teeth bared. Renard locked eyes with him, and while he didn't make a sound, he lowered his arms to his sides, hands open, and he widened his stance. Juliette realized he was preparing to fight.

"Monroe, what are you—" Rosalee reached out to touch him as she spoke, but Monroe batted her hand aside. With a single graceful move, he leaped onto the countertop and crouched there, leaning forward slightly, growling louder.

Rosalee looked to Juliette with an expression of alarm. As far as Juliette knew, Monroe and Renard had nothing against each other. They were hardly friends—little more than acquaintances, really—but they were far from enemies.

It's the Ewig Woge, she realized. It had strengthened Monroe's territorial instincts, and he now saw Renard as an intruder who must be challenged. As for Renard... Juliette knew very little about Zauberbiester, other than that they were reputed to be scheming and calculating, as well as stronger and faster than humans. But even if Renard didn't possess deep-rooted animal instincts prompting his actions while in Wesen form, it seemed obvious that he had no intention of backing down from Monroe's challenge.

Monroe's muscles began to coil, and Juliette knew he was seconds away from springing toward Renard. Not knowing what else to do, she ran forward and put herself between them. An instant later, Rosalee rushed out from behind the counter and joined her. The women stood back-to-back, arms outstretched and hands held palms up.

"You don't want to do this," Juliette said, trying to keep her tone as neutral as possible to avoid setting off either man. "You're both being affected by exposure to the Wechselbalg's hormone. Not only is it keeping you woged, it's making you hyper-aggressive."

"You both need to calm down before someone gets hurt," Rosalee added. "And before my shop gets wrecked even more than it already is."

Rosalee practically growled her words, and Juliette knew that she was fighting her own aggressive feelings. It appeared her "soothing tea" couldn't stand up to a concentrated assault of enhanced woge hormone combined with adrenaline.

Neither Monroe nor Renard appeared to have heard the two women. They continued glaring at each other. Monroe continued growling, even louder now, and Renard made a continuous sound, eerie and disturbing, a cross between a wordless deep tone and a serpent's hiss.

"It's like we're not even here," Juliette said.

"Then maybe we need to work a little harder to get their attention," Rosalee said. She smiled at Juliette, revealing teeth that were less prominent than Monroe's, but just as sharp.

Juliette found her friend's smile disquieting, but she returned it, and then the two women started walking. Rosalee toward Monroe and Juliette toward Renard. Renard didn't look at Juliette as she approached, nor did he react in any way when she stopped within a few inches of him. She raised her hand and then slapped his face as hard as she could. She heard her slap echoed, and she knew that Rosalee had done the same thing to Monroe. Her hand hurt like hell, but she ignored the sting and kept her gaze focused on Renard's eyes. If her slap had caused him any pain, he didn't show it. But he did look at her, his upper lip curled in a snarl, and he raised his hand as if to return the strike.

Juliette showed no fear as she said, "Do it and I guarantee you'll regret it. In all kinds of ways."

Renard continued glaring at her, his hand trembling, and for an instant she thought he would strike her. But then he sighed and lowered his hand. When she was confident the moment of danger had passed, she glanced toward Rosalee and Monroe. He was sitting on the counter now, legs dangling over the side, hugging Rosalee, no longer growling.

The door opened then and Nick and Hank entered. The two men stopped when they saw the tableau before them.

"Uh… Did we miss something?" Nick asked.

Juliette smiled.

CHAPTER EIGHT

"So you've made *no* progress on finding a treatment?" Renard asked, his usually controlled voice tinged with impatience.

Monroe scowled. "Pardon us for not having everything figured out in a couple hours," he said, his voice close to a growl.

Monroe and Renard had remained relatively calm since Nick and Hank's arrival, but the two men had hair-trigger tempers right now. Nick knew it was due to the *Ewig Woge*, but that didn't make it any less irritating.

Everyone had taken up different positions in the spice shop, as if claiming their territory. Monroe and Rosalee remained behind the counter, Renard stood a dozen feet away, and Nick, Juliette, and Hank stood between them, acting as a buffer. At least, Nick hoped they were. The last thing Rosalee needed was for Monroe and Renard to start fighting. There had already been enough damage to her shop tonight as it was. More importantly, Nick feared the two men wouldn't have any restraint thanks to the *Ewig Woge*, and both of them could be seriously hurt if they fought. Nick had no idea who would win in a battle between Monroe and Renard, but he didn't want to find out. He wondered how many similar scenes were playing out in Portland tonight. Family and friends affected by the *Ewig Woge* who were struggling to keep from attacking one another. Struggling, and maybe failing. And while he and the others stood around the shop bickering, the *Ewig Woge* continued to spread.

"This is a disaster," Renard said. "The longer Wesen remain fully woged, the greater the chance we'll be exposed. And if those of us with more... aggressive natures keep getting worse, before long the city will start experiencing a level of violence like it's never seen before."

"You make it sound like it's some kind of Wesen apocalypse," Hank said.

"In a very real sense it is," Renard said. "According to Grimm lore, the *Ewig Woge* last hit in a time when travel wasn't nearly as easy as it is today. People can cross the globe in a matter of hours now. It's conceivable this condition could spread to every Wesen on the planet, and faster than we think."

"Maybe that would be a good thing," Juliette said.

Everyone turned to look at her.

"I mean, Wesen have been keeping their existence a secret from humans... well, forever. The *Ewig Woge* could bring that to an end. Wesen wouldn't have to hide anymore."

"It's a nice thought," Rosalee said. "And there are a lot of modern Wesen who hope that one day we'll be able to live openly among humans."

"But that day's not here yet," Monroe said. "Especially if the *Ewig Woge* makes *some* of us a little hard to get along with." He glanced at Renard.

Renard scowled at Monroe, but he didn't take the bait.

"With all the problems there are in the world today, the last thing humanity needs is to learn that there's been a race of shapeshifting beings living alongside them in secret," Renard said. "We'd be hunted like never before. It'd be like the entire human race had become Grimms."

"Okay, I get the point," Hank said. "So what can we do to keep things from getting that bad?"

"Maybe it's time to start thinking about using the Hafen," Nick said.

Juliette gave him a puzzled look, and he quickly explained to her what a Hafen was.

"Dawn is still several hours off," Monroe said. "It's a perfect time for people to head for the forest. They won't be seen. But a lot of people are going to call in sick to work and school tomorrow, enough to be noticed."

"We can cover it up with a story about a bad flu strain hitting Portland," Renard said. "It's close enough to the truth."

"None of that's important now," Nick said. "First we have to start spreading the word that people need to head for the Hafen."

"That won't be hard," Monroe said. "Each of us has a call list. We call five people, they call five people, and within a couple of hours, Portland's Wesen will be on the road to Forest Park."

"All the Wesen who are on the lists," Rosalee said.

"And who get the call," Juliette added.

"I've got Wesen connections throughout Portland," Renard said. "Uniformed officers, firefighters, paramedics, sanitation workers... They can remain in the city to keep an eye out for any Wesen suffering from *Ewig Woge* who don't get the message to go to the Hafen." He turned to Nick and Hank. "And you two can keep working on trying to track down the Wechselbalg."

Nick nodded.

"You have to do whatever it takes to stop the Wechselbalg," Rosalee said. "I know that. But try your best not to kill it. We may need some of its substance in order to make a cure for the *Ewig Woge*."

"We'll take him alive if we can," Nick said. If it came down to killing the Wechselbalg to save an innocent life, he'd do it, no question. Otherwise, he'd try his damnedest to bring the shapeshifter in alive.

Rosalee nodded. "Okay. While you're out chasing the Wechselbalg, Monroe and I will stay here and keep searching for some kind of treatment for the *Ewig Woge*."

"*After* we call the people on our lists," Monroe said.

Rosalee smiled at him and nodded.

"I can stay and help you," Juliette said, and then she yawned.

"You've been on your feet for almost twenty hours," Nick said. "You should go home and get some sleep."

"All of *you* are tired too," she protested.

"Not really," Rosalee said. "The *Ewig Woge* is acting like a stimulant on our systems. But if we do find a treatment for it, I may need some ingredients that I don't have on hand. That means I'll need someone who isn't an *Ewig Woge*-affected Wesen to go pick them up for me. You should get some rest now, so you'll be more alert later, when we'll need you."

Juliette frowned as she thought it over. Nick knew she hated the idea of leaving her friends during a time of need, but she was an intelligent and practical person. He knew what she'd decide to do.

"Fine," Juliette said. "But you promise to call me the moment you need me, okay?" She looked at Nick. "That goes for you, too."

"Promise," he said. "I'll give you a ride back to the storage facility so you can pick up your car."

"You've got too much to do," she said. "I'll call a cab." After she made the call, she kissed him goodbye. Then with a tired smile and wave for the others, she left the shop.

Nick was glad she was going home. He had no idea how bad the situation in town would become, and he felt better knowing she'd be safe. Juliette was smarter than he was, and brave as hell, but she didn't have his Grimm abilities or Hank's police training. He'd taught her to shoot and she practiced on a fairly regular basis, but she wasn't ready to hold her own in a gun battle yet. He hoped she'd never have to.

"All right," Nick said. "Let's get to work."

Juliette stared at the book open before her on the spice shop counter. She was trying to read it, but the text refused to come all the way into focus. And when it did clear for several seconds, it was a nonsense jumble of letters and weird symbols that weren't letters at all. She didn't recognize it as a foreign language, at least not any that she was familiar with.

She turned the book so Monroe and Rosalee could see it better.

"Hey, do either of you have any idea what..."

Her voice died when she looked away from the baffling pages and toward her friends. They stood behind the counter, fully woged—which should have bothered her, but for some reason it didn't. It seemed almost normal somehow. What did bother her was how *much* they'd woged. Both were far more bestial than she'd ever seen them before. Even in Wesen form they normally remained human-looking, although with certain animal-like features. But while their bodies were still mostly humanoid, Monroe had the head of a brown-furred wolf, and Rosalee an orange-and-white-furred fox. As disturbing as that was, their features were exaggerated versions of those animals.

Sharper teeth, longer tapering canine ears, lengthy lolling tongues, and eyes that seemed to glow with internal light: an angry crimson for Monroe, a baleful yellow for Rosalee. Both Wesen began growling deep in their throats, and they raised wickedly clawed hands and lunged across the counter to grab her.

Juliette stepped back just in time to avoid their swiping claws, but in doing so she lost her balance and stumbled backward. She would've fallen if she hadn't backed into something solid which prevented her. She spun around and realized she'd bumped into someone, a slim man wearing a tailored suit.

"Oh, Sean, I'm so sorry, but—"

She broke off as she looked at his face and saw he'd undergone a transformation even more severe than Monroe's and Rosalee's. His face was covered with open wounds, festering sores, raw scar tissue, and places where the skin had been torn away to reveal gleaming bone. One eye was gone, submerged completely beneath distorted, swollen flesh, and his lips were drawn back from his teeth, giving him a perpetual grimace. His ears were little more than shriveled nubs, and most of his hair was gone, with only a few ragged patches remaining. A terrible smell of rot and infection wafted from him, so strong that it made her gorge rise. Hot acid seared her throat, and it took a supreme effort of will to keep from vomiting.

Renard's lone eye blazed with hatred and he snarled as he took hold of her shoulders with ravaged hands. She screamed, tore free of his grasp, and ran past him toward the door. She heard Monroe and Rosalee come out from behind the counter, growling and breathing hard, and she didn't have to look back to know they were coming after her. Renard, too, in all likelihood.

She threw open the door so hard it slammed against the

inner wall and the bells jangled loudly. She plunged into the night and began running. She didn't consciously pick a direction. She was operating almost entirely on survival instinct now. All she knew was she had to get as far away as possible from the spice shop and the nightmarish creatures her friends had become.

She ran faster than she ever had in her life. For a time during her teenage years, she'd run track, and she still ran whenever she could fit it into her busy schedule. But even at the peak of her training and conditioning, she'd never run like *this*. Her legs flew across the asphalt, her feet blurring. She ran lightly and easily, her heart-rate steady, her breath moving in and out of her lungs slow and even. She felt as if she could keep going like this for hours, maybe forever, her pace never slackening, her body never tiring. Despite the situation, the feeling was exhilarating, and she couldn't help bursting out with a joyous laugh.

But her joy instantly gave way to terror when she heard loud snarling behind her, accompanied by the skittering of claws on the hard surface of the street. She knew she shouldn't look back, but she couldn't stop herself. She glanced over her shoulder, and for an instant, she didn't understand what she was seeing. Two canines were running alongside a twisted, misshapen being that could only generously be referred to as human. Then she realized the canines were a wolf and a fox—not Wesen, but actual animals. The other creature, which ran with lurching, spastic motions because of its malformed limbs, was covered with grotesquely ravaged skin that put her in mind of someone who'd been severely burned over his or her entire body. The creature was naked, but its skin was so mottled by wounds and scars that it almost looked like it was clothed. All three beasts were snarling, teeth gnashing, foam flecking their jaws. She could feel the mindless bloodlust pouring from them, and she knew that if they managed to run her down, they would tear her limb from limb and laugh as they bathed in her blood.

She faced forward and put on a fresh burst of speed, determined to outdistance her savage pursuers. But no matter how fast she ran, they were always there behind her, a little closer each time she looked.

She had no idea how long she ran. It could've been minutes, hours, or days. But just as she feared that she'd never be able to escape the creatures who had once been her friends, a dark figure stepped out from an alley ahead of her, walked into the middle of the street, and turned to face her. She felt a stab of fear upon seeing the figure, but as she drew closer to it, she was almost deliriously relieved to see that it was Nick. He was holding a large object in his hand, and as she neared him, she saw that it was a medieval battle-axe, the polished blade gleaming with a silvery light.

Her seemingly endless energy drained out of her then, and her heart began pounding rapidly. She couldn't breathe, and her arms and legs felt as they were filled with wet cement. She stumbled as she reached Nick, and fell to her knees before him.

"Thank God," she said. Or rather, tried to say. Instead of words, what came out of her mouth was an unintelligible combination of sounds, shrill and high-pitched, wet and gurgly, low and gravelly. She looked at her hands and was horrified to see that they were no longer fully human. Instead of skin, her hands were covered with a patchwork of fur, scales, and feathers, and her slender fingers—which now seemed to possess too many joints—ended in sharp claws, talons, or spines, depending on the finger.

She looked up at Nick, confused and frightened, but instead of seeing loving concern in his eyes, she saw cold cruelty and disgust.

"*Wesen*," he said harshly, almost spitting the word. Then he gripped the battle-axe with both hands and raised it high over his head. Juliette heard snuffling laughter from the creatures that had pursued her for so long, and then Nick swung the axe downward in a vicious strike so swift she didn't have time to scream.

Someone was pounding on the door, hitting it so hard it sounded as if they were trying to batter it down. The sound was so startling that she was up and halfway to the door before she was aware of being conscious. She stopped, momentarily disoriented, and then the details of her nightmare came back to her to a jumble of images, sounds, and emotions. She checked her hands, half-expecting to see them as a conglomeration of various animal species, but she was relieved to find them normal.

The pounding continued, becoming louder and more insistent, the force of the blows making the windows in the front room vibrate. Who in the hell could it be, she wondered, especially this late? Then the last of the sleep fog dissipated, and she remembered the *Ewig Woge*. Maybe Monroe or Rosalee was at the door, maybe they'd tried calling her, and she'd been sleeping too deeply to hear her phone ring. Maybe something bad had happened to one of them, or to Hank. Or Nick.

She hurried the rest of the way to the door, unlocked it, and threw it open wide.

Nick stood on the porch, fist raised, hand red from pounding so hard.

"Juliette," he said.

"What are you doing here?" she asked. "Is everything okay? Did you lose your keys?" She looked past him and saw he was alone. "Where's Hank?"

He didn't answer her at first. He continued to look at her, an unreadable expression on his face. She'd seen him go blank like this before, and it worried her. Was it due to the lingering effects of the Cracher-Mortel toxin? Or was it an aftereffect of the woge hormone the Wechselbalg had injected him with? Worse, could it be an interaction between the two?

She took his hand and pulled him inside. He gave no resistance, and once he was in, she closed and locked the door once more. Since becoming aware of Nick's legacy as a Grimm, she'd become more security conscious than ever. If something had come running out of the night to attack them, she wouldn't have been surprised. After all, it wouldn't have been the first time.

And to think I used to worry about Nick dealing with ordinary human criminals.

She turned to him. "Come on, let's get you onto the couch."

She took his hand once more and led him to the couch where she'd been dozing. He looked around as they walked into the living room, his gaze sweeping over the place, taking in everything. She'd grown used to him surveying his immediate environment wherever they went. His police training and experience made him far more aware of his surroundings than ordinary people, and his observational abilities had grown even stronger since he'd come into his heritage as a Grimm. Usually he was more circumspect in observing whenever he entered a room, and she couldn't recall seeing him observe so intently in his own home.

He sat on the couch and glanced down at the upholstery. He ran his hand over it slowly.

"Are you okay?" she asked again.

"Hmmm? Oh, yeah. I'm fine. A little tired. It's been a long night."

"Yes, it has. Can I get you something to drink?"

"Sure."

When he didn't say anything more, she asked, "Anything in particular you want?"

He considered the question for several moments, an expression of deep thought on his face, as if he were debating a serious matter.

"Whatever I usually have is fine," he said.

She frowned, but said, "Okay." She then started for the kitchen.

She was standing at the fridge, door open, trying to decide whether she should get Nick a beer or a bottled water, when it hit her. The person sitting on the couch wasn't Nick. At least not *her* Nick.

She reached into her pants pocket for her phone, but then realized she'd left it on the end table next to the couch when she'd been sleeping.

"Damn it!" she whispered. She didn't have her keys, either. If she decided to sneak out the back, she'd be forced to go on foot. It wasn't so cold out that she'd need a jacket or shoes, as long as she was outside only for a short time. But she needed to let Nick know the Wechselbalg was here as soon as possible. If she left the house, the Wechselbalg might too. She needed to keep him here until Nick could arrive. More importantly, she needed to keep the creature here so it wasn't running loose and threatening people's lives.

Her mind made up, she reached into the fridge, grabbed two bottles of water, closed the door, and headed back into the living room. Her heart was pounding, and when she held out a bottle for "Nick," she couldn't keep her hand from trembling. The Wechselbalg didn't seem to notice, and he took the bottle from her, twisted off the cap, and took a long drink, polishing off the entire bottle. He then handed the empty to her and took the second bottle. He drained that one even faster.

It made sense. If the Wechselbalg's true form was a semisolid mass of highly evolved woge hormone, it would need a lot of liquid to survive, far more than a human needed. She took the second empty from him, walked over to the end table, put the bottles down, and picked up her phone.

"You really worked up a thirst tonight. I'll go get you some more water." She slipped the phone into her pocket and started toward the kitchen.

"No need," the Wechselbalg said. "I'm satisfied."

She paused and turned back to face him.

"But I'm still thirsty. Be right back, okay?"

The Wechselbalg looked at her for a moment. No longer was there any confusion in his eyes. His gaze was sharp and focused. She wondered if he'd copied Nick's observation skills. Probably. But even if he hadn't, a creature like the Wechselbalg was like a chameleon, only his protection came not from coloration but rather from being a consummate actor. Observation would be a key component in determining if his audience found his act convincing. If they didn't, he'd adjust his behavior quickly and efficiently. And if he still couldn't convince them, he might flee—or kill them.

She was no actress, but she knew enough to know that if she tried too hard to look innocent, it would only make her seem even more suspicious. So she tried not to do anything, just stand there and look back at the Wechselbalg with as little expression on her face as possible.

The Wechselbalg frowned slightly, his eyes narrowing. The expression was one she'd seen on Nick many times. She was certain Nick had no idea that he looked that way when he was concentrating on something he was observing. She found the Wechselbalg's imitation of the expression to be perfect, eerily so. If she hadn't known she was looking at a Wesen shapeshifter, she would've sworn it was her Nick.

Just when she feared the Wechselbalg had figured out she was on to him, he said, "Sure."

She managed a smile before turning and heading for the kitchen once again. She felt the Wechselbalg watching her go, and she suddenly felt awkward, as if she was unbalanced and ungainly. But she made it out of the living room without the Wechselbalg doing or saying anything, and once she was in the kitchen, she took out her phone and began texting Nick. She knew she didn't have long until the Wechselbalg became suspicious and came looking for her, so she kept her message short.

Shapeshifter is here. I'm okay. Come fast.

She hit SEND, then tucked the phone back into her pocket. She got a bottle of water from the fridge and then returned to the living room. The Wechselbalg was no longer sitting on the couch. He was walking around the room, looking at pictures and knick-knacks, a slightly lost expression on his face, as if he was trying to remember them but couldn't. It seemed that while the Wechselbalg had managed to copy some of Nick's memories, he hadn't copied them all.

She wanted to keep a safe distance from him without making it obvious, so she went to the couch, sat, removed the cap from the bottle and took a sip.

"How was work tonight?" she asked.

He turned around and looked at her.

"Why ask me that? You know what I really am. I can see it in your eyes."

Cold fear gripped her as the Wechselbalg started walking toward her.

Nick and Hank had been patrolling the streets of Portland for the better part of an hour. Monroe and Rosalee remained at the spice shop to contact the Wesen on their call lists and continue researching. Renard had left the shop at the same time as Nick and Hank. He was also patrolling the city, while presumably calling his various Wesen contacts to elicit their help. Knowing Renard's somewhat Machiavellian personality, Nick had no doubt the man had any number of contacts in the city—hell, probably across the globe—that he could call on when needed. But whoever they were, Nick feared they wouldn't be enough to cover the whole city.

One encouraging development was the traffic. It wasn't as if the streets of Portland were suddenly clogged with vehicles, but there was a marked difference in the number of cars out compared to a normal night. Then again, Nick thought, there weren't really any normal nights in this city, not since he'd started working as a Grimm.

"Looks like the Wesen are getting out of Dodge," Hank said. "I think we just passed a family of... What do you call the ones that look like rhinos?"

"Dickfellig," Nick said.

Hank chuckled. "I know. I just like to make you say the word."

Nick scowled at him. He was about to comment on his partner's juvenile sense of humor, when a flash of movement on the sidewalk caught his eye. Someone was running down the street, a Seelengut from the look of her. The sheep-like Wesen wore a red hoodie and black yoga pants, but her feet—which were more or less human— were bare. Some Wesen were graceful and powerful when woged. Others not so much. Seelenguter tended to fall into the latter category. The woman was *trying* to run, but her motion was more like a fast shuffle, her arms hanging limply at her sides, as if she feared she might unbalance herself by using them.

Following behind her at little more than a fast walk was

a cat-like Wesen that Nick figured for a Klaustreich. While Klaustreich were technically predator types, they tended to be scavengers rather than hunters. More alley cat than jungle cat. But he supposed that thanks to the *Ewig Woge*, the Klaustreich's feral instincts had been strengthened and brought to the surface.

"Hank!"

"I see them. *Really* see them. Hold on."

Hank yanked the steering wheel hard to the right, and the Charger's tires squealed as the car skidded to the curb. Nick didn't bother complimenting his partner on his parking job. He shoved the door open, got out of the car, and made it onto the sidewalk in time to intercept the Seelengut woman. She let out a bleat of surprise as she bumped into Nick, and he took hold of her shoulders to steady her.

"It's all right," he said quickly. "I'm a police officer. I'm here to help."

But his words didn't seem to reassure her. If anything, they upset her more. She tried to pull free from his grip, turning her head from side to side as she did, as if she were trying to avoid meeting his gaze.

"Don't look at me!" she shouted. "Let me go!"

She's not just afraid of the Klaustreich, Nick thought. *She's also afraid because she knows she can't hide her appearance.*

"I know you're Seelengut, and it's okay," he said. "I won't hurt you."

"But *I* might."

The Klaustreich had slowed his pace to what Nick thought of as an insolent stroll. His fur was black with patches of white above the eyes and around the mouth. The Klaustreichen that Nick had encountered had possessed eyes that looked like a fifty-fifty blend of feline and human. But this one's eyes were all cat. Another sign of the *Ewig Woge*'s effects?

The Klaustreich wore a scuffed black leather jacket, a white turtleneck, jeans, and sneakers. He kept his hands in his jacket pockets as he approached, and Nick heard a soft, throaty rumbling. The man was purring, he realized.

The woman looked over her shoulder at the Klaustreich, and the sight of him so close—he was less than ten feet away—caused her to forget her fear of Nick. She pressed herself against him and said, "Don't let him hurt me!"

"Keep your distance," Hank said in an I'm-a-cop-and-don't-mess-with-me voice.

The Klaustreich gave him an amused look, clearly unimpressed, but he did as Hank asked and stopped walking.

If this had been an ordinary situation, Nick would've gently placed the woman at arm's length, and then he and Hank would've begun questioning her and her pursuer to find out what was going on. But this was nowhere near a normal situation, so Nick allowed the woman to continue clinging to him.

"What's your name?" Nick asked. It took her a moment to reply.

"Allison," she said.

Nick nodded, then turned his focus to the Klaustreich. "What about you?"

"You can call me Sylvester."

"Don't be a smart-ass," Nick said.

Klaustreichen had a reputation for being the jerks of the Wesen community, and it seemed this man was determined to do his best to live up to that reputation.

The Klaustreich let out a long theatrical sigh. "Fine. My real name is Donald."

"That's not much better," Hank said.

Donald shot him a dark look, but didn't comment.

Allison kept sneaking glances at Donald, and Nick felt her tremble in his arms.

"What happened, Allison?" he asked gently.

She kept glancing at Donald as she spoke. The Klaustreich looked equal parts amused and bored.

"I— I was at work when I felt a woge coming over me. Not a regular one, either. This was different somehow. Stronger. I was on drive-thru, so I yanked off my headset, grabbed my hoodie, told the manager that I wasn't feeling good, and got out of there just as the change hit me. I scared a customer who was walking into the restaurant, and that's when I knew everyone could see me. See me like *this*, I mean. I pulled up my hood and kept my hands in my pockets and started walking home. Normally I take the bus, but I couldn't get on when everyone would see me as a Seelengut."

Allison hadn't said where she worked, but it was obviously a fast-food joint of some kind. She could've caught the *Ewig Woge* from a Wesen customer, and then in turn passed it on to other Wesen who came to her drive-thru. At this rate, most of Portland's Wesen community would be infected by sunrise, Nick thought. If not sooner.

Hank turned to Donald. "Where do you come in?"

Before he could answer, a passing motorist honked his horn and shouted, "Kick-ass costumes!" out the window as he drove by.

"Damn it," Nick muttered. Similar scenes were probably playing out across town. Humans spotting fully woged Wesen and taking them as people wearing costumes or—if they got a close-up look—thinking they were seeing monsters. How long would it be before the city had a full-scale panic on its hands?

"I asked you a question," Hank said to the Klaustreich.

"I was out clubbing when the woge came over me. I

rushed out before too many people saw me. Luckily, most of them weren't in a condition to trust their senses, if you know what I mean. So after I left the club, I tried keeping to the shadows while I attempted to get my woge under control—with no luck. And then I saw *her*."

Nick wasn't used to seeing Wesen fully woged when first encountering them. Usually he saw their human aspects first and then witnessed them change. Seeing Allison and Donald like this made it hard to judge their ages based solely on appearance. But now that he'd heard both of them speak, he figured them to be in their late teens or early twenties.

Donald continued. "She was walking on the sidewalk. At first I couldn't tell she was Wesen. Like she said, she had her hood up. But I was intrigued by the way she walked. Or *tried* to walk. She kept wobbling and stumbling, as if her legs weren't working right. I thought she might be drunk or high, but then she stopped to take off her shoes, and that's when I realized *why* she was having trouble walking. She was Seelengut. It was obvious she was struggling to control her woge, and since I was similarly affected, I thought I could help her. And—selfishly—I hoped she might be able to shed some light on what had happened to both of us. But when I approached her, she did a major freak-out. She looked at me as if I was a starving Blutbad, screamed, and ran. Seelengut aren't always the most graceful creatures— especially when they're afraid." He glanced at Allison and smiled. "No offense."

In response, Allison pressed against Nick more tightly.

"Why did you follow her after she ran?" Nick asked. Something wasn't adding up here. If the Klaustreich had the *Ewig Woge*, he should've been displaying signs of increased aggression. But he'd been doing his best to paint himself as a Good Samaritan, and working just a bit too hard at it.

Donald shrugged. "I wanted to see what she'd do."

Nick exchanged a look with Hank before turning back to Donald.

"Explain."

Donald rolled his feline eyes skyward, as if he couldn't believe how dense Nick was being. "I followed *because* she ran. It's an instinct thing. Besides…" The Klaustreich's mouth curved into an inhuman smile, revealing needle-sharp teeth. "I thought I might be able to have some fun with her." As if to demonstrate what sort of fun he was talking about, he took his fur-covered hands from his jacket pockets and extended his claws. "Don't worry. I wouldn't have marked her *too* deeply."

He let out a hissing laugh that made the hair on the back of Nick's neck stand up. Klaustreichen might not be as bloodthirsty as some Wesen, but the *Ewig Woge* had intensified Donald's natural feline curiosity and casual cruelty to the point where he reveled in tormenting Allison. Maybe he was telling the truth about not wishing to kill her. Maybe he was lying. Or maybe once he began spilling her blood, he'd find himself unable to stop, thanks to the *Ewig Woge*. Whatever the outcome would've been if he and Hank hadn't come on the scene, Nick was glad they'd stopped Donald from hurting Allison any more than he already had.

"We should haul your furry ass down to the precinct and book you for assault," Hank said.

"But I haven't done anything," Donald said, his tone all innocence. "Except offer my help to a frightened woman who overreacted."

His smile widened, and Nick found himself thinking of the Cheshire Cat. He didn't think Donald would be vanishing into thin air any time soon. Too bad. It would save them the hassle of dealing with him if he did.

Nick looked at Allison. Normally, he'd ask if she wanted to press charges against Donald, but given the way they both looked at the moment, he couldn't take them to the precinct.

"My partner and I could give you a ride home," he said. Then he looked to Donald. "As for you, I'd go straight home, pack a bag, and head to the Hafen. This... condition is affecting Wesen all over town. We don't know how long it will last or if we can find a cure. Until then, the best thing to do is lie low."

"And keep your claws to yourself," Hank added.

Donald dropped his mocking attitude. "It's *that* serious?"

"Sure is," Nick said.

Allison began to tremble even harder in his arms, and he feared she was on the verge of a full-scale panic attack. If the *Ewig Woge* had intensified the natural timidity of her kind, it could be manifesting as uncontrollable fear.

"It's okay, Allison. Everything's going to be—"

Before Nick could finish, Allison tore free from his arms, spun around, and ran toward Donald. Nick and Hank were so surprised by her actions that they could only stand and stare as she reached Donald, lashed out with one of her hooves, and struck him a solid kick to the knee. There was the sharp sound of bone cracking, and Donald yowled in pain. His leg buckled, and he fought to maintain his balance. But Allison gave him a hard shove, and he fell to the sidewalk, yowling even louder as his knee struck concrete. Allison didn't stop there, though. She began kicking Donald in the face as hard as she could.

Nick shook off his paralysis and ran forward to stop her. He grabbed hold of her and pulled her away from Donald. She managed to get in a last kick before he got her far enough away from the Klaustreich.

"What the hell are you doing?" he demanded as he

turned her around to face him, well aware that by doing so he was risking a hoof to the head. He expected to find her features twisted into a mask of hate by the *Ewig Woge*. But instead he saw wide, terror-filled eyes, flaring nostrils as she breathed rapidly, and trembling lips.

"I won't let him hurt me," she panted. "I won't!"

Nick realized she hadn't attacked the Klaustreich out of anger, but rather from fear. When confronted by danger, all creatures experienced a flight or fight response. Nick had removed the option of flight when he'd stepped in to help her. She'd been left with no other choice but to fight.

The *Ewig Woge* was worse than they'd thought. If it could cause a normally peaceful being like a Seelengut to savagely attack someone, how much more would it do to predatory Wesen? If affected Wesen couldn't control themselves, predators or not, how safe would the Hafen be? The Wesen might well have been safer if they'd remained in their own homes behind locked doors, isolated from one another. Even now dozens, maybe hundreds of Wesen were heading out of town to Forest Park to what they thought was a safe refuge. But instead they could be heading to a killing field.

My God, he thought. *We've made a terrible mistake.*

Hank had moved near Donald and was crouched down, checking the Klaustreich's injuries. He kept several feet back to better avoid a claw strike should the Wesen lash out in pain or anger. Donald moaned, and he was bleeding from his now swollen and misshapen nose, but he sat up and waved Hank away, as if to say he didn't need any help. His claws had retracted—at least for now—which Nick took as a hopeful sign.

Nick was trying to decide how best to handle the situation before it deteriorated any further, when Allison looked at him with dawning recognition.

"You're the Grimm!" she said, voice quavering.

"He is?" Donald jumped to his feet in a fluid motion, only to let out a particularly colorful curse word when he tried to put weight on his injured knee. He narrowed his eyes and extended his claws once more. "You killed those two Skalengeck kids in the alley."

Nick wondered how Donald had heard about the teens' deaths. Maybe their families—distraught and angry—had found the graffiti and spread the word. *The wonders of modern technology,* he thought. Information—too often, incorrect information—spread even faster these days than something like the *Ewig Woge*.

"No, that wasn't me," he said. "In fact, my partner and I were called out to investigate their murders."

"That's right," Hank said.

"Bullshit," Donald said, then spat a glob of blood onto the sidewalk. "You stay the hell away from me!"

He turned and started hobbling away as fast as he could on his bad knee, throwing glances over his shoulder to make sure Nick wasn't following him.

Allison stomped hard on Nick's foot then, and he released his grip on her out of reflex. She ran in the same direction as Donald, now more afraid of Nick than the Klaustreich that had tormented her.

Hank walked over to join Nick.

"That looked like it hurt."

Nick flexed his toes within his shoe and grimaced. "It did. I don't think anything's broken, though."

For several moments the two men watched the Wesen retreat down the sidewalk. Eventually, Donald turned a corner, but Allison kept going straight.

"At least we don't have to worry about those two getting into another fight," Hank said.

"Not with each other, anyway," Nick said, then he sighed.

"The longer this night goes on, the worse things get."

Hank nodded. "It's only a matter of time before the situation gets seriously out of hand—if it hasn't already."

"I think we should check in with the Captain and see what he thinks."

Nick took his phone from his pocket, but before he could call Renard, he saw that he'd received a text. It must've come while they've been dealing with Allison and Donald, or else he would've heard the alert tone. He checked the message and saw it was from Juliette. It was brief, and as he read the words, he felt an icy hand close around his heart.

"What?" Hank said. "Is something wrong?"

Nick didn't answer. He ran toward the Charger, and Hank followed.

CHAPTER NINE

Juliette's first impulse was to jump off the couch and run for the front door, but she didn't give in to it. She knew that there was no way she could outrun the Wechselbalg, especially if he possessed Nick's speed and reflexes. So while she was far from calm inside, she did her best to keep her emotions from showing on her face.

The Wechselbalg walked toward her, a coldness in his eyes like nothing she'd ever seen in Nick—*her* Nick— before.

"I know what it's like," she said.

The Wechselbalg stopped and regarded her, curiosity now joining the coldness in his gaze.

Juliette hurried on. "I don't know how many of Nick's memories you were able to duplicate, but it's obvious that you didn't get all of them. I saw the way you were walking around the room, looking at things, touching them, as if you almost remembered them but didn't quite."

The Wechselbalg continued to look at her in silence. He didn't start advancing toward her again, though, and she was encouraged enough to keep talking.

"I know what it's like to grope for memories that seem

just out of reach. Something happened to me a while back, and I fell into a coma. When I came out of it, I couldn't remember anything about Nick. Not a single detail about our relationship or about him as a person. I felt like something was missing, but I didn't know what. Nick and our friends told me what had happened, and while I believed them, I still couldn't remember Nick. It was so bizarre to meet a stranger who everyone believes is your fiancé. Everyone but you, that is."

She paused to gauge the Wechselbalg's reaction to her words. The shapeshifter's face displayed no sign of emotion, but his gaze showed continued curiosity mixed with wariness. And was there a little hope present as well? Maybe.

Juliette went on.

"My memories of Nick returned eventually, but I still remember what it was like to *not* remember him, if that makes sense. Sometimes it almost feels like I'm two different people, and I'm not sure who the real me is. It must be so much worse for you."

She paused again to give the Wechselbalg a chance to reply. Several moments passed in silence, and she began to think he would never speak. But then softly, hesitantly, he started talking.

"I am always two people, although I try very hard to talk, act, and think like the person whose body I wear. The memories I… acquire from others are never complete, but usually they are sufficient for my needs. But not this time. Nick Burkhardt's memories are incomplete and hazy. Whenever I try to grab hold of them, they squirm out of my fingers, like tiny fish that swim rapidly away. It's most frustrating."

"I imagine it is," Juliette said.

"I am trying to do a good job of being Nick Burkhardt, but without greater access to his memories, it is difficult."

The Wechselbalg brightened. "But you can help me! You are Nick's fiancée. You know him better than anyone. You can remember *for* me!"

He took a step closer, and Juliette had to fight to keep from flinching. She didn't want to show fear. She wanted to keep the Wechselbalg relaxed and talking until Nick got there. She forced herself to smile.

"I'll be happy to tell you anything you want to know."

The Wechselbalg smiled back at her, but then he frowned.

"Something doesn't feel right about this."

Juliette cursed inwardly. The Wechselbalg might be mentally confused, but he still had Nick's instincts and intuition. He could sense her deception, even if he wasn't aware of exactly what he sensed.

"I *am* scared a little," she said. "It's not every day that you meet a Wesen who looks like your fiancé."

A look of concern came over the Wechselbalg's face.

"Please don't worry, Juliette. I wouldn't ever do anything to hurt you. Now that Nick is gone, I *am* Nick." He tried to give her what she assumed was meant to be a reassuring smile, but it seemed artificial and devoid of any real emotion, like a mannequin.

He doesn't know that Nick's alive, she thought. And why would he? Up to this point in the Wechselbalg's life, none of the people it duplicated had survived the process. This was good. The Wechselbalg had no reason to suspect Nick was on his way—she *hoped* he was on his way—and therefore he had no reason to flee.

"I'll try not to be afraid," she said, and managed another smile.

"Good."

The Wechselbalg walked over to the couch and sat next to her. There were only a couple inches between them, and her proximity to the creature made her skin crawl. Her senses told her this was Nick. He looked and sounded like Nick. But her mind knew that he was a killer who stole the form and memories of his victims. And he would've killed Nick if he could have. He thought he had. And now here he was, sitting next to her as if were the most normal thing in the world. She hoped he wouldn't try to touch her. She didn't think she'd be able to stand that.

"I've never had anyone to talk to about these things," the Wechselbalg said. "And I never thought I'd find anyone who understood what it's like." He gave her a tentative, shy smile.

"I promise I'll do my best to understand everything," she said.

"Wechselbalgen live lonely lives, and we live much longer than ordinary humans or Wesen. Because of this, we reproduce rarely. I have no memory of my parents or of any siblings. We rarely encounter others of our kind. I don't think there are many of us."

"How do you recognize each other?"

"We automatically woge in one another's presence if we are close enough. The last time I saw another of my kind was…" The Wechselbalg trailed off as he thought. "In Krakow. Sometime in the early 1800s, I think. I can't recall the exact date."

He fell silent for a time after that, but since Juliette didn't feel any tension from him, she sat quietly and waited to see if he would continue speaking. Eventually, he did.

"All Wesen blend in to survive, but my kind goes a step further. We *become* humans, both on the outside and on the inside. We're so good at it that after a while we almost forget we're Wechselbalgen. Until our bodies begin to return to our natural state. Then we find someone else to join with."

Join? Juliette thought. *You mean copy and kill.*

"It takes years before that happens. Sometimes decades. At least, it used to. It happens faster for me now. Much faster. I'm not sure why. Maybe it's because I'm so old, eh?" He chuckled. "But *this* one—" He slapped his chest so hard that it made Juliette jump. "This body is strong. Sturdy. I think it will last a long time. I hope so, anyway."

If she hadn't known Nick was alive, she would've been sickened to hear the Wechselbalg talk about his duplicated body as casually as this. As it was, it still made her uncomfortable.

"I can think better in this body, too." He frowned. "Not as clearly as I used to, but good. Better than in years. And I can do things I never could before."

Without warning, he leaped off the couch, sprang into the air, came down to perform a graceful somersault, and then rose to his feet. He spun around to face her and raised his hands as if he were a gymnast who'd just finished a particularly difficult routine.

"Ta-dah!" he said, then grinned.

Juliette hesitated for a half second before applauding. She smiled as if delighted by the trick, but inside she was realizing that, at least on one level, the Wechselbalg was little more than a child. It made sense, since humans suffering from dementia often displayed regressive childlike behavior. But when the person who displayed these symptoms was Wesen—and a Wesen who'd duplicated a Grimm's body—that situation couldn't be more dangerous. There was no predicting what the creature might do, or how much further its mental state might deteriorate in the hours ahead. From what the Wechselbalg had said, he'd been burning through bodies rapidly over the last several years. Duplicating Nick's Grimm physiology might make the Wechselbalg's current body last longer than usual, but it wasn't a real Grimm's body, just a copy. And given how much the Wechselbalg had declined over the years, it probably wasn't all that stable a copy. It was only a matter of time before the Wechselbalg began to have a meltdown—literally. The only question was how many people he would kill before then.

"What else can you do?" Juliette asked.

The Wechselbalg shrugged. "I'm not really sure. I haven't had much of a chance to find out."

Without warning, he dove to the floor, pressed his palms on the carpet, and straightened his legs into the air. He held this position seemingly without effort, and Juliette had the impression that he might be able to do so for hours. He then lifted his right arm and stretched it out to the side, supporting himself entirely with his left. Then he reversed the action, holding out his left arm while supporting himself with his right. She could see that holding himself up one-handed did take a bit of effort, but not much. He then put both hands down and allowed his legs to fall backward, and he assumed a standing position once more.

Juliette dutifully clapped. This time the Wechselbalg executed a self-mocking bow, the gesture so like something Nick would've done that it made her gasp.

She felt sorry for the Wechselbalg then. It was one thing to lose a large chunk of memory, as she had for a time, but what was it like to have no identity of your own? To always pretend to be something you weren't? To never be able to share your most private thoughts and feelings without exposing yourself as a monster? The loneliness, the sense of isolation and dislocation, were beyond imagining.

The Wechselbalg returned to the couch and sat next to her once more.

"What do you want to do now?" he asked.

He's like a kid on a playground who's just made a new friend, she thought.

She told herself not to be fooled, though. As a vet, she knew that even the sweetest-seeming animal could turn vicious in an instant, given the right circumstances. The Wechselbalg might not be an animal, but he was a proven killer, and she couldn't afford to let her guard down even for a second.

"We could watch TV," Juliette suggested. "Or maybe play a board game. Nick doesn't like board games as much as I do, but he humors me."

She knew she'd said the wrong thing even before she finished speaking. The Wechselbalg's brow furrowed, and his lips pressed into a tight line.

"*I'm* Nick," he said. His words were spoken softly, and were all the more threatening for it.

"Yes. I'm sorry. It's just that this is all so new to me."

The Wechselbalg continued scowling, and she knew her words hadn't placated him.

"You don't think I'm Nick. You're just pretending you do because you're scared of me."

Juliette struggled to think of something, anything she could say that might allay the Wechselbalg's suspicions, at least for a little longer, but nothing came to her.

She heard the front door open then, and the relief that washed over her was overwhelming.

"Juliette?" Nick—the *real* Nick—called out. "Are you okay?"

She wanted to jump up off the couch and run to him, but she feared what the Wechselbalg might do if she made any sudden moves. So she stayed where she was and called back, "We're in here."

The Wechselbalg didn't react upon hearing Nick's voice, other than to cock his head slightly to the side, like a puzzled dog.

Nick came into the living room, followed closely by

Hank. Both men had their guns drawn and pointed toward the floor. When they saw the Wechselbalg—and especially saw how close he was sitting to her—they stopped. Nick locked gazes with the Wechselbalg, and Juliette saw his eyes widen in surprise upon seeing an exact likeness of himself in his own home.

The Wechselbalg rose to his feet, and Juliette saw that he had a gun tucked into his pants against the small of his back.

"This isn't possible," the shapeshifter said. "You're dead, and *I'm* Nick Burkhardt."

"Wrong on both counts," Nick said.

The Wechselbalg looked at Nick for a long moment, his thoughts unreadable. Then in a single swift motion he drew his gun. Juliette started to cry out, intending to warn Nick. But instead of firing on Nick or Hank, the creature pressed the gun's muzzle against the side of her head.

Juliette stiffened and the Wechselbalg's mouth curved into a cruel smile.

"Your move," he said to Nick.

Nick had known what the Wechselbalg would look like, but *knowing* and *seeing* were two different things. He'd experienced so many strange things as a Grimm, but seeing himself sitting on the couch next to Juliette was perhaps the most bizarre. He experienced an unexpected moment of disorientation, as if he were looking into a funhouse mirror.

The Wechselbalg stood and told Nick it wasn't possible for him to be here. Nick disagreed, but before he or Hank could make a move, the Wechselbalg drew a Glock and pressed it against Juliette's temple.

Nick had heard other cops talk about how time seemed to stand still during a tense or traumatic situation, but it was an experience he'd never had. He always seemed to be able to do what needed to be done without hesitating, and if he had any emotional reaction, it would be later, after the situation was resolved. But now that he was seeing a version of himself holding a gun to the head of the woman he loved, time seemed to slow to a crawl. Even worse, he had no idea what to do. If he made a wrong move—maybe *any* move—the shapeshifter might pull the trigger, and Juliette would die. But he felt another, competing impulse. The Wechselbalg was a threat, not just to Juliette but to anyone unfortunate enough to catch his attention. The shapeshifter might be confused, maybe even mentally ill, but he was a killer and he had to be stopped. The part of Nick that was a Grimm—a part so deep, so essential to who and what he was—urged him to take action and slay the beast. *Now.* His hands tightened on his Glock, and he experienced an almost overwhelming urge to raise his gun and aim it at the Wechselbalg.

As if sensing the struggle taking place inside his partner, Hank said, "Easy, Nick."

Nick nodded almost imperceptibly, and he kept his gun pointed toward the floor.

"He won't hurt me," Juliette said.

The Wechselbalg glared at her. "Be quiet," he said.

Juliette ignored him and kept her gaze fastened on Nick.

"He has too much of you inside him," she said. "He may be an imperfect copy, but he can't hurt me because *you* never would."

"I don't know," Hank said. "He's hurt plenty of people already tonight."

"Trust me, Nick," Juliette said, still holding his gaze.

"Shut up, shut up, shut UP!" the Wechselbalg said, his voice rising with each word.

Juliette was clearly upsetting the shapeshifter, but he

wasn't showing any indication of violence toward her. In and of itself, that wasn't surprising. A violent criminal in the Wechselbalg's position who was seeking to establish control over a situation would be reluctant to kill a hostage, especially with two armed cops standing only a few feet away. Cops who'd start firing at him before his victim could hit the floor. But there was more to the Wechselbalg's agitation that that. He wasn't demanding that Nick and Hank drop their weapons, nor was he insisting that he was serious, he'd really do it, so they better give him what he wanted if they didn't want to see Juliette's brains splattered all over the couch. Instead, his primary concern seemed to be urging Juliette to quit insisting he wouldn't harm her. That, more than anything else, convinced Nick that Juliette was right. The Wechselbalg *didn't* want to hurt her. But that didn't mean he wouldn't, even if only by accident, if this standoff continued any longer.

"I'm going to put my gun down on the floor," Nick said, "and my partner is going to do the same."

"I am?" Hank said, making it very clear from his tone that he did *not* approve of this development. But Nick knew that Hank would back his play, no matter what.

"So just take it easy, okay?" Nick kept his gaze locked on the Wechselbalg as he slowly crouched down and gently placed his Glock on the floor. He didn't take his eyes off the Wechselbalg to check, but he didn't need to see Hank to know he did the same.

Nick straightened. "Your problem isn't with Juliette. It's with me."

The Wechselbalg's gaze shifted back and forth between Nick and Juliette, but his gun hand never wavered.

"She acted like she was my friend. Like she understood me. But she told you I was here, didn't she? How else would you and Hank have known to come here and enter with your weapons drawn? I don't know what she did. Probably called or texted you when she was in the kitchen. It doesn't matter *how* she did it. She did it. She doesn't care about me, and she never did."

The Wechselbalg sounded more hurt than angry, like a child rejected by a beloved adult. But if he truly felt betrayed by Juliette, he might go ahead and shoot her despite whatever emotional programming he'd picked up when he'd copied Nick.

"Your problem with me is much bigger," he said. "Something obviously went wrong with the duplicating process. You look like me, and you have my abilities, but you don't have all my memories. Besides, how can you even hope to become me all the way as long as I'm still alive? The only way you can truly be Nick Burkhardt is to finish what you started."

The Wechselbalg gave Juliette one last look before taking his gun away from her head and pointing it at Nick.

"If I shoot you, there will only be one of us," the Wechselbalg said.

"Yes, but you won't get the rest of my memories then. They'll die with me."

The Wechselbalg looked at Nick for several moments. Nick could see the warring impulses at work on the shapeshifter's face. Nick honestly didn't know which way it was going to go, and he was readying himself to leap to the side if the Wechselbalg started firing. But the shapeshifter tucked his gun against the small of his back again, and he started walking toward Nick, spines extending from his fingertips.

Nick figured he had a fifty-fifty chance of snatching his gun off the floor and putting a bullet into the Wechselbalg before the shapeshifter could reach him. But he wanted to avoid killing his doppelganger if he could. Rosalee had said she might need some of the Wechselbalg's substance to create a cure for the *Ewig Woge*. She might still be able to extract it if the creature was dead, but Nick didn't want to take that chance.

Nick's first priority was to lure the Wechselbalg out of the house and get it away from Juliette and Hank. But before he could turn and run, the Wechselbalg put on a sudden burst of speed and came rushing toward him. Nick intended to repeat one of the moves he'd used on the Wechselbalg when it had attacked him at the Millers' house. He grabbed hold of the Wechselbalg's wrists with the intention of falling backward, planting a foot on the creature's midsection, and using the shapeshifter's momentum to throw it into the air. But it seemed the Wechselbalg wasn't going to fall for the same trick twice. When Nick tried to fall backward, the Wechselbalg braced himself and swung his arms to the left. Nick maintained his grip on the Wechselbalg's wrists, and the creature's momentum pulled him off balance. The Wechselbalg continued spinning to the left, pulling Nick stumbling with it. The Wechselbalg picked up speed, and snapped his arms as if they were whips. The action broke Nick's grip on the shapeshifter's wrists and sent him stumbling toward the wall face-first. He managed to angle his body in time so that his right shoulder slammed into the wall instead of his face, and the impact sent a fiery jolt of pain all the way down to his hand. His arm went partially numb, and he hoped that nothing was broken or dislocated.

Smooth, Burkhardt, he thought.

He turned away from the wall, expecting to see the Wechselbalg coming toward him. But instead he saw that Hank had stepped forward and got the creature in a headlock from behind. Hank was strong, but he was still only human. The Wechselbalg's finger spines remained extended, and he reached up and jabbed them into Hank's arm. The spines passed through the fabric of Hank's jacket and into his flesh without resistance, and Hank cried out in agony. At first he managed to maintain his grip on the creature despite the pain, but then the Wechselbalg savagely yanked the spines free. Hank shouted, blood spurted, and he released the shapeshifter. Nick knew that the Wechselbalg's spines injected a numbing agent, so Hank's pain would pass quickly, but he had no idea whether the creature had injected any of the super woge hormone into Hank. Even if he had, Nick knew the Wechselbalg wouldn't stop his attack there. Hank was a threat to the creature, and therefore had to be destroyed.

Nick started running toward the Wechselbalg as the creature raised its hands for another attack. From the way the creature was standing, Nick figured it planned to swipe the needle-sharp spines across Hank's throat, wounding him so badly that he'd bleed to death.

Juliette didn't merely sit and watch, however. She sprang off the couch and hurried to Hank. She grabbed hold of his shoulder and pulled him backward as the Wechselbalg began to swing one of its needle-hands toward Hank. At the same moment, Nick slammed into the Wechselbalg from behind. The strike's momentum carried them both to the couch. They hit, bounced off, and landed on the carpet several feet apart. They both rolled to their feet and faced one another, each gauging the other, searching for an opening for their next attack. But before either Nick or the Wechselbalg could make his next move, a gunshot sounded loud as thunder. The Wechselbalg spun from the bullet's impact and fell to the floor.

Nick looked toward the shooter, expecting to see it was Hank. But his partner stood cradling his wounded arm. Juliette held one of the Glocks—Nick couldn't tell if it was his or Hank's—in a perfect shooter's stance. Her gaze was calm and focused, and her hands were rock-steady.

Nick felt a great swell of love for her at that moment. He'd always known how strong and fierce she was on the inside, but it was another thing to see it manifested outwardly like this.

I'm the luckiest man in the world, he thought.

Juliette kept the Glock trained on the downed Wechselbalg as she spoke.

"I tried to shoot him in the shoulder. I hope I didn't miss and kill him."

During her shooting lessons, Juliette's aim had started out good and had got even better as time passed. But Nick knew that it was one thing to shoot at an inanimate target on a range and quite another to shoot at a living, breathing person, no matter how much of a threat that person might be. Adrenaline and stress altered people's perceptions and motor skills. Even the best trained and most experienced officer could miss when shooting in a combat situation. And this was Juliette's first time firing a weapon in a fight.

"Keep him covered," Nick said. "I'll check on him."

Juliette nodded.

"Give me a sec," Hank said. His right arm was wounded worse than his left, and he tucked that hand into his jacket pocket as a makeshift sling, grimacing as he did so. The jacket sleeve was dotted with dark splotches, but it didn't look like Hank was bleeding too badly. When his wounded arm was dealt with, Hank walked over to pick up the second Glock from the carpet. Holding it in his left hand, he turned and pointed the weapon at the Wechselbalg. Accuracy declined when a person shot one-handed, let alone when they shot with their weaker hand. But most cops practiced shooting one-handed with both their right and left, just in case. Hank might not win any marksmanship contests shooting with his left hand, but at this range, he'd be able to hit the Wechselbalg if he needed to.

"Ready," Hank said.

Nick gave his partner a nod and then started toward the Wechselbalg. He knew he was taking a risk going so close to the creature. The Wechselbalg wanted the rest of his memories, and he wanted to be the only Nick Burkhardt. But the shapeshifter had remained still since Juliette had shot him. His eyes were closed, and more importantly, his fingers spines had retracted. If he wasn't dead, there was a good chance he was unconscious. *Or playing possum,* Nick thought. Only one way to find out.

He continued toward the Wechselbalg, trying to ignore the eerie feeling that he was approaching his own corpse. His senses were on high alert, searching for any sign of life or activity from the shapeshifter. He could detect no breathing, but that didn't mean anything. The Wechselbalg could simply be holding its breath, and for all Nick knew, the creature might be able to do so longer than a human. He saw no sign the Wechselbalg was bleeding from his wound—no widening dark splotch on the carpet beneath him. Nick had approached many dead bodies during his career in law enforcement, and one thing they all had in common was a terrible stillness to them. Nick was a rational man, and he didn't know if something like a soul existed. But he did know that a dead body was definitely missing something vital it had possessed when alive. Something more than could be accounted for by biological processes alone. It was this absence, this lack, more than anything else that Nick was looking for as he drew near the fallen Wechselbalg. It wasn't something you could see so much as something you sensed. Whatever it was precisely, he didn't see it now. The Wechselbalg was definitely alive.

But before he could act on this knowledge, the Wechselbalg leaped to his feet, shoved past him, and ran toward the front door. Nick caught a glimpse of blood on the creature's left shoulder, and then both Juliette and Hank fired. If either of them hit the fleeing Wechselbalg, it didn't slow him down. Within seconds, he was through the door, out of the house, and back into the night.

Nick hurried over to Juliette and she handed the Glock to him.

"Go get him," she said.

He gave her a quick kiss, and then headed for the door. Hank followed, right hand still tucked into his pocket to keep his wounded arm steady. Nick wanted to tell him to stay behind and take care of his wound, but he knew Hank wouldn't pay him any more attention than he would've paid to Hank if their situations were reversed, so he said nothing.

Nick's own arm was still somewhat numb from when he collided with the wall, but its condition was improving with every passing moment. He had no trouble maintaining his grip on the Glock as he ran outside. He half-expected the Wechselbalg to be lying in wait to attack him the instant he emerged from the house, but there was no immediate sign of the shapershifter. Nick ran out onto the sidewalk, sweeping his gaze back and forth as he searched for the Wechselbalg. Hank joined him a moment later, breathing harder than usual, and Nick wondered if his partner had lost more blood than he'd thought.

"Taking one in the shoulder doesn't seem to have slowed him down any," Hank said.

"Yeah." If the Wechselbalg had left a blood trail, Nick wondered if Monroe would be able to track it. Probably not, he decided. If the Wechselbalg didn't have a scent normally, there was a good chance his blood—or whatever substance oozed from his wounds in place of blood—wouldn't have a scent either. With Wechselbalgen, it was all about staying hidden. Unless of course they were suffering from their version of Alzheimer's and had demented to the point where it was almost impossible for them to act rationally and remain unseen.

Nick almost wished this Wechselbalg was still mentally healthy. If he had been, he would only kill when he needed to assume a new identity. And while that was bad enough, at least he wouldn't be on a killing spree right now.

The two men were standing less than a dozen feet from the Charger, and as they cast their gazes around the area searching for the Wechselbalg, at one point they both turned their backs to the car. And that's when the Wechselbalg struck.

At the sound of rapid footsteps on asphalt, Nick turned and saw a handful of needle-spines slashing toward his face. He leaned back in time to avoid getting hurt, but Hank wasn't so lucky. The spines struck the bicep of his good arm and sank deep. The Wechselbalg yanked them free, an expression of savage triumph on his face. Hank took in a hissing breath, and his fingers sprang open. His Glock fell to the sidewalk, and Hank went down on one knee, moaning in pain.

Nick stepped forward and swung his gun butt toward the Wechselbalg's head. The creature tried to avoid the blow, but he didn't move fast enough. The butt of the Glock slammed into the side of his head, and the impact staggered him. Nick knew better than to give the shapeshifter so much as a second to recover. He moved forward, intending to strike the Wechselbalg a second blow. But the shapeshifter jabbed his finger spines forward and stabbed Nick's gun hand. There was an instant of pain before an almost pleasant sensation of numbness began to spread through his hand. The Glock slipped from his fingers, but right then the loss of his weapon was the last of his worries. When the Wechselbalg had initially duplicated him, he'd plunged the finger-spines into Nick's neck. Nick had no idea if the Wechselbalg could copy his memories through another part of his body, but he didn't want to find out.

He curled his left hand into a fist and hit the Wechselbalg as hard as he could, driving his knuckles into the shapeshifter's nose. Cartilage ground and a clear liquid gushed in place of blood. The Wechselbalg's head snapped back, and his finger spines pulled free of Nick's right hand. Despite the numbness in that hand, Nick made a fist, stepped forward, and struck the Wechselbalg with a hard right cross to the jaw. Because of the numbness, Nick couldn't judge the strength of the blow, but from the way the Wechselbalg staggered to the side, he figured he'd hit him hard enough.

Nick moved forward, intending to press his advantage, but the Wechselbalg—perhaps knowing Nick well enough now to guess what he'd do in this situation—met Nick head-on. He charged forward, wrapped his arms around Nick, and lifted him off his feet. Nick head-butted the shapeshifter before he could do anything, and the creature's head snapped back once more. His grip on Nick slackened, allowing Nick to break free.

The Wechselbalg was looking pretty wobbly by this point, and Nick figured he could knock out the creature with one more solid blow. But before he could advance on the shapeshifter, the Wechselbalg drew his Glock and pointed it at Nick. The creature might've been unsteady on his feet, but there was nothing wrong with his aim.

Nick froze, fully expecting to hear the sound of a gunshot blast and feel the punch of a bullet striking him.

But before the Wechselbalg could fire, Hank slammed his shoulder into the shapeshifter, knocking him sideways. The blow caused the creature to drop his Glock, but either he wasn't as weak as Nick had surmised or he'd recovered quickly, because he grabbed hold of Hank, spun around, and shoved him toward Nick. Then he took off sprinting.

Nick caught Hank, but the Wechselbalg had pushed him so hard that both men went down in a heap. A Jeep Cherokee was parked at the curb several dozen feet away from where Nick had parked the Charger. When the Wechselbalg reached it, he quickly climbed in, started it, and roared away from the curb.

Nick stood and helped Hank to his feet. They watched the taillights of the Cherokee as it sped away.

"I didn't get the plate," Hank asked. "You?"

Nick shook his head. "Too dark."

"And here I thought you had special Grimm vision or something."

Nick smiled. "Guess it's offline tonight."

He turned to his friend. Hank still had his right hand tucked into his jacket pocket. The blood splotches on his sleeve were wider and darker now. He carried the Glock in his left hand, but it hung limp at his side. He looked tired as hell, and Nick didn't blame him. It had been a long night, and it was far from over.

Juliette came running across the lawn to join them. She wrapped her arms around Nick, and he put his arm around her shoulders and held her close.

"At least we know what vehicle he's driving," Nick said.

"You're going to go after him," Juliette said. It wasn't a question.

"Just as soon as we get Hank patched up." He glanced at his wounded hand. Most of the numbness had worn off, but it was still bleeding from several pinprick-sized holes. Nothing serious, though.

The three of them turned and started back toward the house. In the distance, they heard the sounds of approaching police sirens.

"One of the neighbors reported the gunshots," Hank said.

"More than one, probably," Nick said. He sighed and pulled away from Juliette. "You take Hank inside while I try to think of a cover story to tell whoever shows up."

Juliette nodded, then turned to Hank. "Don't worry, I've got plenty of medical supplies in the house. I stocked up so I could take care of Nick."

"He *does* tend to play a little rough sometimes," Hank said.

Nick headed to the end of the driveway as Juliette and Hank returned to the house. The sirens grew louder. Wouldn't the neighbors just *love* that noise on top of the gunshots? If this sort of thing kept up, he and Juliette would have to start looking for a new house.

As he waited for the responding officers to arrive, he tried not to think about how the Wechselbalg had escaped, where he might be going next, and worse, what he might do when he got there.

CHAPTER TEN

"Damn, damn, damn!"

The Wechselbalg hit the steering wheel with the palm of his hand as he swore, as if to punctuate the words.

He was driving far too fast for a suburban neighborhood, but he didn't care. He wasn't worried about Nick... No, he *was* Nick! He wasn't worried about the *Other* giving pursuit. He would remain behind, at least long enough to make sure his partner was okay, which would give the Wechselbalg more than enough time to flee. He'd broken off the battle not because he'd been disarmed, but to give his injuries a chance to heal. His kind healed far faster than humans and even most Wesen, but it still took time. It was the fact that he *was* fleeing which upset him so. That, along with the Other still being alive. The Wechselbalg had tried to kill him twice now, and both times he'd failed. It was beyond maddening! He hurt from the injuries he'd sustained while fighting the Other, and while the wound to his shoulder was the worst, he was more upset by his nose. It throbbed in time with his heartbeat, and he wondered if it was broken. The thought made him even angrier. He'd only had the nose for a few hours. The damned thing was practically brand new!

But all of his pain paled in comparison to the turbulent emotions that roiled inside him. A major part of a Wechselbalg's survival strategy was to adapt as quickly as it could after assuming a new form. That meant shedding an identity that he'd lived with for a long time—years, perhaps decades—and adopting an entirely new one almost instantly. But his incomplete memories were impeding the process, and now that he knew the Other still lived, all of his instincts screamed at him to kill the man. How could he fully assume the identity of Nick Burkhardt if he... if the *Other* still existed? He considered turning around and going back to the house—the house that was supposed to be *his*—and trying again to kill the Other so he could be rid of him once and for all, even if he wasn't currently at his full strength. The Wechselbalg almost did it, but he heard the sound of approaching police sirens, and instead of pulling the Cherokee into a U-turn, he continued going straight. He did not, however, decrease his speed.

Two cruisers appeared, coming toward him from the opposite direction, lights flashing, sirens blaring. He stiffened in his seat and gripped the steering wheel tighter, afraid that the officers were coming for him. But the fear passed quickly. The Other would never report that he had an exact double running around town. He would want to protect his identity as a Grimm, as well as keep the secret of the Wesen's existence.

The Wechselbalg watched the cruisers go past, realizing they were probably on their way to the house, responding to a report of gunfire. Good. Let the Other deal with them. It would give him time to come up with a plan to—

The Wechselbalg ended that line of thought when caught sight of one of the cruisers turning around.

That's when he realized how fast he was going, and he smacked the steering wheel again in frustration. Of *course* he looked suspicious, speeding away from an area where shots had been reported. If he hadn't been so upset by his encounter with the Other, he would've anticipated this and driven more slowly. Why was it always so damned hard for him to think?

He briefly considered stomping on the gas and trying to flee, but he wasn't about to run from an ordinary *human* police officer. He took his foot off the gas pedal and let the Cherokee slow down. It didn't take long for the cruiser to catch up, and the Wechselbalg pulled over to the curb. He sat quietly behind the wheel while the officer called in the stop and the Cherokee's license plate number. Then the officer stepped out of the cruiser and approached, hand on his weapon, but the gun still holstered.

Big mistake, the Wechselbalg thought.

The shapeshifter watched the officer's reflection in the side-view mirror as he approached. He was a Hispanic male in mid to late thirties, fit, and he moved with a confidence born of both training and experience. He was alert, but not nervous, and the Wechselbalg knew this made him dangerous.

As the officer leaned down to the driver's side window, he said, "License and reg—" He broke off as he noticed the Wechselbalg's broken nose and shoulder wound. The Wechselbalg knew the man would draw his weapon and demand he exit the vehicle. But the shapeshifter wasn't going to give him that chance. His fist blurred through the open window and slammed into the officer's face. He put all the strength he could into the blow, and the officer flew backwards, hit the asphalt, and didn't get up.

The Wechselbalg glanced out the window to make sure the man wouldn't be rising anytime soon. The officer lay motionless on the ground, his nose broken and bloodied. The shapeshifter smiled. At least he wasn't the only one with a bloody nose now. He didn't know if the man was alive or dead, and right then he really didn't care, just as long as the man was no longer an annoyance.

The Wechselbalg got out of the Cherokee, removed the officer's Glock to replace the one he lost back at the house, then got back in his vehicle. He pulled away from the curb and left the officer and his cruiser with the lights still flashing. He was careful to drive more slowly this time.

Striking the officer had taken the edge off his frustration, but it quickly rebuilt to its previous level and kept mounting. He wanted more than anything to return to the Other and kill him once and for all. But even in the midst of his fury, he knew couldn't do that. The Other would be on his guard now, and he would alert his allies as well. The Wechselbalg would need to find a way to catch him off guard—and that would take thought and planning. Both traits which, admittedly, weren't the easiest for him at that moment. He supposed he should find someplace to hole up for a while, somewhere he'd have peace and quiet, where he would be able to concentrate more effectively while he finished healing.

But Nick Burkhardt wasn't the sort of man to go off by himself when he had a problem. He thought better when he kept moving, kept working. So that's exactly what the Wechselbalg would do. The Other had grown soft over the last few years, treating Wesen not only as if they were human, but even calling some of them friends. The Other had become a poor excuse for a Grimm, and the Wechselbalg had a lot of work ahead of him in order to put fear back into the heart of Portland's Wesen. And he knew of a good place to begin rectifying the Other's mistakes.

Now if he could only remember where Bud Wurstner lived...

* * *

Both Monroe and Rosalee still found the shop to be oppressively hot. Rosalee continued wearing a T-shirt, but Monroe had removed his shirt entirely. His muscles were larger, more defined, and harder than when he was in human form. His skin was covered with a light coat of dark brown fur, and she found the whole primitive look appealing. But she did her best to ignore how he looked. Too many people were depending on them to find a cure. Besides, they'd already fooled around once tonight. That should be enough. Right?

She snuck a look at Monroe, who was paging through another in a seemingly endless supply of old books. She bit her lip and quickly returned her attention to her own book.

"This is driving me *insane!*"

Monroe gripped the large leather-bound book, his claws dimpling the cover and threatening to pierce it. He'd already damaged a half-dozen books, either by clawing their covers or throwing them around the shop, which in turn caused all kinds of other damage.

Her feelings of physical attraction toward him were swept away by a wave of irritation so intense it bordered on fury. Rosalee didn't think she could take much more of his temper tantrums. And she *knew* she couldn't take him damaging any more books—especially this one.

"Be careful," she said, trying to keep the words from coming out as a growl. "That book—which you are dangerously close to shredding—used to belong to my great aunt. It's been in the family for generations."

Monroe didn't put the book down. Instead, he gripped it harder, looking at her in defiance, as if daring her to press the issue. Rosalee, however, was not in a mood to back down.

"It's *special* to me," she said, emphasizing the word by lowering her voice to a throaty near-growl. But Monroe gave no indication that he picked up on her message.

"It's bad enough that it's written in German," he said, "but the type is so tiny, you practically need a microscope to see it."

"I'll look through it then. Maybe you should take a break."

This is like Umkippen, she thought. If Wesen forced themselves to woge over and over, there was a danger that the Wesen side could take over, leaving them at the mercy of their most primitive instincts. The longer the *Ewig Woge* kept them in Wesen form, the more their control over their bestial sides would erode until nothing would be left but pure, savage animal drive.

She reached for the book, moving slowly so as not to trigger the beast that was increasingly taking him over. He didn't snap or snarl at her, but he did take a step away from her and angle his body, as if to block her reach.

"I'm fine," he said. "If either of us needs a break, it's *you*."

Rosalee raised her eyebrows.

"Really?"

"Yeah. You've been getting kind of growly over the last half hour or so."

Rosalee tried to hold it in, she really did, but she just didn't have the control right then.

She swept her arm through the air, intending to make a gesture taking in all the damage that Monroe's temper had caused. She already had her next words framed in her mind.

Look at this place! You're the one responsible for this mess, and you have the gall to say that I'm the one who needs a break?

But she misjudged the distance, and instead of passing

close to Monroe's bare shoulder, her hand—more specifically, her claws—grazed him. Her claws might not have been as long or sharp as Monroe's, but they could do some serious damage of their own, especially when backed by the strength of her anger. A deep scratch appeared on Monroe's skin, and beads of dark blood welled forth.

At first he only looked at the scratch, as if he wasn't certain what it was. But then his head snapped around to face her, eyes burning with anger. He bared his teeth, and he began breathing faster, oxygenating his blood in preparation to fight.

Rosalee hadn't meant to hurt him, but she had. Sure, it was only a scratch, but in the grip of the *Ewig Woge*, even something as minor as an accidental scratch could feel like a deliberate attack. Still, that was no reason for him to act like a big baby about it. He was a big, bad Blutbad, wasn't he? About time he started acting like it.

With a start, she realized that she'd been giving in to her own inner beast without even being aware of doing so. The loss of the rational self was the ultimate nightmare for most Wesen, and Rosalee was no exception. For a time—too *long* a time—she'd been hooked on Jay, a drug that had no effect on humans but was highly addictive for Wesen. She knew all too well what it was like to lose herself in pure sensation that felt like it was real, but which was actually just an artificially induced lie. The *Ewig Woge* was the same thing: it was a hormone imbalance that mimicked a disease, but it *felt* as if her animal side was fighting and clawing its way up from the depths of her being, determined to be free of the flesh-prison that had kept it caged for far too long.

She could feel herself teetering on the edge, on the verge of losing control. She used every ounce of mental and emotional strength she possessed and employed the same fierce willpower that had finally allowed her to walk away from Jay and never touch it again.

I'm not an animal, she told herself. *I'm not.*

She gave it everything she had, but in the end it wasn't enough.

She returned Monroe's snarl with interest and took a swipe at his head, intending to claw deep furrows into his cheek and jaw. His reflexes were too good, though, and he raised the book he was holding and used it as a shield. Her claws struck the back cover and took a chunk out of the leather. This drove him even further into a rage, and she reversed the direction of her hand and knocked the book out of Monroe's grip with a backhanded blow. Deep inside, she recoiled at further damaging the heirloom, as she watched it fall to the floor, but the beast inside her felt only a surge of gleeful satisfaction at having deprived Monroe of his pathetic makeshift shield.

Monroe roared and reached for her with his clawed hands, but Rosalee wasn't about to let him get hold of her. She spun around and ran toward the back room, where she'd have more room to maneuver. Fuchsbau might not be as strong or as bloodthirsty as Blutbaden, but they were fast, sly, and clever. As far as Rosalee was concerned, intelligence could beat primitive savagery any day—as long as you kept moving, that is.

The back room was where the shop's bulk supplies were kept—large canisters of spices and dried roots, huge jugs filled with liquid extracts and essential oils, jars of dehydrated vegetables, bags of nuts and seeds, and more. Rosalee was a firm believer in having supplies on hand at all times, and the shelves were so full, they bowed from the weight of the contents. There was also a large refrigerator/ freezer for those materials that needed to be kept fresh, and it too was jam-packed.

She knew she had only seconds before Monroe caught up with her, so she ran to one of the shelves, grabbed a canister, and spun around just in time to see Monroe claw past the curtain that separated the front of the shop from the back. Snarling, he fixed his gaze on Rosalee. She saw no sign of the man she loved in those blazing crimson eyes, saw no hint of anything even remotely human. Monroe as she knew him was gone, and all that remained was an angry, violent beast. This didn't upset her, though. In many ways, she was little more than a beast herself right then. But there was one difference between them. She was a beast who was prepared. She jerked the lid off the canister, cast it aside, and as Monroe charged toward her, she hurled the canister's contents in his face.

The ghost pepper was reputed to be one of the hottest chiles in the world, and Monroe got an industrial-sized blast of it dried and ground. He howled in pain and doubled over, coughing and rubbing furiously at his eyes. He started wheezing as his throat began to swell, and tears streamed from his reddened eyes and dripped onto the floor. The ghost pepper powder would've caused anyone who was attacked with it to react violently, but the effect was a thousand times more intense for Monroe, given his heightened Blutbad senses. For him—at least in terms of pain—it was almost like being splashed in the face with sulfuric acid.

The beast in Rosalee felt malicious triumph at having neutralized an enemy so thoroughly, but the woman in her felt only horrified guilt at having hurt the man she loved.

Strike now, while he's helpless, her beast told her.

All she had to do was rush forward, extend her claws to the fullest, and slash them across the Blutbad's throat. It didn't matter how strong and fierce he was. Once he started bleeding, it would all be over in seconds. She had to do it. It was the only way to make sure she'd be safe.

You could run, Rosalee thought.

He'd only give chase, her beast replied. *And after what we did to him, he'll be so furious he won't stop until he's caught us, clawed us open from neck to crotch, and is feasting on our entrails.*

Monroe would never do that, Rosalee told herself. Except he wasn't Monroe any more, was he? At least not all the way. No more than she was Rosalee Calvert. She was Fuchsbau, she was speed and guile, and she would survive, no matter what it took.

She didn't give in to the beast so much as it took control of her, and she moved toward Monroe, growling softly, claws raised.

Monroe was still wheezing and tears continued to fall from his eyes. He dropped to his knees and fell forward. His hands splayed in the chile powder and nearly slipped out from under him. Rosalee's mouth curled into a cruel smile at the sight of his humiliation. The mighty Blutbad, brought low by a sniffer full of ghost pepper!

Now that he was on all fours, she wouldn't simply finish him off with a single swipe of her claws. She would grab hold of his hair, lift his head to expose his throat, sink the claws of her free hand into his flesh, get a good grip, and tear—

Before she could go any farther, Monroe jumped to his feet and pressed his hands, both of which were covered with chile power, to her face, one hand over her mouth, the other her nose. She inhaled from surprise before she could stop herself, and fire exploded inside her nasal passages, and her throat felt as if it was filled with blazing hot shards of broken glass. She tried to push Monroe's hands away, but he held them firmly against her face. Tears gushed from her eyes, and she tried to cough, but since

Monroe's hand covered her mouth, no sound came out. She thought he intended to smother her to death, and she started beating and clawing at his chest. But then he pulled his hands away and stepped back.

Now that she was able to breathe, she attempted to draw in deep lungfuls of air, but her throat had swollen to the point where it felt like she was breathing through a straw. She gasped, wheezed, coughed, and choked, and all the while two miniature Niagras gushed from her tear ducts.

The entire time this was happening, Monroe stood and watched. His eyes were still red and swollen, but they weren't as teary as they had been. His breathing was harsh and ragged, but steady enough, and he no longer coughed.

"Sorry," he said. "I know it's not much fun."

"Not… much… *fun*?" she gasped out. "It feels like I inhaled… gasoline, and then… swallowed a lit match!"

She hurt like blazes. Who the hell actually ate ghost peppers on *purpose*?

It took several more moments for the worst of her physical reactions to pass. When they did—when she was able to more or less breathe freely again—she realized something.

"I can think clearly again," she said.

Monroe, despite still being in Blutbad form, seemed like his usual sweet self, without any sign of the bestial rage that had gripped him. She remained in Wesen form as well, but she too felt no anger and no pressure to act on instinct.

"It's the ghost pepper!" she said, almost giddy with excitement. "Something in the powder helped counter the effects of the *Ewig Woge!*"

"Some of them anyway," Monroe said. "We're both still pretty hairy." He gingerly touched the claw marks Rosalee had left on his shoulder. "And by the way, *ow*!"

She stepped forward, put her hands on his shoulders,

and kissed him. His lips tasted like chile powder, but at this point, she didn't find the sensation of heat unpleasant, not in the slightest.

"Sorry," she said.

He put his hands on her waist.

"*I'm* the one who should be sorry. I can't believe I—"

She kissed him again to shut him up.

"It wasn't your fault," she said. "It's the *Ewig Woge*. But at least now we have a place to start looking for a treatment: the ghost pepper, the hottest chile in the world!"

"Actually," Monroe said, "that's up for debate. In 2013, the *Guinness Book of World Records* decided the Carolina Reaper was—"

Rosalee kissed him again, and this time they didn't break apart for several minutes.

When they separated, Monroe sighed. "Back to work?"

Rosalee grinned, feeling hope for the first time in hours.

"Back to work,' she said.

Bud had spent the last hour or so trying to settle on a hiding place. He'd found several good ones in the basement, attic, and crawlspace, but they were all occupied by his family. The Eisbiber had a saying: *Strong together; safer apart*. They tended to scatter when they had to make it more difficult for predators to find them. When you hid in a group, you gave off more body heat, scents were intensified, and the sounds of respiration were louder.

He was proud of his family's skill at hiding, but unfortunately, they hadn't left him with many choices for his own hiding place. He currently stood in the living room, considering his remaining options. He was contemplating hiding in the garage, or maybe going old school and digging himself a hole in the backyard, when his phone rang. He was so full of anxiety at that point that he actually jumped several inches into the air when he heard the ring. Grateful that no one had been around to see him overreact, he answered the phone.

It was his friend Roscoe. Roscoe was just as nervous as Bud, and words poured out of him so fast that Bud—no stranger to speaking fast himself—had trouble following what Roscoe was saying. He gathered Roscoe and his family had also been affected by whatever-it-was that kept Wesen in a state of perpetual woge. He caught the word Hafen.

"Gottagoothercallstomake," Roscoe said, and then disconnected.

Bud understood what was happening, and it was bad. *Really* bad. This woge condition was spreading among Portland's Wesen community, and without any kind of treatment available, the affected Wesen were getting out of the city. But he had his own list of people to call in such an emergency. His first instinct was to gather his family together and tell them to start packing, but the protocol in such situations was crystal clear. Call first, flee second. Word had to be spread as fast as possible.

Bud began making his calls, and he was in the middle of the third one when someone began pounding on the front door.

"Gotta go, Natalie. Someone's at the door."

He disconnected and tucked the phone in his pocket. The pounding continued without cease, getting louder with each second. His whiskers quivered. Always a bad sign. He wanted to hide—not that there were any good places left—but he stayed where he was. It could be someone he knew, someone who was in trouble. Then again, if any Wesen could be affected by the woge sickness, the predators would be too. And if they gave in to their animal urges… well, no one would be safe. Maybe it *was* a predator at the door… but maybe it *wasn't*. Maybe it was someone who needed help.

Throwing his fears aside, Bud rushed to the door and put his hand on the lock. But before he did anything more, he called out, "Who is it?"

"Burkhardt!"

"Nick?"

Bud quickly unlocked the door and started to open it. But before he could open it more than a couple inches, the door burst inward. The knob tore out of his hand, and he found himself looking at a man he barely recognized. Part of the problem—a big part—was his nose. It was swollen and caked with... something. Whatever it was, it didn't look like blood. It was slightly crooked, too, or at least Bud thought it was. As Bud looked closer, he saw it move back into place with a soft click. Did Grimms heal like that? He had no idea.

Even more worrying than the damage to Nick's nose was the stain on his left shoulder. His jacket had a ragged hole in it, and from the amount of discoloration, it looked as if he'd lost a lot of leakage from whatever wound he'd sustained there. Knife blade? Gunshot? Bud had no idea, but whatever had happened, it looked bad.

But it wasn't just the nose or the shoulder. Mostly, it was the eyes. They were cold, dead, and empty. Looking into them was like gazing into two bottomless pits of darkness, and Bud couldn't help shivering in fear.

This is Nick, he told himself. *He's a friend.*

But Bud's instincts told him that a predator had indeed come to his home, and that predator had a name: *Grimm*.

Bud was better able to control his anxiety than most Eisbiber—although they preferred to regard their nervousness as common sense. But his control had been shaky at best since he'd become stuck in his Wesen form, and what little remained vanished when Nick drew his gun. Bud didn't ask why Nick was acting like this, didn't plead with him to keep the gun down. He spun on his feet and ran. He had no conscious thought other than to lure the Grimm away from his family. If he could make it to the back door and lure him out into the yard...

But before he could get more than a few feet, he felt Nick grab hold of his shirt collar and yank him backward. Off-balance, he stumbled, and then Nick pulled downward, even harder this time, and Bud fell to the floor. Before he could rise, Nick let go of his collar, stepped where Bud could see him, crouched down, and pressed the muzzle of his gun to Bud's forehead. Bud's heart pounded so rapidly that he couldn't feel any space between the beats. If he hadn't been in Wesen form, he would've feared he was having a heart attack.

"You're Bud," Nick said. "Bud Wurstner."

Bud's throat was so dry, it felt as if he'd swallowed a bucket of sand. It took him several attempts to respond.

"Yes, yes, I am. And may I say, you pronounced my last name superbly. A lot of people hit the T too hard, but not you. You put just right amount of emphasis—"

He broke off when Nick pressed the muzzle harder against his head.

"You're Wesen," Nick said. "An Eisbiber."

Though the majority of his mind was occupied by sheer terror, a small but still rational part wondered why Nick was talking like this. Maybe whatever or whoever had busted his nose had hit him hard enough to scramble his brains a little. If that were true, it could explain Nick's bizarre behavior. With any luck, he'd soon shake off the effects of the blow and return to normal. But in the meantime, he'd be a confused and—if Bud's current predicament was any indication—extremely dangerous man.

Bud struggled to ignore the feeling of metal pressing

into his skin and get his fear under control. Not so much for himself, but for Phoebe and the children.

"If anything's wrong, Nick, I want to help. Just tell me what it is, okay?"

Nick frowned. "What's wrong? This whole *town* is what's wrong! It's *crawling* with Wesen! You're like… like…"

"Ants? Cockroaches? Grasshoppers? Wait—that last one doesn't work, does it?"

Nick ignored him.

"Something needs to be done about all of you. The Other has failed to live up to his heritage. He's a disgrace!"

"I'm, uh, sure he is."

Wow, whatever hit him must've hit him really *hard.* Or maybe the blood loss from the shoulder wound was to blame for Nick's strange behavior. Heck, Bud practically fainted whenever he cut himself.

"That's why I'm here. He needs to be taught a lesson. He's been sloppy. Lenient. Worse, he's been *fraternizing.*" Nick said this last word as if it were a euphemism for a particularly obscene and degrading act.

Bud tried to frown, but the gun muzzle pressed to his head prevented him from doing so.

"I'm sorry, Nick, but I really don't have any idea what you're talking about. I'd really appreciate it if you would take the gun away from my head, though. It's making me kind of nervous, you know?"

Nick went on as if he hadn't heard him.

"I have to clean up his mess, tidy up the loose ends he's left behind, send him a message. There's a new sheriff in town."

Nick smiled the cruelest smile Bud had ever seen—and he'd once witnessed a Schneetmacher grin.

"I don't know exactly who you're planning on sending a message to—and pardon me for adding this, but I have to say that sounds like a particularly ominous phrase—but if there's anyone who can send a message and make sure it's well and truly sent, it's Nick Burkhardt."

Nick's smile fell away, not that Bud was sorry to see it go. He fixed Bud with an appraising look, and when he spoke next, his voice was low and intense. "What did you call me?"

Bud tried to swallow past the lump in his throat, but it was the size of grapefruit on steroids, and he couldn't do it. He managed to find his voice anyway.

"You mean your name?"

Nick nodded. "Say it again."

Feeling equal measures confused and creeped out by the request, Bud nevertheless fulfilled it.

"Nick Burkhardt."

Nick looked at him for a few moments after that, face expressionless, gaze unreadable. Bud had the sense he was thinking something over, weighing his options. He wasn't sure he wanted to know what those options were.

Nick finally seemed to come to a decision. He smiled and removed the gun muzzle from Bud's head

"Yes. I am Nick Burkhardt." He stood, tucked his gun away, and held out a hand to help Bud to his feet.

Bud didn't trust Nick right now, but he didn't want to make him angry, either. So he took Nick's hand and let the man help him up. And if his grip hurt and he yanked Bud's arm too hard, so what? At least Nick wasn't holding a gun to his head anymore.

The two men regarded each other in awkward silence for a moment. Nick was the first to break it.

"I should be going. I have a lot of work to do."

"Sure, sure," Bud said. He had no idea what Nick was talking about, but he was too relieved that Nick was leaving to care.

Nick's manner turned serious once more. "Stay in tonight. It's dangerous out there, and it's only going to get worse."

"I know," Bud said. "I got the call." When Nick frowned, Bud continued. "The call to go to the Hafen?"

"Yes, the Hafen. Which is…"

"In Forest Park," Bud said. "I told you that before, remember? When you were here the last time? Well, I didn't *tell* you exactly, but you guessed."

Nick nodded. "Right. And the city's Wesen are gathering there now?"

"Yeah. All the ones that are stuck in full woge, anyway."

Nick nodded again. "Good," he said, and then added, "*Very* good. How about you, Bud? Are you going?"

"I have a couple more calls to make—folks I need to tell about heading to the Hafen. And then I'm going to pack the family in the truck and head for the park." He let out an uncomfortable chuckle. "If I can get them to leave their hiding places, that is."

"Okay," Nick said. The smile he gave Bud this time was more normal than before, but it still held a hint of cruelty. "See you there."

After Nick left, Bud closed and locked the door. He knew it wouldn't keep out Nick if he was determined to get back in, but it made him feel better. He took several deep breaths to calm himself, then took his phone from his pocket and made his next call.

"Jerry? It's Bud. Are you—yeah, me too. The whole family, yeah. We're heading to the Hafen in a bit, and you should too. Yeah. Right. Oh, one more thing: if you see Nick Burkhardt you should steer clear of him. Yeah, I know I told you he's my friend, and he *is*. Or at least, he was. But something's happened to him, and I don't think…" Bud frowned. "No, I didn't hear about any Skalengeck teenagers. Why?"

As the Wechselbalg drove away from Bud's house, he was glad that he'd been merciful and spared the Eisbiber's life—for now, at least. His luck, it seemed, had finally taken a turn for the better. Portland's Wesen were doing him the favor of gathering in a single place outside the city. That would make his work so much easier. He was going to need more weaponry for a job this big, though. Specialized weaponry, too, as some Wesen were more resistant to gunfire than others.

A piece of the Other's memory—one he'd searched in vain for earlier—finally emerged then, an image of an old-fashioned travel trailer, located in a facility called… Forest Hills Storage. He couldn't recall the address, but now that he remembered the name, he should be able to find it. He was a police detective, after all.

He smiled. By the time the sun rose, the ground in Forest Park would be soaked in Wesen blood. It was going to be glorious.

De Groot sat at his desk, daylight streaming in the window behind him. The window provided a picturesque view of the city, one suitable to put on postcards to sell to tourists, but he rarely took the time to turn around and enjoy it. He was a busy man with much to do. Too much to waste time looking out windows.

He appeared to be a human male in his sixties, balding, with a full white beard that might've made him look a little like St. Nicholas if it hadn't been for his dark, severe eyebrows which were furrowed in a constant frown. And his eyes, of course. Behind his wire-frame glasses they glimmered with a hard intelligence that marked him as a man who knew the seriousness of his job and intended to perform his duties to the utmost of his ability—regardless of the cost.

In his well-tailored suit he resembled nothing so much as an old-world European banker, and in many ways, that wasn't too far off the mark. He spent his days doing calculations and risk assessments, but as a high-ranking member of the Wesen Council, the currency he worked with was not euros or dollars, but rather lives.

He was looking through a report regarding a group of Hadosheru suspected of planning a takeover of the Yakuza when there was a knock at his office door. Without looking up from the report, he said, "Come."

After a moment's hesitation, the door opened and one of his assistants entered. It was Adelbert, and De Groot knew at once that the man was bringing bad news. His hesitation before entering was a telltale sign.

De Groot looked up from the report then. Adelbert was thin, blond, in his late thirties, and had much to learn about mastering his emotions. De Groot could see the tension in his eyes and in the tight line of his mouth. He was the most junior of De Groot's assistants, but if he didn't acquire more self-control, he'd soon be looking for a new position. As far as De Groot was concerned, self-control was the single most important quality for a Wesen to cultivate. It was, after all, the core of the Code of Swabia, was it not?

"What is it, Adelbert?" As always, De Groot kept his voice soft and his words measured.

"We've received a communication from America. From Portland, Oregon, to be precise."

Despite himself, De Groot's pulse quickened. Recently,

Portland had become an area of special interest to him, and any news from there had his complete attention. He closed the folder in front of him and motioned for Adelbert to come all the way into his office. He did not, however, give the man any indication that he wanted him to sit, and Adelbert remained standing.

Without any further encouragement, Adelbert began speaking. De Groot listened intently and with increasing concern. When his assistant finished, De Groot sat back in his chair and clasped his hands on top of his desk. He thought silently for a time, and Adelbert remained standing where he was, nervously quiet.

At length, De Groot spoke once more, and only someone who knew him exceedingly well would've detected the note of worry in his voice.

"I want our best agents on a plane to Portland within the hour. They are to do whatever is necessary to deal with this situation."

De Groot knew he didn't have to explain further.

Aldebert bowed his head.

"At once, sir."

Aldebert started for the door, stopped, and turned back to De Groot.

"How many agents, sir?"

De Groot's ever-present frown deepened into a scowl.

"All of them."

CHAPTER ELEVEN

Nick told the responding officers that Juliette had been cleaning her gun when it accidentally went off. He didn't like blaming the disturbance on her, but he knew there was no way the officers would believe a police detective would make that kind of mistake. As it was, they barely believed Juliette had. Besides, who cleans guns this late at night? But eventually they left, and Nick returned to the house, relieved.

Juliette had taken Hank to the bathroom to tend to his injuries. She called for Nick to join them, since he was banged up, too, but he told her to take care of Hank first. He knew she wasn't happy with his response, but she didn't insist. As far as Nick was concerned, he only had a few scratches and cuts, and they'd heal soon enough on their own. Right now, he wanted to check in with Captain Renard. He tried calling, but he got Renard's voicemail. He left a quick update, then disconnected. Renard was probably busy patrolling the city, just as Nick and Hank had been. Nick hoped he hadn't run into any trouble he couldn't handle. Renard was highly intelligent, emotionally controlled, and tough as hell in a fight. The man could more than take care of himself one on one. But against an entire city of fully woged and panicking Wesen? That might well be a different story.

He went into the kitchen, got three bottles of water out of the fridge, and took them to the bathroom. Hank sat on the toilet lid with his shirt off, while Juliette sat on the edge of the tub, wrapping tape over a large gauze pad she'd applied to his arm.

"The Wechselbalg's finger spines sank deep into the muscle," Juliette said, "but I don't think they did any lasting damage. My primary concern is making sure the wounds don't get infected."

She glanced up at Nick.

"Which is why I wanted you in here in the first place. Grimm or not, your cuts and scrapes should at least get treated with alcohol wipes and antibacterial cream."

Hank smiled. "Juliette, you know I love you, but you need to work on your toilet-side manner."

"You know why I became a vet? Because my patients don't talk back."

She finished with Hank's dressing, examined it, then nodded, satisfied.

"You're good to go. Try not to get punctured again."

"I'll do my best."

Hank's shirt was draped over the towel rod. He pulled it off and slipped it back on. He moved a little stiffly, but otherwise he seemed all right. Nick was glad. Not only because Hank was his friend and partner, but because they needed all hands on deck tonight. They couldn't afford to have a single one of them out of commission.

Juliette patted the toilet seat. "Your turn."

Nick wanted to tell her that he'd be fine, that he and Hank needed to get back out on the street as soon as possible. But the look in her eyes told him she wasn't going to tolerate any protests, so he removed his shirt and handed it to Hank. She worked quickly, cleaning and dressing his pinpoint wounds with swift, efficient motions. She used small adhesive bandages on him instead of the gauze pad she'd used on Hank.

"How come he's not getting the full treatment?" Hank asked. "You two have a lover's spat I don't know about?"

"Since Nick heals faster than ordinary humans, this is all he needs," she said. "Plus, it's about all I can get him to sit still for."

She gave Nick a loving smile to take the sting out of her words, and he returned it. He didn't argue, she was right. As usual.

He stood, Hank handed him his shirt, and he put it on. Juliette put the leftover supplies in the medicine cabinet, washed her hands, and then opened the water bottle Nick had brought her and took a long drink. When she was finished, she said, "Now what?'

Before either Nick or Hank could answer, loud knocking came from the front door.

She looked at Nick and Hank.

"You two answer it. The last time I did, it didn't go so well."

Renard sat down on the couch, then reached over and turned off the lamp on the end table so his distorted features were no longer so clearly illuminated. Nick had never seen the man display any obvious signs of vanity before, and he was a bit surprised that Renard would feel a need to hide his Zauberbiest face from them. Then again, he seemed to relax once the light was out. Maybe too much illumination irritated him or hurt his eyes, especially since he remained stuck in his Wesen form. It was a reminder of how little Nick knew about Zauberbiester and

Hexenbiester—and especially about Sean Renard.

Nick, Juliette, and Hank remained standing. Renard gave off a prickly energy, as if he was working hard to project a façade of calm, while inside his nerves were jangling. One of his feet tap-tap-tapped the floor, while a hand gripped the sofa arm, clenching and unclenching.

"Are you all right?" Nick asked.

Instead of answering the question, Renard said, "I got your message. Sorry I didn't pick up when you called. I was… occupied at the time."

Nick didn't like the way Renard hesitated before saying *occupied*.

Renard continued. "Until the current situation is resolved, I think it would be best if I stayed with you. That way, you can keep an eye on me. Make sure I—" his already malformed lips twisted into a sneer "—behave myself."

"What did you do?" Juliette asked.

"Nothing. It's what I *almost* did. While I was patrolling I came across a Hundjager taunting a group of Mauzhertzen. I don't think he actually wanted to hurt them, so much as… play with them. I stopped my car and got out, intending to break it up."

"But instead you lost control and broke the Hundjager," Hank said.

"Pretty much," Renard said. "If I hadn't managed to restrain myself toward the end…" He looked up at Nick. "If I do lose control and it looks like I might harm an innocent, promise you'll stop me. Whatever it takes."

Nick understood what Renard was asking. He'd want the same thing if their positions were reversed.

"I promise."

Renard nodded, seeming almost relieved.

"So… you encountered the Wechselbalg," Renard said. "Tell me about it."

For the next several minutes, Nick, Juliette, and Hank took turns speaking as they filled in the Captain on what had happened. When they finished, Renard said, "How are Monroe and Rosalee doing on finding a treatment for the *Ewig Woge*?"

"Still working on it," Nick said.

"I was afraid of that. Well, I have one piece of good news. I contacted some friends of mine in Europe, and they were able to find more information on the Wechselbalg."

"Friends?" Nick asked.

"Friends," Renard repeated. "And that's all you need to know about them. They were able to find their way into certain protected databases to retrieve the information we needed."

"Those databases wouldn't happen to belong to the Wesen Council, would they?" Nick asked.

"Breaking the security of the Wesen Council would be considered an act of major aggression and would be dealt with swiftly and harshly," Renard said. "Only the most skilled of computer experts could even attempt such a feat, and even then, they'd only do so in the most extreme of emergencies."

"That isn't a no," Hank said.

Renard continued without acknowledging the point. "According to what my friends learned, if Wechselbalgen are forced to burn through the lifeforce that they've stolen, they weaken. They can then be killed before they have the opportunity to steal another identity. Once dead, their bodies should be burned to prevent them from regenerating into a new creature."

"That last part makes sense," Juliette said. "When the Wechselbalg was here, he drank a lot of water. I think he's primarily a liquid-based lifeform that needs to stay hydrated."

"How do we get it to use up its lifeforce?" Hank

asked. "Other than sitting around and waiting for it to grow old like the rest of us?"

"I don't know," Renard admitted. "From what I gather, Wechselbalgen are extremely rare, and there's been little information gathered about them."

"We need to tire it out," Nick said. "Push it to the point of exhaustion and beyond."

The others looked at him, and he tried to find a better way to explain what he meant.

"Think of lifeforce energy as a kind of fuel. The more active the Wechselbalg is, the more energy he uses. Once he's out of energy—or close to it—he needs to find a new victim."

"And this one is very old," Juliette said. "Even for his kind. He couldn't hold onto Mrs. Webber's identity. He only managed to maintain Nick's form for so long because he's a Grimm."

"And that's the unknown factor in all this," Renard said. "Whatever he managed to copy from Nick has changed him somehow. He might have too much energy for us to deplete."

"We have to try," Nick said.

"Of course we do," Renard said. "I just meant that it's not going to be easy."

"When is it ever?" Hank added.

Just then, Nick's phone vibrated. He took it out of his pocket and saw Rosalee was calling. He answered.

"Please tell me you've made some progress," he said.

"One word," Rosalee said, her voice excited. "Endorphins."

"Endorphins?" Nick asked.

Everyone was back at the spice shop. They were in the side room now, Juliette and Monroe sitting on the couch. Monroe had his arm around Rosalee, and they were also holding hands. It seemed to be more than mere affection, though. There was an intensity bordering on desperation in the way they held onto each other.

Juliette and Hank sat in chairs, but Renard was too jittery to sit. Nick remained standing near Renard, just in case he needed to be calmed down, Grimm-style.

"Yeah," Monroe said. "Remember when you guys were in earlier and you caught Rosalee and I, uh…"

He trailed off, suddenly uncomfortable. Rosalee and Juliette grinned at him.

"*Anyway*, we were both more in control of our Wesen sides for a while after that," he said. "It wore off after a while—"

"And we tried to kill each other," Rosalee said. "Well. Technically Monroe was the one who wanted to do the killing. At least at first."

"I'm really sorry about that," he said. "Blutbaden. What can you do?"

Rosalee laughed.

Nick glanced at the others to see if they were finding this conversation as weird as he was. From their expressions, it looked like they were.

There were a dozen or so burning candles placed throughout the room, filling the air with the mingled scents of vanilla and lavender. Monroe's phone sat on the coffee table, plugged in to an external speaker from which issued soft instrumental music. Next to the phone sat a bowl filled with individually wrapped pieces of chocolate. From time to time, Monroe and Rosalee would take one of the chocolates, unwrap it, and then eat it, chewing slowly, savoring each bite. There was also a bowl filled with pale roots with long bodies and tailing tendrils that reminded Nick a little of squid.

"When we were fighting," Rosalee said, "I threw some chile powder at him."

"*Really* hot stuff," Monroe added. "I got it in my eyes, nose, and mouth. Man, for a couple moments there, I couldn't even breathe. But then I started to feel calmer, more like myself again…"

"So I tried to kill *him* then," Rosalee said. "Purely out of self-preservation, of course."

"Naturally," Monroe said.

"And he got some chile powder on his hands and gave me a good strong dose of it. And, wow, was it powerful! But it did the trick and calmed me down, too."

"Eating spicy foods releases endorphins," Juliette said. "And with your enhanced senses, they probably work even better on you in Wesen form than they would when you're human."

"That's the reason for the rest of this stuff," Renard said. "The candles, the music, the chocolate, the ginseng root…"

So that's what that is, Nick thought.

"The scents of vanilla and lavender are calming," Rosalee said. "And eating chocolate and ginseng produces endorphins, too."

"As does exercise," Monroe said, "And, uh, other types of activity."

"And laughing," Rosalee said, grinning at him.

Nick understood now why Monroe and Rosalee were being so cuddly. They were trying to keep their endorphin production as high as they could.

"At this point, I'll try anything." Renard reached forward, grabbed several chocolates, unwrapped them, and popped them into his mouth.

"So this is the cure?" Hank said. "We just get affected Wesen to sit around smelling candles, listening to tunes, eating chocolate, chewing ginseng, watching comedy DVDs, and getting busy?"

Rosalee shook her head. "These are merely treatments

for the extreme behavior the *Ewig Woge* causes. But now that I know endorphins are key, I think I can make something that will counter the condition. But I'm going to need two things to do it."

"The Wechselbalg," Nick said.

Rosalee nodded. "That's right. And you."

Before Nick could ask what she meant, her phone rang. She pulled it out of her pocket and answered it.

"Bud? What... Hold on a minute. You're talking too fast!" She listened for several moments, confusion and disbelief on her face. "That's not possible, Bud. Nick's right—" She broke off. "Bud? *Bud?*" She lowered her phone. "He disconnected." She tried calling back, but when he didn't answer, she left a quick voicemail telling him that the person he'd told her about was the Wechselbalg and not Nick. When she finished, she disconnected and put the phone on the coffee table.

"Bud said 'Nick' came to his house and held a gun to his head," Rosalee said. "From what I gathered, nothing happened, but Bud was calling to warn us that Nick had, as he said, 'lost it big-time.'"

"Poor Bud," Juliette said. "I hope he and his family are okay."

Nick was angry with the Wechselbalg for terrorizing his friend, but he was also worried about Bud's reaction. "Want to bet that you're not the only person Bud called to warn?"

"I won't take that bet," Renard said. He took another chocolate, unwrapped it, and tossed it into his mouth.

"I've worked hard to gain the trust of the Wesen community in this town," Nick said. "And in one night, the Wechselbalg's destroyed it. How am I supposed to help people if they're scared of me?"

"It's a setback, no question," Monroe said. "But you've

got to remember how deep the fear of Grimms runs in Wesen. It wouldn't take a lot to bring those fears to the surface."

"Especially now, with the *Ewig Woge* affecting them," Rosalee added.

"I guess." Nick knew his friends were right, but he couldn't help feeling that if he'd only worked harder at reaching out to the Wesen community over the last few years, things would be different now. It was funny, in a way. Earlier tonight he'd been uncomfortable when the server at Blind Bill's had treated him as if he were her friendly neighborhood Grimm. Now he wished he'd accepted that role and even cultivated it, if for no other reason than it would allow him help the Wesen more effectively.

He looked around at his friends. When he'd first learned of the existence of Wesen, he'd thought of them as something other than human. Now he thought of them as human-plus, not so much different than special. His life was so much richer for having been allowed to become even a small part of their community. And while he supposed he could never fully become one of them, he would do his best to serve and protect them as well as their human brethren. Not because he was a Grimm, or even a cop. Because he was Nick Burkhardt.

But that brought up an interesting question. What did the Wechselbalg think *he* was right now? A man named Nick or a Wesen-killing machine called a Grimm?

"You've been awfully quiet," Juliette said, reaching out to take his hand.

"Just thinking. From the way the Wechselbalg's been behaving, he's trying to fulfill the role of a Grimm, or at least what in his current mental state he *thinks* a Grimm should be."

"He killed those two teenage taggers," Rosalee said.

"He attacked Nick and me," Hank said.

"And me," Renard added.

"He didn't kill me." Juliette pointed out. "Or Bud."

"Knowing Bud, he probably talked his way out of getting killed," Hank said.

"Maybe the Wechselbalg couldn't hurt Bud because he's my friend," Nick said. "Who knows how much of my personality he copied?"

"Not enough," Renard said. "He doesn't have any problem killing other Wesen for no reason. No rational one, anyway. So if he's going to play out his sick fantasy of what a Grimm is like, he's going to start hunting down Wesen."

"But most of the city's Wesen are heading to the Hafen," Monroe said. "If they aren't already there."

"Which means the Wechselbalg will go to the Hafen, too," Nick said.

"Damn," Hank said. "It'll be like shooting Wesen in a barrel."

"And we sent them there," Rosalee said.

"So not only are they in danger from each other," Monroe said, "because the *Ewig Woge* is causing them to lose control, but they're also at risk of getting sliced up by an insane Wesen that's acting like some kind of Grimm serial killer."

"We need to go to the Hafen," Juliette said. "We have to keep the Wesen calm so they don't start fighting among themselves."

'We have to make the cure for the *Ewig Woge*," Rosalee said, "and get it to the Wesen in the Hafen as soon as possible."

"*And* we have to stop the Wechselbalg," Hank said.

Renard sighed. "That's quite a to-do list."

"Then we'd better get started," Nick said.

* * *

The Wechselbalg felt pleased with himself. He'd found the storage facility without any problem. And although he didn't have a key to the trailer, the door proved no real obstacle. Now he drove down the street, a pair of ancient weapons on the seat next to him—a double-headed battle-axe and a curved sword called a talwar, once used in India. He'd had a difficult time selecting what to bring as he wasn't sure what the various implements of destruction had been designed for. The Other's memories were little help as he'd only used a handful of the weapons in battle before. In the end, the Wechselbalg had chosen the two weapons he had simply because they looked the deadliest as well as the easiest to use. Sharp edges, solid metal. Sturdy and dependable, with the weight of history and tradition behind them. Proper weapons for a true Grimm. He couldn't wait to get to the Hafen and try them out. Not only would it be amusing, it would be good practice for the next time he faced the Other.

No, not the next time. The *last* time.

The Wechselbalg knew the Hafen was located in Forest Park—the Eisbiber had told him this—but he wasn't sure where the park *was*. Once again, he searched the fragmentary memories he'd obtained from the Other for the park's location, but he came up blank. Traditionally Hafens were established outside a village or city in woodland areas, although given how large some of the world's cities had grown over the last few centuries, some places had multiple Hafens, often within the city itself. Portland wasn't that large, however, and the Wechselbalg was willing to bet that the Hafen—and thus, Forest Park—lay outside the city. The question was where?

The Other's police training suggested the Wechselbalg look for vehicles heading out of the city, indicating fleeing Wesen. But while the Wechselbalg did pass the occasional vehicle, the night streets were mostly empty. Either he was in the wrong part of the city or the majority of the Wesen had already departed. He needed to come up with another plan.

A short time later, he saw a black Kia parked on the side of the street in front of a twenty-four-hour burger joint. The vehicle sat at an odd angle, lights on, and the driver's side door open. The restaurant's parking lot was empty, except for a trio of bird-like creatures standing around a man with features resembling a rodent's.

Geier, he thought. *And a Reinigen.*

He pulled the Cherokee behind the Kia, turned off the lights and cut the engine. He looked over at his newly acquired weapons, considered for a moment, then chose the battle-axe.

He got out of the Cherokee and started walking toward the three Geier and the Reinigen. At first, none of them noticed him approaching. The vulture-headed Wesen were completely focused on the rat-like Reinigen. The man looked from one Geier to another, his head jerking in sharp, nervous gestures. The Geier kept flexing their taloned hands, as if eager to slice them into the Reinigen's flesh, but so far he appeared to be unharmed. The Wechselbalg doubted the rat-man would remain that way much longer, however.

The Reinigen wore a dark-blue suit jacket over a white shirt, collar unbuttoned, no tie. Reinigen—because of their low standing in the Wesen community—sometimes tried to compensate by dressing nicely, although this Reinigen's faded jeans and old sneakers didn't do much to add to his ensemble. The Geier were dressed more simply—pullover sweaters, light jackets, and jeans. All dark colors, of course. The better to blend into the shadows.

The Wechselbalg's own memories told him that Geier didn't have any better of a reputation than Reinigen, which was one of the reasons the vulture creatures picked on them. They wanted to feel superior to someone. Geier did serve a function in the Wesen community, although it was a dark one, and most Wesen—at least those who considered themselves civilized—wanted nothing to do with them. The Geier harvested human organs and bodily fluids and sold them for use in various medicines and "enhancements." Humans had done the same thing with animal parts throughout history— and in some cultures still did—although in the Wesen's case, human ingredients actually worked.

The Reinigen raised his hands in what the Wechselbalg assumed was meant to be a placating gesture. All it did was make the Geier laugh. The sound was unpleasant, harsh and grating, and the Wechselbalg spoke to cut it off.

"How are you four this evening?"

They all turned to look at him, the Geier with angry surprise, the Reinigen with desperate hope. Then they took note of the battle-axe he carried at his side.

"Who the hell are you?" one of the Geier demanded. "Paul Bunyan?"

The other two laughed.

"I'm Nick Burkhardt," the Wechselbalg said. "The one and only."

The three Geier scowled, but the Reinigen's face lit up.

"The Grimm!" he said.

The Wechselbalg smiled. "That's right."

"You ruined the organ trade in this town," another Geier said. "The best we can do now is snatch the occasional homeless person off the street and sell the parts out of the back of our van."

"Keeping them fresh is a real pain in the ass," the third said.

"Hardly any money in it at all," said the first. "Not like in the old days."

So the Other had broken up a Geier organ-selling ring? At least he'd done *something* right.

"Why bother with the Reinigen?" the Wechselbalg asked. "And why three on one? You boys scared of him or something?"

The three Geier lowered their heads and extended their necks in a very bird-like display of aggression.

"Reinigen may not be human," the first Geier said.

"Hell, they may not even be fully Wesen," the second added.

"But you can make a few bucks off their organs," the third said. "If you know who to sell them to."

"Not much profit in it," the first said. "But these days, we can't afford to be too picky."

"Of course, now that *you're* here," the second said, "we might change our mind about the rat."

"Grimm organs are rarer than rare," the second said. "We could name our price."

"And then double it," the third said.

"Triple it," the first added.

Without further warning, the Geier came running toward the Wechselbalg, talons held high. The Wechselbalg grinned, raised the axe, and stepped forward to meet them.

It didn't take long.

When it was finished, the Wechselbalg leaned down and wiped the axe head clean on one of Geier's corpses. There wasn't much he could do about the blood covering him, but he'd worry about that later. Besides, he kind of liked it.

The Reinigen had watched the Wechselbalg kill the Geier in horrified fascination. Now the Wechselbalg walked toward him, kicking a Geier head out the way as he approached. In death, a woged Wesen normally resumed its human appearance, and while that process was occurring, it was taking much longer than usual with the Geier. The head he kicked still retained a good portion of its avian qualities, and the grotesque thing bounced across the asphalt, leaving blood splotches as it went.

The Reinigen trembled and tried to draw in upon himself, as if hoping to appear less threatening. "P-please don't hurt me. *Sir*," he added quickly.

The Wechselbalg liked that. *Sir*. Very nice indeed.

He held the axe down at his side so as not to intimidate the Reinigen any more than necessary.

"Where is Forest Park?" he asked.

The Reinigen stared at him. "Um… what?"

The Wechselbalg took a step closer, and the Reinigen flinched.

"Forest Park—where the Hafen is. How do I get there?"

The Reinigen blinked several times, as if he was still having trouble understanding. The Wechselbalg considered brandishing the axe to loosen the man's tongue, but then the Reinigen finally began speaking. He gave the Wechselbalg clear, concise directions, and the shapeshifter committed them to memory.

"Thanks," he said. He turned to go, but then he stopped himself, and turned to face the Reinigen once more. "You're still woged."

He glanced at the Geier's bodies. Although they were dead and returning to their human aspects, the process was taking far longer than normal for all of them. He remembered his conversation with the Eisbiber. He hadn't taken note of it at the time, but the little man had stayed woged the entire time they'd talked. The Wechselbalg looked at the Reinigen once more.

"How is this possible?"

"I don't know,' the rat man said. "Whatever it is, it's happened to a lot of us. It's some kind of sickness, I guess. No one seems to know. It's why everyone's headed to the

Hafen. I was on my way there myself when these three—" he nodded to the dead Geier "—stepped into the street and forced me to pull over." He shook his head. "I can't believe I was so stupid. I should've just run them over and kept going."

The Wechselbalg narrowed his eyes. "Do you truly mean that?"

"Hell, yeah! Lousy carrion-eating bastards."

"Then you're one of the *bad ones*."

Before the Reinigen could react, the Wechselbalg raised the battle-axe, swung it in a swift horizontal strike, and lopped off the rat-man's head. Blood fountained, the body collapsed, and the head—still wearing an expression of surprise—hit the ground, bounced, and rolled to a stop.

The Wechselbalg watched as the Reinigen's head slowly began to assume human features. He experienced a mild wave of dizziness, and sweat broke out on his forehead. He drew the back of his forearm across his head, and the dizziness passed.

Must be getting tired, he thought.

He wiped the blade clean on the Reinigen's clothes, then turned and walked back to the Cherokee. This had been a good warm-up. Now he was looking forward to the main event.

He climbed in the vehicle, started the engine, and headed toward the Hafen.

Nick's night vision had always been good, and it had sharpened considerably since he'd come into his heritage as a Grimm. But he still felt almost blind compared to Monroe. The man moved through the forest with a swift, silent confidence that Nick struggled to emulate. Monroe wore his jacket once more, but he'd removed his shoes. *Need to stay connected to the Earth, you know?*

He'd said before they'd started.

Nick *didn't* know, not exactly, but as the two men made their way toward the Hafen, Nick began to fall into a rhythm with Monroe, his initial awkwardness melted away, and he began weaving between trees and moving through underbrush with newfound ease.

Monroe continually scented the air as they traveled, his inhalations and exhalations indistinguishable from the gentle night breeze. It was important they move as silently as possible, in order to avoid alerting any of the Hafen's outer guards. As Monroe and Rosalee had explained it, Portland's Hafen was located in a clearing created and maintained by Wildermanner, the nature-loving Wesen responsible for the stories of Bigfoot and other legends of bestial wild men. Once people began arriving at the Hafen, volunteers would guard the clearing's inner perimeter, while other Wesen would patrol the woods surrounding the Hafen. This set-up was standard procedure, and although in this case the Wesen sought refuge because of the *Ewig Woge* rather than as protection from human hunters—*or Grimms,* Nick thought—they still maintained guard. Nick was glad they were cautious. As difficult as their wariness was making it for him and Monroe to approach the Hafen, it would hopefully do the same for the Wechselbalg.

Monroe held up a hand. Nick froze and listened. He heard Monroe breathing, along with the muffled sound of the Blutbad's heart. It pounded faster than when Monroe was in human form, but Nick had been around a woged Monroe enough to know that was normal. He heard the wind gently rustling leaves, but that was the extent of the night sounds. He heard no animals moving, no birds chirping. It was possible their presence had frightened the forest creatures into silence, but it was equally possible that someone else had scared them, too. Someone Nick would rather avoid meeting.

The two men listened for several moments, and just when Nick had decided it was a false alarm, a shadowy figure moved between a pair of trees less than a dozen yards ahead of them. It happened so fast that at first Nick wasn't sure he'd seen anything. But then Monroe leaned his mouth close to Nick's ear and breathed a single word.

"Lowen."

Nick tensed, and his senses sharpened even further as he strained to detect the lion-like Wesen. Lowen had an especially keen sense of smell, almost equal to that of Blutbaden, and if the wind had been blowing in a different direction, the Lowen would've scented them by now. Nick wasn't worried about a single Lowen. Well, not much. He and Monroe could handle the lion-man. The problem was the amount of noise they'd make in the process. They'd alert any nearby patrolling Wesen to their presence, and they'd swiftly converge on them. Nick wanted to avoid hurting anyone if at all possible. These Wesen were simply trying to keep themselves safe while they suffered from the *Ewig Woge*. But the condition had likely heightened the Lowen's bestial nature and made him or her highly aggressive. If the Lowen detected them, it would attack first and pause to ask questions only after they were dead. Nick was here to stop the Wechselbalg from killing. He didn't want to add to the night's already high body count.

Several moments passed without any sight of the Lowen, and Monroe turned to Nick and gave him a thumbs up to indicate they were in the clear.

That's when Nick heard the twig snap behind them.

CHAPTER TWELVE

"Let me do the talking," Rosalee said.

"No problem,' Juliette replied.

The two women walked side by side down the path, Hank and Renard following behind. Neither man said anything, and although Juliette couldn't see them, she attributed their silence to wariness. Both were no doubt scanning the woods on either side of the path, alert for the least sign of trouble.

Renard had driven them to Forest Park, and he'd parked his vehicle at the end of a long line of cars, pickups, SUV's, and motorcycles. The other vehicles were covered by foliage and tree branches, placed so expertly that Juliette wouldn't have been able to detect them if she'd hadn't been so close. As they'd disembarked, a fully woged Wildermann emerged from between a pair of trees as if materializing out of thin air. He emitted a not altogether unpleasant odor of fresh green leaves and rich soil. Juliette wondered if he smelled like this because of how much time he spent in the woods, or if his scent was natural protective camouflage. He carried an armful of branches and leaves and immediately began concealing Renard's vehicle. The

Wildermann said nothing, but he gave Juliette and Hank a scowl before setting to work.

All of them carried various supplies. Rosalee and Juliette carried cloth bags filled with jars containing a special endorphin-enhancing paste that Rosalee had made. Juliette wasn't sure what was in it, but she understood much of it was comprised of ingredients that were especially effective for elevating endorphin levels in Wesen. Hank wore a backpack and Renard carried a large plastic cooler, both containing supplies Rosalee needed to make a cure for the *Ewig Woge*. Concealed within a hidden pocket inside Hank's backpack were Hank and Renard's guns. Rosalee had said that weapons were forbidden in the Hafen, and there was no way any of them would be permitted to enter if even one of their party was armed.

Both Rosalee and Renard had a small amount of endorphin-enhancing paste smeared beneath their noses, and while the treatment helped keep the worst emotional effects of the *Ewig Woge* at bay, it could only do so much. Renard carried the heavily laden cooler with ease in his Wesen form, but his brow was wrinkled in a constant frown, and he ground his teeth as they walked, both signs that he was struggling to keep a rein on his aggressive feelings. Rosalee seemed to fare better, but her nose kept twitching, and her breathing was even more rapid than usual for her while she was in full Fuchsbau mode. Juliette feared that both Rosalee and Renard—and presumably Monroe as well—were getting close to reaching their breaking points, when their control would snap and their Wesen halves would assume full control. If everyone in the Hafen was in similar condition, they had little time remaining to act. As bad as it would be if the Wechselbalg started killing Wesen in the Hafen, it would be nothing compared to the wholesale slaughter if the Wesen turned on one another.

The tree canopy grew thicker the farther they walked, until it blocked the night sky. Juliette could see almost nothing as they continued walking through the forest, and she assumed the same was true for Hank. Rosalee—and maybe Renard—had better night vision in Wesen form, and she trusted them to spot any potential danger. Still, it was nerve-wracking walking through darkness, knowing they were approaching a group of woged Wesen on the verge of being overwhelmed by their savage sides.

They walked for a quarter mile or so before the path narrowed to a trail; they continued down it, walking single file now. After a time, Juliette became aware of the smell of campfire smoke, and she saw what she thought were hints of orange-yellow light between the trees.

She was startled when a shadowy figure detached itself from the surrounding darkness and stepped onto the trail ahead of them. As first she feared it was the Wechselbalg, but then she smelled green leaves and turned earth, and she knew the being that confronted them was another Wildermann. There was an additional scent—a lighter, almost fruity one—and Juliette wondered if this was a female Wildermann. A Wilderfrau?

The Wildermann stood silently and waited. Rosalee stepped forward, bowed her head, then whispered a phrase in German. The Wildermann's reply came in English, his—or her—voice deep and gravelly.

"Who are they?"

The Wildermann didn't say the word *humans*, but Juliette knew that's what was meant.

"They are Kehrseite-Schlich-Kennen," Rosalee said. "They've come to help me cure the woge sickness."

The Wildermann blinked in surprise. "Can you really do that, Rosalee?"

Juliette was only a little surprised that Rosalee and

the Wildermann knew each other. Even near-hermits like Wildermann had medical needs.

"I hope so, Lee."

The Wildermann nodded, then pointed at Rosalee's bag, and she held it out for inspection. The Wildermann took a quick look, and then did the same for the others. The Wildermann gave Renard a scowling look before inspecting the cooler. Juliette didn't know if that was because the Wildermann knew Renard was a member of the Royal Family or because he was a Zauberbiest. There were several tense moments as the Wildermann examined the contents of Hank's backpack, but the guard spent no more time checking it out than the others, and Juliette did her best not to look relieved.

The Wildermann stepped aside, took hold of a low-hanging branch of what appeared to be an ordinary tree, and pulled. The tree—along with the underbrush that surrounded it—slid easily across the ground, revealing a narrow opening. Firelight spilled through, illuminating the Wildermann's features. He—or she—was tall, broad-shouldered, well-muscled, and just as shaggy as the one they'd encountered when they'd parked. But the Wildermann moved with a certain grace that strengthened Juliette's suspicions that it was female. In the firelight, Juliette could see that the tree the Wildermann had pulled to the side wasn't full length. It had been cut off at ten feet and mounted on a flat wood-and-metal framework. Juliette assumed the tree had been hollowed out as well to make it easier to move. But then again, it might not be hollow. Wildermanner were *very* strong, after all.

The four of them stepped through the opening and into a clearing. Juliette glanced back over her shoulder to watch the Wildermann replace the camouflage. Once it was in place, she couldn't tell it apart from the trees on either side of it.

The clearing appeared to be almost perfectly circular, and the trees that ringed its circumference were in their prime—thick, tall, and stately. The spaces between them were filled with dense underbrush, including wicked-looking thorn bushes. In the center of the clearing was a large stone slab, carved so that its top and sides were flat and smooth. It looked like some kind of platform or dais to Juliette, and according to Rosalee, it was a place for a speaker to stand and address the Hafen. Small campfires dotted the clearing, and groups of woged Wesen stood around them, watching the flames silently or talking in hushed voices. Juliette was surprised that the Wesen would take the risk of alerting potential enemies to their presence by lighting fires. But then she realized that these Wesen had come here not to hide from a threat, but rather as a kind of quarantine, to have a place to conceal from the outer world the effects of the *Ewig Woge*. A serious situation to be sure, but—as far as they knew—not an immediately dangerous one. So why not have a few fires for warmth, light, and whatever psychological comfort they might bring?

A number of tents had been erected, and sleeping bags were spread out on the ground. No one was lying down, though, and Juliette would bet that most of the tents were empty, too. Everyone would be much too anxious to remain confined in small spaces. She had never seen so many woged Wesen before, and though she tried not to stare, she couldn't help herself. She recognized some types. Blutbaden, of course, along with Fuchsbau and Eisbiber. Others she'd only heard about, such as Bauerschwein, Mauzhertzen, Seelenguter, Skalengecken, and Jagerbaren. But there were many others that she didn't recognize, some of which bore only a passing human resemblance. Seeing them all together like this was like something out of a nightmare, and although Juliette reminded herself that these were intelligent beings much like she or Hank, she couldn't help feeling afraid.

There were just as many children as adults, if not more. Most of the young Wesen stood in small cliques or sat cross-legged on the ground, playing games on their phones or tablets. Seeing them alleviated some of her fear. No matter the species, kids were kids. Some of the younger children were still in human form. Wesen developed the ability to woge in youth, but it hit some earlier than others. Obviously, those children who hadn't started to change yet had been unaffected by the *Ewig Woge*.

The atmosphere in the makeshift camp was already thick with tension, and Juliette and the others only made it worse with their entrance. Heads turned as they walked into the Hafen, brows furrowed, eyes glared, lips curled back from teeth, and the air filled with growls, hisses, and snarls.

It's because of Hank and me, she thought, and she wondered if it would've been better if the two of them had remained behind.

A Bauerschwein stepped forward and blocked their way. He was short and stout, but while he had a bit of a pot belly, he looked like he was made of more muscle than fat. His brow was thick and pronounced, he was bald, and he possessed a porcine snout and ears. His lower teeth jutted out almost like tusks. He wore a dark blue uniform with stitching on the right breast that identified him as an employee of First-Rate Security. Juliette glanced to see if he carried a gun, but all he had was a flashlight holstered to his belt. That was a relief.

The Bauerschwein gave Juliette and Hank a dark look before addressing Rosalee.

"What are these two doing here?"

"*These two* have names," Hank said.

The Bauerschwein snorted, but didn't look away from

Rosalee. Before she could answer his question, though, he sniffed the air, and his scowl—which Juliette believed was likely a permanent part of his expression—deepened.

"You smell of Blutbad." His tone made it sound like an accusation.

Pigs had a tremendous sense of smell, Juliette knew, and it seemed Bauerschwein were no different. Bauerschwein also had a longstanding antipathy to Blutbaden. Not a good combination.

Rosalee's lips drew back from her teeth.

"You smell like a lot of things, but I'm too polite to mention it."

It wasn't like Rosalee to snap like that—not that Juliette blamed her.

A second Wesen stepped forward to join the Bauerschwein. The woman wore a faded jean jacket over a white T-shirt, tight jeans, and worn boots. Juliette didn't recognize the type of Wesen she was. Some sort of feline variety, and from the tawny fur on her face and hands, Juliette guessed she was related to the cougar. She had a long mass of curly brown hair that spilled over her shoulders. But instead of making her seem more human, the hair only accentuated her animal appearance.

"No humans allowed in the Hafen," she growled. "Everyone knows that."

"Not even Kehrseite-Schlich-Kennen?" Juliette asked. She took a quick glance around the clearing. "Looks like there are a few of us here."

"Close friends and family," the Bauerschwein said. "That's different."

Juliette wasn't sure, but she thought the man's lower teeth grew longer and thicker as he spoke.

"Right," the cougar-woman said. "Who vouches for you two?"

Juliette wanted to point out that the Wildermann guards had let them enter and that should be good enough. But given how hostile these two Wesen were being, thanks no doubt to the *Ewig Woge*, she doubted they would care.

"I do," Renard said.

The two Wesen turned to look at him, as did others in the immediate area. Juliette felt the tension in the air increase dramatically, and she feared that if they didn't play the next few seconds just right, violence would break out. If that happened, it could set off the entire Hafen, and the results would be catastrophic.

Renard put the cooler down and stepped forward to stand in front of the Wesen. Juliette could see his struggle to maintain control of his anger in the set of his jaw and the narrowing of his eyes. Normally, the two Wesen might've taken a step back from an angry Zauberbiest, but they were in the grip of the *Ewig Woge*, and that made them step closer to Renard, hands bunched into fists.

"This is ridiculous," Juliette muttered to herself.

She put her bag on the ground, removed a jar and unscrewed the lid. She dipped a finger into the light-purple paste inside and then stepped in between Renard and the two Wesen. The Bauerschwein and cougar-woman glared at her, but in a tone of voice she used to calm both frightened animals and their anxious owners, she said, "Hold still now." She then applied a dab of paste around the Bauerschwein's snout and beneath the cougar-woman's nose. The Wesen were so stunned by her actions that they stood still and let her work. When she finished, she stepped back and the man and woman both inhaled deeply through their noses. The effect was immediate and dramatic. The tension drained from their bodies, and they visibly relaxed.

"What is this stuff?" the cougar-woman asked, inhaling again.

"Lavender and vanilla," the Bauerschwein said. "Among other things." He too inhaled again.

"Well. Whatever it is, it's *great*," the woman said. A moment later, she began purring.

Juliette turned to Rosalee and grinned. Rosalee smiled back.

The first step was to begin distributing the endorphin-enhancer to every Wesen in the Hafen to help keep them calm and relaxed. After that, Rosalee could begin mixing the cure for the *Ewig Woge*. But in order for it to work, she needed a very important final ingredient—and that's where Nick and Monroe came in.

Her smile fell away. Somewhere out there was the Wechselbalg—and in all likelihood, it too was heading for the Hafen. The question was, who would get here first? And what would happen then?

Nick didn't waste time thinking. He stepped to the side just as the Lowen lunged for him. He spun around, grabbed the back of the Lowen's head, and shoved him toward the nearest tree. The Lowen hit face-first, let out a muffled *oof!* and went limp. Nick caught him before he could fall and lowered him gently to the ground. He checked the man's pulse and was relieved to find it strong. He'd put a lot of muscle into that shove, but he hadn't wanted to hurt the man, just keep him from raising the alarm.

Nick straightened and Monroe leaned close to his ear to speak.

"Man, you're a bad-ass when you're being sneaky," he whispered.

Nick smiled and the two men continued toward the Hafen, Monroe once again leading the way. They didn't encounter any more roaming guards, but neither did they run across the Wechselbalg. *Too bad,* he thought. Things would've been simple—and probably a lot less messy—if they could've confronted him outside the Hafen.

Eventually Nick could smell campfire smoke and see glimmers of light ahead. As he and Monroe drew closer, the underbrush began to get thicker, and thorns snagged his jeans and hoodie, scratched his face and hands. Monroe had warned him that it would be like this close to the Hafen, and they slowed their pace, doing their best to keep the thorn damage to a minimum as they proceeded. Both men took in soft, hissing breaths as they were scratched, but eventually they made it to the edge of the clearing.

Monroe leaned close and whispered in his ear once more.

"Try not to get too close to anyone. They might smell the blood from your scratches and get suspicious."

Nick nodded. He pulled up his hood to conceal his features. The two men then entered the Hafen.

The clearing was filled with people standing around small campfires or near tents. Nick estimated there were a couple of hundred people present, and from what he could see, almost all of them were woged. The air practically vibrated with tension; he felt as if he'd just stepped into a room full of high explosives, and all it would take was a single match to set them off.

He and Monroe had agreed it was best not to enter the Hafen with the others so that Nick could hide his presence from the Wechselbalg until he was ready to confront the shapeshifter. But it was equally important to avoid causing an outbreak of violence. The last thing the Wesen needed was to see a Grimm in their midst—especially since some of them believed he'd gone insane and started killing Wesen at random. Even if they hadn't been suffering from the *Ewig Woge,* his presence could've provoked them to attack. So the longer he remained concealed, the better.

No one seemed to have noticed them enter the Hafen. No one turned to look in their direction, and better yet, no one shouted to raise the alarm. Nick and Monroe started walking toward the center of the clearing, Nick sticking close to his friend's side. Monroe had told him that a lot of the Wesen would keep to themselves, some because they tended not to play well with others, and some because they were trying to maintain control of their aggressive urges. So as long as Nick kept his hood up, looked down at the ground, and kept his hands in his pockets, no one would give him a second look—they hoped. Monroe's Blutbad scent would help mask Nick's human scent, but Monroe had cautioned that it still would be best to avoid getting too close to anyone they didn't know, just in case. So they steered clear of Wesen as they walked, and no heads swiveled in their direction, no one sniffed the air, no one pointed and shouted, "Human!" or worse, "Grimm!"

Nick was on edge, but not because he feared discovery. He'd never been in the presence of so many Wesen before, certainly not so many that were woged, and his instincts urged him to attack the creatures that surrounded him. They were monstrous, unnatural beasts, and they had to be stopped before they could cause harm.

Nick gritted his teeth and fought the compulsion to grab the nearest Wesen and beat them to a pulp. The experience brought a newfound respect for Monroe. Walking among all these Wesen, Nick had a much better idea of the battle Monroe fought every day—it was a battle he wasn't sure he'd win if their position had been reversed.

On the other side of the clearing, Nick saw Juliette, Hank, Rosalee, and Renard talking with a pair of Wesen. He was glad to see the others had reached the Hafen safely, but it looked like they weren't receiving the warmest of greetings. Nick felt an urge to go over and help, but he knew he'd only make matters worse if he interfered. Besides, they could take care of themselves. But he planned to keep an eye on them nevertheless.

"Any sign of him?" Nick asked softly as he and Monroe walked.

"No, but if he was here, wouldn't we be able to tell by all the screaming and bleeding?"

Monroe had a point. The Wechselbalg might have been something of a chameleon in his prime, but right now he wasn't one for subtlety. If he was here, he'd be fighting—and killing.

Unless he's walking around in disguise and looking for you, so he can steal the rest of your memories and finally eliminate the competition.

Nick struggled to predict the Wechselbalg's next move. He could be in the Hafen right now, hunting Nick while Nick was hunting him. Or he could've decided Portland wasn't big enough for two Nick Burkhardts, and he could be on the road headed anywhere. Maybe to New York, where Nick had grown up...

He quickly shut down that line of thought. Not only was it counterproductive right now, his instincts told him the Wechselbalg would be here. He just had to keep looking, keep waiting. It was only a matter of time.

Nick and Monroe continued making a slow circuit of the Hafen. Juliette and the others managed to get past their welcoming committee, and now headed toward the stone slab in the center of the clearing. Monroe had told him it was called the Speaking Stone, and anyone who stood on it had the right to address those who'd sought shelter in the Hafen. Whoever held control of the Speaking Stone was allowed to talk as long as they wanted—until a minimum of three Wesen called for them to step down. If they refused, they were "encouraged" to shut up, violently if necessary. When she was ready, Roslaee would step onto the stone and address the assembled Wesen. And then... well, they'd see what happened.

As Rosalee and the others set down their supplies and started to unpack them, Nick caught sight of Bud standing near a tent, talking to another male Eisbiber that Nick didn't recognize. He caught Monroe's eye and nodded in Bud's direction, and the two men headed toward the tent. As they drew closer, Nick was able to make out what Bud was saying.

"—couldn't believe it! I mean, I've known him for a couple years now, and I'd come to consider him a friend. But after tonight, I don't know—" He broke off as he noticed Nick and Monroe approaching. He looked suddenly nervous. Even more so than usual, Nick thought.

"Monroe! What a surprise! I mean, it's not really a surprise, since just about everyone's here and you're definitely part of everyone." He gave Monroe an uneasy smile.

At first Nick wasn't sure what Bud's problem was, but when the man Bud had been talking to got a good look at Monroe, he turned without saying a word and walked rapidly away. Nick got it then. Monroe in human aspect might not be threatening, but in full woge? He was a Blutbad, and no one was comfortable around them, especially Eisbiber.

"Relax," Monroe said. "I've still got it under control." His words came out in a half-growl, and they did little to comfort Bud. If anything, the man looked even more frightened than before.

"Who were you talking about?" Monroe asked. "Whoever it was, it sounded pretty serious."

"I was talking about Nick," Bud said. "Word going around the Hafen is that he killed a couple Skalegenck kids for spraying graffiti. And when he came over to my place, he was acting as if something was really wrong with him. I mean, he held a gun to my head! I feared for my life, I really did!" He shook his head. "I think the Grimm part of him finally took over, you know?"

"Aw, man," Monroe said. "Didn't you get Rosalee's voicemail?"

Bud frowned. "Rosalee called me? Sorry, I've been so busy getting the family to the Hafen that I haven't looked at my phone since leaving the house."

Nick didn't know exactly what had happened at Bud's house, but he knew who was responsible—the Wechselbalg. He raised his head so Bud could get a better look at his face.

Bud looked at him, but the closest campfire was twenty feet away, and it took a moment for him to make out Nick's features.

"Nick?" he said, the word coming out almost as a shriek of alarm.

Up to this point, the tent flap had been open, but now it was zipped closed from the inside with single swift motion.

"Let me guess," Nick said. "Your wife and kids are inside."

Bud's whiskers began twitching so fast, they became twin blurs on either side of his face.

"No, they decided they'd be safer at home. Wait, did I say they were still at home? I meant they left town, but they didn't tell me where they were going, so there's no point in asking me."

The words tumbled out of Bud's mouth even faster than normal, so fast that Nick had trouble making them out. But he didn't need to catch Bud's exact words to know the man was terrified of him.

"It's okay, Bud," Nick said, trying to keep his voice down so no one would overhear.

"Sure. Sure, it's okay. Everything's okay. Always has

been, always will be. Well, it was good seeing you, but I'm sure you've got some important official business to take care of, and I don't want to keep you from it. Never let it be said that Bud Wurstner obstructed justice. So take it easy, and I'll see you later, all right?"

Bud starting backing away, but he continued facing Nick, as if afraid to turn his back on him.

"It's *me*, Bud. Nick. The *real* one."

"It's true," Monroe said. "He's the one and only. Well, maybe not *only* these days, but he is the original, that's for sure."

Bud stopped backing up, and his furry brow knitted into a frown. He looked at Monroe.

"Have you gone crazy, too?" he asked. He held up his hands. "No offense."

Nick stepped closer to Bud so he wouldn't have to speak louder to be heard. Bud stiffened, and for an instant Nick thought the man would flee, but he held his ground. Monroe stayed by Nick's side.

"Earlier tonight, when Hank and I visited, do you remember me asking about a Wechselbalg?"

"Sure, but that's not the visit that concerns me. It's when you came back later, alone, that—" Bud broke off, eyes widening in realization. "That wasn't you the second time, was it? He sure looked like you, but he didn't act like you." He let out a short laugh. "Man, what a relief! I should've realized you'd never do anything like that. Not our Nick."

Bud spoke in a normal tone of voice, and Monroe put a finger to his lips to shush him.

"Keep it down. We're trying to be incognito."

"Right," Bud said, although it was clear from his tone of voice that he had no idea what Monroe was talking about.

"Did the Wechselbalg hurt you or your family?" Nick asked.

"No. He scared me a little, that's all. Well, he scared me a *lot*, but no permanent harm done. So he's the one who killed those teenagers, right?"

Nick nodded.

"It's a good thing you haven't shown yourself yet," Bud said. "Word spread fast about what you—*he*—did to those poor kids." Bud hesitated. "And I might've told a few people about how you came back to my home and threatened me. Sorry."

By a *few* people, Nick figured Bud really meant every Wesen he'd come in contact with tonight. When Bud was nervous, he talked. And the more anxiety he felt, the more often he talked. By this point, the entire Hafen probably thought Nick Burkhardt had become a homicidal maniac. *Great.*

"I take it there's been no sign of the Wechselbalg so far," Nick said.

Bud suddenly looked nervous again. "No. Why? You think he's going to come here?"

"That's what we're counting on," Monroe said.

"That would be bad," Bud said. "*Really* bad. Everyone here is on edge, and some of them are on the verge of losing it altogether. If the fake Nick suddenly showed up and started trying to kill people…"

"Ka-pow," Monroe said, miming an explosion with his hands.

"Yeah," Bud said.

"We'll just have to do our best to make sure that doesn't happen," Nick said.

"No offense, Nick," Bud said. "You're good, but I don't see how even you can keep this pot from boiling over sooner or later."

Nick glanced toward the center of the clearing and saw Rosalee step onto the Speaking Stone.

He smiled.

"Good thing I don't have to do it alone," he said.

The Wechselbalg did his best to move silently through the woods, but it wasn't easy with the battle-axe in his right hand and the talwar in his left. He still had his Glock tucked into the back of his pants, but he was beginning to wish he'd selected weapons from the trailer that were a little easier to maneuver with through underbrush.

The weapons felt increasingly heavy as he walked, and his legs began to feel thick and awkward, as if his muscles were made of rubber. Sweat ran down his face and neck, trickled along his spine. For the first time since he'd become Nick Burkhardt, he felt himself growing tired, growing weaker. No, not the first time. He recalled the short dizzy spell he'd experienced after slaying the Geier and the Reinigen. Panic stabbed him in the gut as he realized what was happening. This body, which had started out so strong and vital, was beginning to wear thin.

Not again! He'd had such hopes for this body, and despite a few difficulties, he was really enjoying being Nick Burkhardt. He didn't want it to end—not this soon, at any rate. All of his long life, he'd been careful to avoid standing out, labored to be just another face in the crowd. It felt good to someone special for once, to be a *hero*. And he didn't want to give that up. Maybe if he—

A rustle in the underbrush off to his left. Not loud. Could be a small animal, frightened by his passage. But his instincts told him it was something else. Something bigger.

The Wechselbalg swung the talwar outward in a sweeping horizontal arc. He felt no resistance as the blade passed through empty air, but he sensed as much as heard someone jumping back to avoid the strike. He spun to his side, raising the battle-axe before him like a shield. He found himself looking into the cold, fierce eyes of a bird-like Wesen, a… Raub-Kondor, Nick's memories provided. Strong fighter, excellent night vision. No wonder this Wesen was guarding the Hafen's outer perimeter. With those eyes, he could see better than a soldier equipped with night-vision goggles.

The Raub-Kondor stared at the Wechselbalg for a long moment before uttering a single word.

"Grimm."

The Wechselbalg smiled, all traces of his previous weariness gone, as if hearing that word alone had restored his vitality. The Wechselbalg expected the Raub-Kondor to raise his taloned fingers and attack, but instead the bird-man tilted his head back. In a flash, the Wechselbalg understood what the Raub-Kondor intended to do— sound the alarm.

The Wecheselbalg hurled the axe, and it sank into the Raub-Kondor's chest with a solid *thunk*. The man's eyes widened in shock, and the only sound that emerged from his beak-like mouth was a soft, wet click. The Raub-Kondor was one of the hardier breeds of Wesen, and it remained alive long enough to take three shaky steps away from the Wechselbalg, the axe still embedded in its chest, before it pitched face-first to the ground.

The Wechselbalg stepped over to the Raub-Kondor's corpse, shoved it onto its back with a foot, then bent down to pull the axe free. He wiped the weapon clean on the man's clothes, and by the time he'd finished, the Raub-Kondor was well on his way to resuming human form once more.

The rush of adrenaline from the unexpected encounter had done much to wipe away the Wechselbalg's weariness, but it wasn't entirely gone. It was because the Other still lived. He needed to complete the duplication process and fully become Nick Burkhardt. Once that was accomplished, the Other would be gone, and his physical condition would stabilize. Everything would be fine then. Just fine. Especially if he got to kill more Wesen along the way.

He continued moving through the forest.

CHAPTER THIRTEEN

Juliette watched as Rosalee stepped onto the Speaking Stone, feeling as nervous as if she were the one about to address a camp full of frightened, aggressive, fully woged Wesen. Rosalee didn't say anthing at first, and no one seemed to notice her standing there. But slowly, one person at a time, then by twos and threes, people realized what she had done, and they quieted and turned to face her until she had the full attention of everyone present.

"My name is Rosalee Calvert. Some of you know me. Some of you knew my brother, Freddy. I run the Exotic Spice & Tea Shop in town, and many of you have been our customers at one time or another."

She paused and a number of Wesen nodded, acknowledging her words. But not everyone was willing to let her talk.

"You forgot to mention that you're friends with the Grimm!" shouted a female Lausenschlange. The snake-woman followed her statement with an angry hiss.

Several of the assembled Wesen called out their agreement with the Lausenschlange, and a couple even shook their fists in the air, as if parodying an angry mob from an old black-and-white movie. But this was no joke. Juliette knew how on edge the Wesen were, and more than a few of them were no doubt looking for a target to take out their fear and anger on. Juliette hoped Rosalee wasn't in the process of making herself such a target.

Rosalee continued as if the Lausenslange woman hadn't spoken.

"All of us have been exposed to… well, it's not exactly a disease per se, but it functions like one. It's called the *Ewig Woge*, and as the name implies, it traps us in our Wesen forms. The longer we remain in them, the harder it becomes to control our emotions and natural, instinctive behaviors."

While everyone else was watching Rosalee, Juliette noted that Hank and Renard were watching the crowd, keeping an eye out for the Wechselbalg as well as anyone who might be tempted to give in to their "instinctive behaviors."

"We've found a treatment for the *Ewig Woge*," Rosalee said, "but it's going to take some time to prepare it. In the meantime, we have this."

That was Juliette's cue. She took one of the jars of endorphin-enhancer and handed it to Rosalee.

"We need to keep our endorphin levels high to counteract the emotional effects of the *Ewig Woge*. A little of this—" she lifted the jar high so everyone could see it "—applied directly under the nose will help. The first thing we need to do is make sure everyone gets some. That way we can all remain calm while I work on the treatment."

"What the hell is that stuff?" someone shouted.

"A mixture of lavender and vanilla," Rosalee said, "along with a few other substances that will intensify the effect on us."

The crowd was silent for a moment, and then a Drang-Zorn man called out, "You mean we're supposed to *smell* ourselves calm?"

Laughter spread throughout the crowd, but before Rosalee could respond, the Bauerschwein security guard stepped forward. He raised his hands to get the crowd's attention, and even though he wasn't on the Speaking Stone, they gave it to him.

"I know it sounds crazy, but it works," he said. "Before Rosalee gave me some of the stuff I was so angry, I was ready to tear her and her friends apart."

"Like to have seen you try it," Hank murmured softly, and Renard gave him a smile.

"But as soon as I got a whiff, my anger started draining away. I'm still not all the way back to normal, but at least I'm not looking for a fight anymore."

The cougar-woman came forward and joined the Bauerschwein.

"It worked the same for me," she said. "How many fights have broken out since we came here? A half-dozen? And how many more *almost* happened?"

No one responded.

Rosalee jumped back in then.

"You all know how hard you've been working to control your Wesen side, and you know how close you've come to losing that control over the last few hours. Believe me, I've been there, too. It's only a matter of time before you can't hold on any longer. And when that happens, someone's going to get hurt. Maybe even killed. You can't let that happen. *Please* don't let that happen!"

No one said anything for several moments, then one by one, people came forward and started lining up in front of the Speaking Stone.

Juliette felt the first real sense of hope since this mess had started. Now if everything else worked out as planned...

If.

Juliette, Hank, and Renard assisted Rosalee, and the

four of them each opened a jar of the endorphin-enhancing paste and began applying it to the Wesen in line. Juliette knew it wasn't right, but she couldn't help feeling like she was at work, applying medicine to sick animals.

They managed to get through only a handful of Wesen, however, before a Skalengeck woman rushed forward and slapped the jar out of Juliette's hand. The impact from the lizard-woman's thick claws caused the jar to shatter, and a mass of shards and paste fell to the ground. Startled, Juliette stepped back, but the Skalengeck woman followed, leaning her scaly face forward in what Juliette recognized as an aggressive stance.

"You damn humans!" she hissed. "I've never like your kind, and I've always hated having to pretend to be one of you. You think you're so smart, so strong. But you're nothing compared to us. Nothing!"

Renard stepped forward and put himself between Juliette and the angry Skalengeck.

"I'm not human," he said, his voice low and menacing.

The Skalengeck drew her head back when she saw him, but she didn't retreat.

"Zauberbiest. You're not much better than human. But you know what's even worse? Grimms! My daughter and her boyfriend were killed by one tonight. You know why? Because they were spray-painting graffiti. Big-time criminals, huh? My poor girl." She shook her head. "The things he did to her…" The lizard-woman's voice broke and her inhuman eyes glistened with tears.

Juliette felt sympathy for the woman, and if Renard hadn't been standing between them, she would've stepped forward and tried to comfort her. But given the state the woman was in, she probably would've killed Juliette if she'd made the attempt. So all things considered, she was glad Renard was there.

A Seelengut woman came forward then.

"The Grimm tried to kill me, too. I was lucky to get away."

From deeper in the crowd, a Klaustreich called out, "It's true! I was there and he almost killed me, too!"

"Us too!" a young Jagerbar shouted. Another Jagerbar standing at his side nodded vigorously. "We weren't doing anything when he attacked us!"

A dozen yards from the Jagerbaren, a Luisant-Pêcheur stepped forward.

"Seriously?" the otter-woman said. "You guys were going to tear up my bar because you were fighting over a woman who didn't want either of you. You're lucky Nick didn't beat you up any worse than he did."

The Jagerbaren glared at the Luisant-Pêcheur and bared their deadly-looking teeth. She glared right back at them, defiant.

Juliette knew that the Hafen was about to explode into violence, and she feared there was nothing they could do to prevent it. She looked from Rosalee, to Hank, and to Renard, but they all appeared just as uncertain as she was.

"Can I have a turn to talk?"

Juliette couldn't help smiling as Nick appeared, walking through the crowd toward the Speaking Stone. Wesen drew back as he approached, some wary, some fearful, some looking absolutely terrified. Many snarled, hissed, and growled, but many more remained deathly silent as they watched him pass. Monroe and Bud followed behind him, Monroe fixing his crimson-eyed gaze on those few Wesen who looked as if they wanted to rush forward and attack Nick. Bud glanced back and forth, whiskers vibrating with fear. Someone else might've thought the Eisbiber looked cowardly, but Juliette knew how hard the man had to fight against his kind's natural timidity to stand with Nick, and she thought she'd never seen anything braver.

As they reached the center of the clearing, Nick headed for the stone while Monroe and Bud joined the others. Rosalee had already stepped down from the Speaking Stone to administer the endorphin-enhancer, and as Nick stepped up onto it, he looked at Juliette and whispered, "I have no idea what to say."

She smiled. "You've got this."

He smiled back. "Let's hope."

Then he turned to face the crowd, took a deep breath, and began to speak.

Nick was normally a confident, decisive man. Some of that was due to his natural personality and his police training, but a lot of it was due to how his Aunt Marie had raised him. And he supposed a good portion of it was due to his being a Grimm. After all, you wouldn't last long in a fight against a predatory Wesen if you couldn't make quick decisions. But standing there on the Speaking Stone beneath the night sky, looking out at a mass of Wesen faces illuminated by the glow of firelight, he didn't feel very confident. The men and woman gazed back at him with a mixture of fear and hatred, and he was well aware that if they chose to rush him all at once, there was nothing he could do to prevent them from tearing him limb from limb.

Talk about a tough crowd, he thought.

The plan had been for him to remain unnoticed while he searched the Hafen for the Wechselbalg. But given the way the situation had begun to deteriorate for Rosalee, he felt he had no choice but to step in. He hoped he wasn't making a mistake.

He had no idea where to begin, so he took a deep breath and just started talking.

"My name is Nick Burkhardt, and yes, I am a Grimm. But I'm not like the Grimms in the stories you've heard all your lives. I'm not a monster any more than any of you are. We're all people. As different from the rest of humanity as we are from each other, maybe, but in all the ways that truly matter, we're the same. You want to live your lives in peace. I want to help make that possible. It's why I became a police officer, and it's what I hope to accomplish as a Grimm. I want to make peace possible—for both Wesen and humans."

He paused to gauge the crowd's response to his words. He couldn't tell what they thought about what he was saying, but they all appeared to be listening. He chose to take that as a good sign.

But before he could start speaking again, the Skalengeck woman whose daughter the Wechselbalg had killed stepped up to the Speaking Stone and glared up at him.

"Is killing teenagers your idea of keeping the peace?" she demanded. "The only peace your kind is interested in showing us is the peace of the grave!"

She bared her teeth at him, and the gill slits on the sides of her neck opened and closed, as if she were breathing heavily.

"I didn't kill your daughter or her boyfriend," Nick said. He was careful to meet the woman's gaze and keep his tone calm and even. Even without the influence of the *Ewig Woge*, she would've been devastated by the loss of her child. But under the *Ewig Woge*'s influence, it wouldn't take much to goad her into attacking him.

"It's difficult to explain," he continued, "but a shapeshifting Wesen called a Wechselbalg made itself into a duplicate of me. That's who killed your daughter." He paused, then added, "If I'd managed to stop the Wechselbalg when I first encountered it, your daughter would still be alive, and for that I'm truly sorry."

When he spoke the word *Wechselbalg*, many Wesen in the crowd looked at each other, confused. But recognition showed on a number of faces, and Nick caught a few quick snatches of conversation.

"Could it be true?"

"I thought they were only a legend."

"My grandmother said she met one once."

The Skalengeck woman flexed her clawed fingers.

"I thought Grimms were supposed to be smart," she said. "Do you really expect me to believe a ridiculous story like that?"

"Honestly? No. But it's the truth. And I can think of only one way to prove it to you." He reached around his back and drew his Glock. The Skalengeck woman's eyes widened in horror, but before she or anyone else could react further, he turned and held the weapon out to Juliette. She hesitated before taking it, eyes filled with worry. But she took hold of the gun and, after a second of thought, laid it on the ground.

Nick faced the Skalengeck woman once more.

"I'm unarmed," he said. He got down on his knees and clasped his hands behind his back. "All it would take to kill me right now would be one solid strike with your claws. You could tear my throat out before I could react."

"Nick, no!" Juliette said.

Hank stepped to her side and put a hand on her shoulder, as much to hold her back as to comfort her, Nick knew. Hank might not like what he was attempting any more than Juliette, but Nick knew his partner would back his play, regardless.

For her part, the Skalengeck woman seemed confused. He could still feel anger radiating from her, but it was tempered by a struggle to understand what was happening.

"If I had killed your daughter, if I was the monster so

many Wesen believe me to be, why would I have come to the Hafen in the first place? And why would I offer myself to you like this? If you truly believe there's no chance at all that I might be telling the truth about the Wechselbalg, then go ahead. Kill me."

And with that, Nick closed his eyes.

The entire Hafen fell silent. Nick could hear people breathing, and he thought he could almost hear their hearts beating as well. He could feel the emotional atmosphere in the clearing shift from stifling, pent-up aggression to surprised disbelief.

"Kill him!" someone shouted, but the words lacked conviction, were almost a question.

Several moments passed in silence after that, and then Nick heard the Skalengeck woman whisper softly, "I don't know. I just don't know."

Nick opened his eyes, but before he could say anything to the woman, he heard a rustling noise, followed by a series of grunts and then a cry of pain. A section of the foliage that enclosed the clearing was shoved violently aside, and an instant later a figure was hurled into the clearing. The body hit the ground hard and slid several feet before coming to a stop. He could see it was a Wildermann female. The back of her coat was stained with blood, and the spot widened as Nick watched. He hadn't heard a gunshot, so she must've been stabbed by something big and nasty from the look of it.

He got to his feet, but before he could rush to the woman's side to check for a pulse, another figure entered the Hafen. This one strolled in with an easy confidence, as if he owned the place, and Nick was not surprised to see the Wechselbalg had finally arrived. They'd already fought two times. Nick was determined the third would be last.

"There's the shapeshifter," Monroe said, pointing to

the Wechselbalg. "Now do you believe Nick?"

With a dark gleam in his eyes and a cruel smile on his face, the Wechselbalg looked like a storybook Grimm plucked from the nightmares of Wesen children and made flesh. He was splattered with blood from head to toe and carried a pair of wicked-looking ancient weapons. Nick recognized them, and he knew the creature had paid a visit to Aunt Marie's trailer. The axe was designed for swift, efficient decapitation of Wesen with dense bone structure, while the curved sword was a talwar. It was a weapon from India, used to dispatch a variety of small-statured Wesen that were related to Indian red scorpions, which were tiny but considered to be the most deadly scorpion in the world. The talwar was slick with blood, and the Wechselbalg held up the curved blade and examined it, as if fascinated.

"I've never seen blood by firelight," he said softly, as it to himself. "It's actually quite beautiful."

Their plan had worked, but at a terrible cost. The Wechselbalg had been drawn out into the open, but the woman guarding the entrance to the Hafen had paid with her life.

The assembled Wesen looked to each other, fear and confusion on their inhuman faces. As emotionally fragile as they were under the *Ewig Woge*, the sight of another Nick Burkhardt—one who looked like the bloodthirsty Grimms of legend—might cause them to flee the Hafen in terror. They couldn't afford to have that happen. Once the Wesen dispersed it would be difficult, if not impossible, to round them all up and administer Rosalee's cure. He had to find a way to keep them calm.

"You don't have to be afraid!" He spoke loudly so he could be heard throughout the Hafen. "None of you are in any danger. It's *me* the Wechselbalg wants. He wants to finish duplicating me before the body he's wearing burns out."

The Wechselbalg kept his gaze fastened on Nick as he walked further into the clearing. He passed by the body of the Wildermann female, but he paid it no attention. It was as if she had ceased to exist for him, or had never existed in the first place. The Wechselbalg might be mentally ill and ultimately not responsible for his actions, but upon seeing him walk past the woman he'd killed without even a hint of acknowledgment, Nick vowed that whatever else happened here tonight, the Wechselbalg would not hurt anyone else, even if he had to sacrifice his own life to make certain.

The Wechselbalg positioned himself between the crowd and the Speaking Stone. He slowly swept his gaze over the gathered Wesen, and more than a few averted their eyes or took several steps backward. Then he turned to face Nick.

"Nice try, *shapeshifter*," the Wechselbalg said. "But of the two of us, which one seems more like a true Grimm? You? You knelt before that *creature*—" he used the talwar to gesture at the Skalengeck, who remained standing close to the Speaking Stone "—and offered your life to her. Is that the sort of thing a real Grimm would do?"

Most of the Wesen remained silent, but some looked doubtful, and a handful began to whisper among themselves.

"It's exactly the kind of thing he would do," Juliette said. She gave Nick a smile, and he returned it.

The Wechselbalg turned to face Juliette. "He has you fooled, too? I'd hoped you of all people would be able to tell the difference between us." His voice was that of a man trying to contain his sorrow and disappointment.

"You can cut the crap," Hank said. "Nobody's buying it."

Nick wasn't so certain of that. The vast majority of Portland's Wesen knew him only by reputation. It was one thing to hear that a different kind of Grimm lived and worked in town. It was another to believe it, especially given the well-earned reputation Grimms had made for themselves as merciless killers over the centuries.

"He's telling the truth about one thing," the Wechselbalg said. "I have no interest in any of you here. Not tonight, anyway. I've only come here for *him*."

He leveled the talwar at Nick to emphasize his words.

Nick noticed something then. The Wechselbalg was sweating. Nick didn't remember seeing him do that before. *His body is already starting to burn out,* Nick realized. If he could get the creature to expend its dwindling energy reserves, he'd have a chance to defeat it. Assuming he could exhaust the Wechselbalg before it killed him.

The Wechselbalg continued. "As long as the rest of you stay back and don't interfere, no harm will come to you."

"Sheesh," Monroe said. "Do you come up with that corny dialogue all by yourself, or is there a special website you download it from?"

The Wechselbalg shot Monroe a venomous glare, and the Blutbad's eyes became a deeper crimson, and he began growling softly.

Rosalee put a hand on Monroe's arm. "Don't," she said.

Monroe scowled at her, but he stopped growling.

Nick stepped down from the Speaking Stone. Juliette leaned closer and whispered, "Do you want your gun?"

He shook his head. They needed to capture the Wecheselbalg alive. Besides, if he simply shot the shapeshifter as he attacked, he'd look like a cold-hearted executioner to the assembled Wesen. If he wanted them to trust him, he was going to have to do this the hard way. He then looked at Rosalee. "Start getting the cure ready."

She nodded. "Be careful."

He smiled. "That's the plan."

Both Hank and Renard inclined their heads at him, a sign of respect and encouragement. Bud gave him a nervous smile and a thumbs-up.

"I should be going out there with you," Monroe said. He fixed his red-eyed glare on the Wechselbalg and bared his teeth.

Nick put a hand on his friend's shoulder.

"Maybe next time."

Juliette gave him quick kiss, and it did more for him than any verbal encouragement ever could. Her eyes wished him good luck, and then he turned away from her and started walking toward the Wechselbalg.

"I don't suppose you're going to give me one of those weapons and make it a fair fight," he said.

The Wechselbalg grinned. "I thought heroes liked to have the odds stacked against them."

Nick noted the slight strain in the Wechselbalg's voice, saw his arms tremble slightly from the effort of holding both the axe and sword. He stopped just outside the Wechselbalg's striking range. He knew it was useless, but he had to try reasoning with the Wechselbalg one last time.

"Please let us help you," he said. "You're sick, and I'm not just talking about how you feel physically. You're not thinking clearly. You get confused easily, forget things. You aren't sure who you really are."

As Nick spoke, the Wechselbalg's expression became uncertain, but then it hardened into a mask of implacable hatred.

"You're wrong. I know exactly who I am. I'm Nick Burkhardt. And you're not."

The Wechselbalg let out a cry of rage, raised his two weapons, and came charging toward Nick. The weight of both weapons threw the Wechselbalg off balance, making his charge a clumsy one. It was a simple matter for Nick to step out of the way and avoid a sword strike. But the Wechselbalg's attack was so slow and awkward, Nick could've remained motionless as a statue and still the creature would've missed.

The Wechselbalg stumbled as he tried to regain his balance, and Nick took advantage of the opening. He stepped forward, planted a foot on the Wechselbalg's rear, and shoved. Hard. The shapeshifter stumbled even farther, then one of his feet slipped out from under him and he fell. He managed to twist as he went down, avoiding getting wounded by his own weapons. He landed on his right side, and the breath was driven out of his lungs with a harsh burst of air.

Nick moved forward, but the Wechselbalg rolled onto his back and hurled the battle-axe at Nick. The weapon spun end over end toward him, but he didn't attempt to get out of its way. Nick's hand became a blur of motion and he snatched hold of the axe handle and caught the weapon easily.

"I see you changed your mind about sharing," Nick said. "Thanks."

The Wechselbalg snarled in frustration. Sweat poured down his face, and his skin reddened, as if he'd somehow been exposed to a day's worth of unshielded sunlight in the last few minutes. Nick lunged again, intending to thump the Wechselbalg on top of the head with the butt of the axe handle, hopefully rendering him unconscious. But despite looking like he was on the verge of collapsing, the Wechselbalg jumped to his feet in a single fluid motion and swung the talwar at Nick's neck. The ancient Romans had called Grimm *Decapitari*, and it seemed like the Wechselbalg intended to live up that heritage. Nick leaned back and brought up his newly acquired axe at the same time. Metal clanged on metal, and he felt the jolt of the blow all the way up his arm and into his shoulder. Had the Wechselbalg only been acting as if he were weakened in order to lull him into overconfidence? No, the physical signs of the shapeshifter's exhaustion were real. Nick understood then that the Wechselbalg was drawing on his last reserves of energy. That made him desperate, which in turn made him all the more dangerous.

The Wechselbalg put on a surprising burst of speed and spun around in the opposite direction. Halfway through the maneuver, he took a two-handed grip on the talwar to put more power into his strike. Nick was equally as fast, though, and he dropped to a crouching position. The sword blade cut through the air above his head, and the Wechselbalg—not anticipating the lack of resistance— became unbalanced once more. Nick swept his left leg out and knocked the Wechselbalg's legs out from under him. The Wechselbalg crashed to the ground, but he managed to maintain his grip on the sword. Nick rose to his feet and brought the flat of the axe down, intending to give the Wechselbalg a solid enough blow to the head to knock him out. But the Wechselbalg rolled away as the axe came down, and the only thing Nick managed to strike was a patch of grass-covered earth.

That's exactly what I would've done, he thought.

The Wechselbalg might not have been an exact copy of him, especially when it came to personality, but in terms of reflexes and fighting skill, it was like he was battling himself. How could he get an advantage over a being who could match his speed and strength?

By exploiting his one weakness, Nick realized.

The Wechselbalg came out of his roll and rose to his feet in a single graceful move. He spun around to face Nick, talwar brandished to defend against the next attack. But Nick made no move toward the Wechselbalg. Instead, he spoke.

"You're sweating a hell of a lot. Are you all right?"

The Wechselbalg frowned, and his gaze became calculating. When he didn't reply, Nick went on.

"Me, I feel fine. I'm barely winded, in fact. I could keep on going like this for hours."

The Wechselbalg glared at him and ground his teeth.

"But I suppose that's because I'm a Grimm. A *real* one."

The Wechselbalg bared his teeth and let out a savage snarl that was more animal than human.

"And you're…" He trailed off, frowning. "What is it you are again?"

"I'm. Nick. *Burkhardt!*"

The Wechselbalg's voice rose to a scream. He dropped the talwar and came running toward Nick, spines extending from his fingers. He let out an inarticulate cry as he ran, and the bright light of madness blazed in his eyes. Sweat poured off of him like water, and Nick wouldn't have been surprised if the creature's entire body liquefied and splashed to the ground where it would be absorbed by the soil.

Nick had no idea if the Wechselbalg would be able to complete the duplication process if he managed to sink those spines into his flesh again, but he wasn't going to give the creature the chance to find out.

He waited until the Wechselbalg was almost upon him, and then he sidestepped and swung his axe. Once more, he used the flat of the blade, and he struck the shapeshifter on the side of the head. The Wechselbalg's momentum kept him running several more feet before he veered to the right and collapsed. The Wechselbalg, blinded by rage and pain, hadn't noticed he'd been headed toward one of the campfires, and as he fell, his right hand landed directly in the flames. Nick thought he had hit the Wechselbalg hard enough to render him unconscious, but the pain from his burning hand must've shocked him instantly back to full awareness. He shrieked, yanked his hand out of the fire, moved into a sitting position, and cradled the damaged hand to his chest, as if to protect it from further injury.

The Wechselbalg threw Nick a hate-filled look.

"What have you done to me?" he demanded, his voice low and surprisingly calm. He then slowly held up his hand to examine it, and Nick saw that it had become a charred, blackened lump. Not only had the finger spines been burned away, but the fingers themselves had been reduced to uneven nubs.

Nick didn't understand. The Wechselbalg's hand had only been in the fire for a split second. Sure, he should be burned, seriously so, but there was no way he could've sustained that amount of damage. He looked toward Juliette, and she also seemed puzzled. But then her expression brightened.

"The Wechselbalg's body is made up almost entirely of woge hormone," she said.

"Yes!" Rosalee said. "He's mostly liquid."

Nick thought of how hard the shapeshifter had been sweating during their fight. He hadn't been perspiring. He'd been losing a portion of the fluid that made up his body. And that was the reason his ancestors advised burning a Wechselbalg's body after killing it: its chemical make-up was highly reactive to flame. Nick knew then what he had to do.

But before he could put his plan into motion, the Wechselbalg sprang to his feet and came rushing toward him, arms extended. His right hand might've been a charred ruin, but the fingers on his left—and the spines extending from them—were just fine. The creature came at him with truly inhuman speed, faster than Nick could move, faster than he'd ever seen any Wesen move. It was as if he were propelled by a combination of hatred and desperation to survive. The Wechselbalg blurred toward him, and it was only out of instinct that he was able to raise and swing the axe before the shapeshifter reached him. He didn't have time to aim, and all the axe blade did was shear off the tips of the Wechselbalg's last two fingers. Nick barely registered this before the Wechselbalg slammed into him. The impact caused him to lose his grip on the axe, and the two of them fell to the ground. The Wechselbalg still had three finger spines remaining, and he jabbed them toward Nick's unprotected throat. Nick grabbed hold of the Wechselbalg's wrist with both hands to keep the spines from plunging into his neck. But the Wechselbalg was oozing clear liquid from every pore now, and it was almost impossible to maintain a grip on his slick flesh.

The shapeshifter's features began to deform, as if he were a melting wax statue, and when he spoke, his voice was thick and gurgly.

"Give me what's mine!"

Nick struggled to keep hold of the Wechselbalg's wrist. He could feel the flesh and bone give slightly beneath his grip, as if the shapeshifter was on the verge of complete structural collapse. But the Wechselbalg's finger-spines seemed unaffected by his worsening condition, and despite Nick's best efforts, he managed to push them forward inch by inch, until Nick could feel their sharp points dimple his skin.

He looked into the Wechselbalg's eyes and saw madness and hate, and more than a little fear.

"I'm sorry," Nick said.

He rocked back, drew his legs up beneath the Wechselbalg, planted his feet solidly on the shapeshifter's midsection, and shoved as hard as he could. The creature flew backward through the air, arms and legs flailing, only to land upon the same campfire in which he'd burned his hand.

The Wechselbalg's screams filled the Hafen. He thrashed within the fire, body wreathed in flame, skin blackening, as he struggled to pull himself free. A horrible nauseating stench filled the air, foul beyond anything Nick had ever experienced. Hot bile splashed the back of his throat, and a number of Wesen possessed of a highly developed sense of smell, including Monroe and Rosalee, moaned and gagged as the stink of burning Wechselbalg suffused the clearing.

The shapeshifter managed to crawl out of the fire, but it was too late. The damage had been done. He had become a featureless charred mass that possessed only the most rudimentary resemblance to a human form. As he crawled, smoldering bits and pieces of his body broke off and fell to the ground, where they collapsed into small mounds of black ash.

The Wechselbalg continued to shed bits of itself as it crawled toward Nick, losing mass until its body was no larger than that of a small child. When the Wechselbalg was within several feet of Nick, it raised a featureless black face to him, and reached out with a fingerless stump of a hand. A dry, whispering voice emerged from what was left of its throat, the sound like two autumn leaves being rubbed together.

"I am… I am…"

It continued reaching, reaching, before finally falling away to ash completely.

Nick stared at the black mound that was all that remained of the Wechselbalg. The Hafen was totally silent, save for the soft crackling of the campfires. And then, one by one, the Wesen gathered there began to cheer.

CHAPTER FOURTEEN

The cheering continued as Juliette joined Nick, and he slipped his arm around her, grateful for her comforting presence. Part of him—the part he thought of as Nick Burkhardt—regretted the loss of the Wechselbalg's life and wished he'd been able to find another way to stop him. But another part—the *Grimm* part—felt a cold, steely satisfaction at having rid the world of another monster. In that moment, he knew there was, in some ways at least, not much difference between himself and the shapeshifter, and the realization caused him to draw Juliette closer. As if sensing his inner conflict, she wrapped her arms around him and held him tight.

The others soon joined them, and the cheering died away. Nick was glad for that. Hearing the Wesen cheer was better than hearing them howl for his blood, but he didn't feel like a hero at the moment. Not in the slightest.

Hank clapped him on the shoulder, and Renard gave him a nod and said, "Nice work."

Nick nodded back to acknowledge the Captain's words. Although Renard was a good man—at least, Nick thought he was—he could be a cold pragmatist at times.

Nick looked once more at the Wechselbalg's ashes, and he wondered if one day he would be as cold as Renard. He hoped not.

"Man, that looked like touch and go for a while there," Monroe said. "There were a couple times I didn't think you were going to make it."

"Not me," Bud said, grinning to reveal his two large square front teeth. "I knew he'd come through okay. Well… I *mostly* knew. Okay, I *hoped*, but that's kind of the same thing as knowing, right?"

Nick continued staring at the Wechselbalg's ashes and felt a growing sense of defeat.

"I was supposed to avoid killing him if I could. Rosalee said she needed some of his substance to make the cure for the *Ewig Woge*." He sighed. "It doesn't look like there's much of him left."

"Maybe she can use the ashes," Monroe said, although he sounded doubtful.

"No, the ashes won't work," Rosalee said. She hadn't joined the others earlier, but she came walking toward them now. "But this just might." She smiled as she held up a small pink object. It took Nick a second to realize what he was looking at: the severed tip of one of the Wechselbalg's fingers.

Rosalee set up a makeshift kitchen-cum-lab next to a campfire, different from the one that had killed the Wechselbalg. With Monroe and Juliette's help, she mixed ingredients in a metal pan and then, using a small towel as a potholder, she held the pan over the fire. While the others worked on the cure, Nick, Hank, and Renard worked on distributing endorphin-enhancer to the rest of the Wesen in the Hafen. They were still in the grip of the *Ewig Woge*, and it was important to do everything possible to keep them calm and relaxed until Rosalee had finished her work.

Not all of the Wesen were happy to receive the paste from a Grimm, a Zauberbiest, or a human, but accept it they did. By the time Rosalee announced, "I think it's ready," everyone in the Hafen was inhaling the mingled scents of vanilla and lavender.

Juliette slowly poured the contents of the pan into a large mug and carried it over to Nick. Juliette and Monroe accompanied her.

Nick frowned when the saw the mug. "That's all?"

"What are you going to do?" Hank asked. "Dispense it with an eyedropper?"

"Not quite," Rosalee said. "The *Ewig Woge* is caused when Grimm physiology tries to shed woge hormone, setting off a reaction in any nearby Wesen."

"Yeah," Nick said. "So?"

"So we have to cure it in a similar way," Rosalee said. She held out the mug to Nick. "Bottoms up."

Nick took the mug from her and examined the contents. The liquid looked thick as tar and had a greasy film on the surface. And it smelled like something that had crawled into a sewer to die. He looked up at Rosalee.

"You've got to be kidding." He thought for a moment. "You said you needed the Wechselbalg alive to make this. Isn't a severed fingertip technically dead?"

"It was alive enough," she said. "Let's hope so, anyway."

Hank leaned close to Nick.

"Since she used part of the Wechselbalg to make that stuff, if you drink it, does that mean you're a cannibal?"

Nick's stomach gave a queasy gurgle.

"Do me a favor, Hank?"

"Sure thing."

"Shut up."

Hank unsuccessfully tried to stifle a grin. "Shutting up."

It took Nick several minutes to get the entire mugful down, and a few more until he was fairly certain he was going to keep it down. There was a lumpy residue at the bottom of the mug, but he wisely avoided looking too closely at it.

"How long until it starts working?" Nick asked.

"Not long," Rosalee said.

"So what do I do?"

"Touch anyone who's affected," she said. "A handshake might do the trick, but a hug would probably be best."

Nick glanced at the crowd of Wesen. While Rosalee had been working, most had stood or sat quietly watching. Now all eyes were on him. Some of them had fear in their gazes, some anger and resentment. But some—far more than Nick would've expected—looked at him with hope.

He couldn't help smiling as he wondered what his ancestors would think of that.

"All right then," he said. "Let's get started."

"Me first!" Bud hurried forward, wrapped his arms around Nick, closed his eyes, and hugged him tight.

Feeling awkward, Nick returned the hug and tried to ignore his friends' amused smiles.

The first light of dawn tinted the sky by the time the last affected Wesen approached Nick. The campfires had been extinguished, the tents taken down and the sleeping bags rolled up. The Wesen, including Bud and his family, had departed as they were cured, and now the only ones remaining in the Hafen were Nick, Juliette, Hank, Monroe, Rosalee, and Renard—the latter three relieved of the *Ewig Woge* and looking quite human once more. And, of course, there was the final Wesen Nick needed to cure.

The mother of the dead Skalengeck teenager had held back the entire time Nick had been curing the others. He'd noticed, of course, and he'd wondered if she'd be able to bring herself to let him help her. Even though Nick hadn't been responsible for her daughter's death, her killer had been an almost exact duplicate of him. He wouldn't blame her for not wanting to come near him.

The woman finally approached him. She stopped short of coming into arm's reach of him, though. Since becoming aware of the existence of Wesen, Nick had become skilled at reading their facial expressions when woged. But he couldn't read her now.

"What's your name?" he asked gently.

The question seemed to catch the woman off guard. It took him a moment to respond. When she did, she said, "Jessica."

"I'm sorry for your loss, Jessica."

She regarded him for several seconds before speaking again.

"At least you got the bastard who killed my girl."

She stepped forward and gave him a stiff, awkward hug. He held her, and after a moment, she relaxed into his arms. It didn't take long for the *Ewig Woge* to release its hold on her. She assumed her human aspect—a brown-haired woman in her early fifties—and then pulled away from Nick.

She gave him a tentative smile, and then turned and departed the Hafen.

Nick looked around. Wildermanner had tidied the clearing and removed their companion's body. There was no sign anyone had ever been here. You couldn't even see where the campfires had been. Even the Wechselbalg's ashes were gone, leaving no evidence the creature had ever existed in the first place.

"Do you think we got everyone?" Hank asked. "I mean,

there could still be some affected Wesen in town who didn't make it to the Hafen for one reason or another."

"It's possible," Renard said. "I'll have my contacts keep an eye out for them."

"And word will get around about how to cure the *Ewig Woge* pretty fast," Monroe added.

"I saved enough of the 'special ingredient' to make more of the cure," Rosalee said. "Just in case."

"Well, I hope we don't need anymore," Nick said. "I don't know everything that was in that stuff, and I don't want to know. But I've got a pounding headache and my mouth feels like it's lined with cotton."

"Your system's been through a lot in the last twelve hours or so," Rosalee said. "Go home, get some rest, drink lots of fluids, and you should be fine."

Nick smiled. "Thanks, Doctor."

"Don't worry, Rosalee," Juliette said. "I'll take good care of him."

Nick grinned at her. "When you say 'take good care…'"

She smiled. "I'll leave that to your imagination."

"Looks like we avoided a repeat of the Killing Time," Renard said.

"People *did* die," Juliette said.

"But it wasn't a wholesale slaughter," Monroe pointed out.

"I guess so," Juliette said. "I still can't help feeling sorry for the Wechselbalg. Do you think there are any more out there somewhere? Ones as old or even older than the one we encountered?"

"Impossible to know," Renard said. "We'll just have to hope that this one was among the last."

They started walking toward the Hafen's entrance then, Hank carrying the talwar and Monroe carrying the battle-axe. Monroe couldn't help giving the weapon a couple experimental swings, but he stopped when Renard and Hank both gave him warning glances.

As they left, Nick couldn't help feeling they were forgetting something, but he couldn't think of what it might be. He was bone-weary and his heard hurt, and all he wanted to do was go home, take a shower, crawl into bed, and sleep for a week. He figured whatever he was trying to remember would come back to him if it was truly important.

De Groot was sitting at his desk reading an email from a Council operative in Japan regarding the Yakuza situation when there was a knock at his door. While he appreciated his assistants' good manners, sometimes he wondered how much of his work day he wasted giving them permission to enter.

"Come," he said.

Adelbert opened the door, stepped into the office, and closed it behind him.

"Sir, about that matter in Portland…"

"Yes?"

"We've just received word that the Wechselbalg has been killed and those Wesen exposed to the *Ewig Woge* have been cured."

De Groot raised an eyebrow. "The Grimm?"

Aldebert nodded.

De Groot contemplated this development for several moments, Adelbert standing quietly by as he thought. At length, he said, "Very well. Recall our agents."

"Yes, sir." Without another word, Adelbert departed.

De Groot leaned back in his chair, folded his hands over his stomach, and thought about Nick Burkhardt. The man was resourceful, even for a Grimm. He might prove useful in the future. Quite useful.

De Groot leaned forward once more, returned his attention to his computer monitor, and resumed his work.

The morning was overcast in Portland, and a light rain began to fall. In the Hafen, hidden within a small clump of grass where even the sharp-eyed Wildermanner had missed it, a lump of flesh and bone—the tip of the Wechselbalg's finger, sheared off with Nick's axe—absorbed the moisture that fell upon it. Little by little, it began to swell, to grow, its surface edging away from charred pink as it assumed a silvery cast. It twitched once, twice, and then, moving slowly at first, but with increasing speed, it began crawling toward the forest in search of life. An insect, or perhaps a rodent—anything would do, really.

All it needed was a place to start.

ACKNOWLEDGMENTS

Thanks to Cath Trechman for inviting me to play in Portland, and to Natalie Laverick for picking up the ball and running with it. And a huge thanks to Cherry Weiner for her friendship and wise counsel.

ABOUT THE AUTHOR

Shirley Jackson Award finalist Tim Waggoner has published over thirty novels and three short-story collections of dark fiction. He teaches creative writing at Sinclair Community College and in Seton Hill University's MFA in Writing Popular Fiction program. You can find him on the web at www.timwaggoner.com.

GRIMM
THE ICY TOUCH

JOHN SHIRLEY

When a torched body is found in an underground tunnel, Portland police captain Sean Renard takes one look at the victim's burned claws and assigns the case to homicide detectives Nick Burkhardt and Hank Griffin. They soon discover that a criminal organization known as The Icy Touch is threatening Wesen into joining their illegal drug-smuggling operation, and brutally murdering those who refuse. But as Nick closes in on the gang's charismatic and ruthless leader, the Grimm uncovers an ancient—and deadly—rivalry...

A brand-new original novel set in the *Grimm* universe.

GRIMM
THE CHOPPING BLOCK

JOHN PASSARELLA

When a pile of bones is discovered in a Portland forest, severed and stripped of flesh, homicide detectives Nick Burkhardt and Hank Griffin quickly rule out an animal attack, but suspect the killer is something other than human. Soon more skeletal remains are unearthed, and tests reveal that the bones were cooked before burial. As the body count increases, Nick, Hank, and reformed Blutbad Monroe must track down a Wesen with a taste for human meat, before the killer can butcher their next meal…

A brand-new original novel set in the *Grimm* universe.

GRIMM
AUNT MARIE'S BOOK OF LORE

As his Aunt Marie is dying, homicide detective Nick
Burkhardt discovers he is descended from an elite line
of criminal profilers known as "Grimms," who keep the
balance between humanity and mythological creatures.
As well as inheriting the "gift" from his aunt of being able
to see the creatures' true forms, he also inherits useful
artefacts, including the Book of Lore.

An in-universe book exploring the weapons, potions and
creatures of *Grimm*.

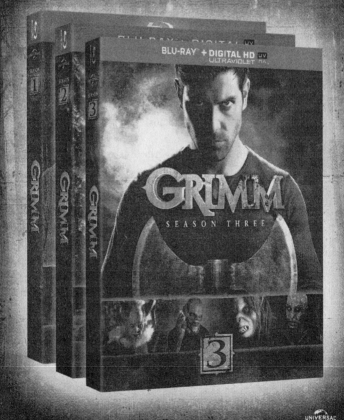

GRIMM

PRODUCTS BASED ON CHARACTERS AND STORIES FROM THE HIT SHOW!

GRIMM

AVAILABLE AT YOUR LOCAL COMICS SHOP

For more fantastic fiction, author events, exclusive excerpts, competitions, limited editions and more

VISIT OUR WEBSITE
titanbooks.com

LIKE US ON FACEBOOK
facebook.com/titanbooks

FOLLOW US ON TWITTER
@TitanBooks

EMAIL US
readerfeedback@titanemail.com